Praise for *Where Earth Meets Water* and Pia Padukone

"Smart and insightful.
A worthy addition to the burgeoning field of new Indian literature."
—Gary Shteyngart, author of *Absurdistan* and *Little Failure: A Memoir*

"Padukone offers a gripping tale of one man's haunting sorrows,
the wounds that bind a people, and the redemptive power of love.
An unforgettable debut by a very promising young writer."
—Patricia Engel, author of *It's Not Love, It's Just Paris* and *Vida*

"Pia Padukone adeptly captures the aspirations
and heartbreak of her engaging characters—how tragedy marks them,
love drives them and need makes them ruthless."
—Manil Suri, author of *The City of Devi*

WHERE *Earth* MEETS *Water*

PIA PADUKONE

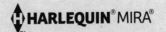

Recycling programs
for this product may
not exist in your area.

ISBN-13: 978-0-7783-1597-1

WHERE EARTH MEETS WATER

Copyright © 2014 by Pia Padukone

"Could Have" from VIEW WITH A GRAIN OF SAND: SELECTED POEMS by Wisława Szymborska, translated from the Polish by Stanisław Barańczak and Clare Cavanagh. Copyright © 1995 by Houghton Mifflin Harcourt Publishing Company. Copyright © 1976 Czytenik, Warszawa. Reprinted by permission of Houghton Mifflin Harcourt Publishing Company. All rights reserved.

For questions and comments about the quality of this book, please contact us at CustomerService@Harlequin.com.

Printed in U.S.A.

First printing: May 2014
10 9 8 7 6 5 4 3 2 1

For both my grandmothers, who have loved me intensely:
my Anamma, Vrinda Padukone, with her quietly creative inspiration
&
my Ajji, Nalini Nadkarni, whose fierce loyalty
and passion for the written word always fueled me forward.

WHERE

Earth

MEETS

Water

COULD HAVE

It could have happened.
It had to happen.
It happened earlier. Later.
Nearer. Farther off.
It happened, but not to you.
You were saved because you were the first.
You were saved because you were the last.
Alone. With others.
On the right. The left.
Because it was raining. Because of the shade.
Because the day was sunny.
You were in luck—there was a forest.
You were in luck—there were no trees.
You were in luck—a rake, a hook, a beam, a brake,
A jamb, a turn, a quarter-inch, an instant...
So you're here? Still dizzy from
another dodge, close shave, reprieve?
One hole in the net and you slipped through?
I couldn't be more shocked or
speechless.
Listen,
how your heart pounds inside me.

Wisława Szymborska

Karom

~

From the first morning that Karom awakes in Gita's grandmother's house, he can tell that their time in Delhi is going to be different from the rest of their trip. They arrive late at night from Agra, and as they drag their suitcases up to the second floor, Gita caresses the nameplate outside Ammama's apartment lightly, leaving a small wake in the dust with her fingers. "Huh," she says. "That's new." Kamini Pai, it reads. Before Karom has a chance to ask what she means, they are tumbling into the small flat, sandy from road silt and Indian rail travel, blinking under the fat fluorescent tube lights like a pair of bears emerging from a long winter's hibernation. After formal introductions and sleepy smiles, they fall into bed, Karom in the living room, Gita in her grandmother's room, surrendering to sleep miles away from any nettlesome insect buzzing or monotonous calls to prayer that echo through the compound. The night passes swiftly, gathering snatches of reality and combining them with fancy, translating and then siphoning them into their ears so that they dream vividly, solidly.

But then, in the early morning, in fact for each of the mornings for the six days they stay with Ammama in her small flat, a gong rings somewhere outside that sounds like a frying pan being hit with a metal spoon. Karom cautiously opens one eye to peer at his vintage Rolex, perched carefully on the chair he is using as a bedside table. Five forty-five. This is when Ammama pads into the sitting room, where Karom sleeps on the hard wooden pallet, his legs tangled in the threadbare sheets, his skin cool and clammy from nightly sweats. She presses a damp cloth on his forehead and he feigns sleep, unsure of how to react, rigidly aware of Gita asleep in the next room. She lowers herself onto the slate floor beside him with a towel under her knees. She swipes a line of vermilion across the hollow in her throat, directly in the center of her clavicle and, depending on how Karom is situated, mirrors the gesture on him. She closes her eyes, reopens them immediately to ensure that Karom is still sleeping, sucks in her breath and lets out a slew of Sanskrit. Karom yearns for the sweet, strong cold coffee that she places inches away from him—he can smell the chicory as the fan gathers the scent into the air—but is afraid that Ammama will see him awake and either make him participate in her ritual or scurry away in embarrassment.

He is touched that she has remembered his love for cold coffee, that it is a sacred thing in India. Back home in New York City, there is only iced coffee: simply ice dumped on top of coffee that becomes immediately diluted and insipid. Cold coffee is creamy, strong and pure. He waits until she finishes mumbling her indecipherable words, heaves herself to her feet and leaves the room. It is only once he hears the crescendo of the bucket being filled for her bath that he dares to reach for the drink, beads of sweat gathered around the base of the brass tumbler.

On their third day in Delhi, he tells Gita as they step out into the street and the blinding light of the premonsoon summer.

"She comes into my room in the mornings," he says. "With a tray of perfectly ripe bananas, a glass of cold coffee and a cold compress that she puts on my forehead. She kneels down next to my bed and mutters under her voice. It's hard to tell with the whirring of the fan, but I'm pretty sure she's praying."

"Get *out*," Gita says, hitting him playfully on the chest, smiling broadly. "What do you do?"

"Nothing," Karom says, stepping over an open sewage grate. "I pretend to sleep. What else am I supposed to do?"

Gita chuckles.

"It's not funny," he says. "She's so sweet, but the whole thing is incredibly awkward."

"It's only for three more days," Gita says. "Hang in there. She's a sweet old lady who's attached to her rituals. I'm sure she's only doing it out of love."

The perfectly ripe bananas don't escape Gita. She won't eat a banana with even a spot of brown on it, and Ammama presumes this condition extends to Karom. But it irks Gita that each day, the only bananas that remain on the breakfast table are either the ones from the day before, which Ammama will eventually turn into *halwa,* or those that are still green and will leave a film on Gita's tongue and a waxy taste in her mouth long after she's eaten one.

"You're not going to say anything to her?" Karom asks.

"What could I possibly say to her, Karom?" Gita responds. She is still thinking about the new nameplate outside the door. It's the first time during all her years of traveling to India that she has seen her grandmother's name proudly proclaiming her ownership of the apartment; previously it held her grandfather's name, a grandfather she's never met.

Karom knows there are some skeletons in Ammama's dusty closet, unopened for years. Gita has danced around the details of Ammama's past, but Karom understands that there is more to the old lady than even Gita is aware of. This became apparent when they originally discussed visiting India months before their trip.

"Visiting India," Gita had said at brunch in New York, "involves seeing my family. There's no way I could avoid it."

"And I'm thrilled about it," Karom had replied. "I wouldn't have it any other way."

"It's not that easy. Visiting together, like this, for the first time…" Gita struggled for words as her eyes flitted over Karom's plate. "You know how people think over there."

"Let them think," Karom said, spearing a large bite of stuffed French toast onto his fork and holding it out to Gita. He knew that she would take it without a fight, that it was a naughty departure from the egg-white omelet that sat in front of her. He knew it would keep her quiet while she chewed, giving him time to take control of the conversation. But it was she who managed to reveal a new side of her family.

Karom cut up another square of his French toast as Gita was chewing, layering it onto his fork into levels until he could no longer see the tines. He held it dangerously close to Gita's mouth, the cream cheese touching her lip. She looked at him and then the food, back and forth like a cross-eyed little girl.

"You're such a tease," she said, before taking the bread in one bite. "Ammama won't judge us, though. She's safe."

"Safe?"

"Life was hard in India over there back then," Gita proclaimed matter-of-factly, forking the remainder of his French toast onto her own plate, cutting and chewing between sentences.

"How do you mean?"

"Ammama is living proof of a marriage gone wrong. She's lived alone most of her adult life. She's what the rest of my family calls 'a freethinker.'"

En route to Ammama's house, they'd stopped at the Taj Mahal. Karom had wanted to spend the whole day at the mausoleum, watching the arc of the sun travel over the domed eggshell marble. He'd read a *National Geographic* article about how the sun changes the color of the marble depending on its angle throughout the day. The photos displayed the dome over twenty-four hours: pink, prenatal and shy in the dawn hours, citrine-yellow at midmorning, blinding white at high noon. It appeared as a completely different structure each moment, and Karom loved the unpredictability of it. The same ubiquitous structure that the world knew so intimately displayed so many different personalities. Had Shah Jahan meant to capture his beloved wife's multifaceted character? Her casual morning softness, her dour depression at having lost seven of her children, while constantly displaying the fierce, unfailing love she had for her husband? What made the Taj so emotional, changing over the course of the day depending on its mood? How had this feat been accomplished so many hundreds of years ago, when just the building of an edifice of this size had seemed impossible? Karom couldn't wait to watch its metamorphosis right before his very eyes.

But the train to Agra hadn't shown, and the Jaipur station from which they were departing had been overflowing with passengers, occupying all the benches or peering uselessly into the distance over the tracks. Karom watched Gita approach a tour guide who was playing games on his cell phone. She smoothed her hair behind her ears and spoke to him for a few minutes before she returned to Karom and told him about the strike.

"I saw an STD booth over there," he said. "I'm going to call Lloyd. I'd forgotten that he's leaving for his bachelor party one of these days. I hope I can catch him." She watched him lope off toward the dusty shack set back from the railroad platform, where he opened a glass door and slid inside.

When he returned, the two of them sat on the platform, leaning their backs against one another for support, summoning the strength for the wait that loomed ahead. Karom unhooked his watch and reread the inscription on the underside of the face. It felt like a brand-new gift each time.

Together we learn there's nothing like time.

The strength he drew from this little mantra had made it possible to get through grueling days of struggling with the right word for a headline at the advertising agency where he worked, made it a little easier to stomach shelling out three figures for underwhelming plays and frustrating tiffs that he and Gita always managed to spark just before bedtime. The words rolled over in his mind and across his tongue when he needed something to concentrate on, while he was training for his first road race, and then a 10K, and then a full marathon. And during those moments, when he had to stop and check his patient pulse, when he could feel it bleating slowly but capably under the thin skin of his under-wrist, he repeated these words to himself.

Karom looked down at the platform beneath him, spackled red with *paan* spit. He traced one of the spatters with the toe of his sandal. *Animals on safari,* he thought. *There's the elephant trunk, holding on to a hippo's tail, an alligator? No, a gecko, one of the household varieties that Gita screamed at until I chased it out of our tent in Jaisalmer.*

Back home, in the subways of New York City, Karom liked to peer over the edge of the platform into the depths of the tunnels, waiting diligently for that crescent of light to appear reflected on the sheen of the tracks, holding until the headlights finally appeared and the silver cars careened into the station. At times, when the tunnel was long without any hidden curves, he could see the train's headlights a full station away. He could watch it amble down the stretch toward him, teasing him with its proximity. But most of the time, the delightful snatch of light wouldn't give itself away until the last minute, when it came peeking around the bend. Karom loved this dance with the train but simultaneously worried himself over how long it would take to appear. Most nights, when service was delayed or curtailed, he paced back and forth, his ears perking up at the faintest of rumblings, which sent him scurrying to perch his toes over the perimeter of yellow paint that warned passengers not to cross this line.

Once, the transit police who were loitering up and down the platform had approached him as he peered down the tunnel. "Sir," the officer had said. "I'm going to have to ask you to step away from the platform edge. It's for your own safety."

When they'd first taken the subway together years before, Karom's platform behavior had made Gita nervous.

"You stand so close to the edge," she'd said, tugging at his hand. "Please come back."

"It's just a game," Karom had said. "I lean over until I have to lean back."

"Well, I don't like it."

People lived in those tunnels, in the dank recesses, venturing out only to forage for food. Mole people, as he had heard them referred to, though he thought this term disrespectful and embarrassing. He couldn't imagine living that far underground, though he'd read that the tunnels spread so far below the surface of pavement that it was possible to venture seven or eight stories deep. He had joked to Gita that one day real estate would be at such a premium that well-appointed condos with marble countertops and bamboo floors would have no choice but to spread to the netherworld that lay beneath them. Doormen would stand at attention at the mouths of stairwells that meandered far below the sidewalk, and the former valuable measurement of natural light would be replaced by mold-repellant abilities.

"Just wait," Karom had said, "until the most sought-after apartments are those that are farther below the surface. Humans always need one-upmanship."

After two hours of waiting on the Jaipur station platform, Karom stood up suddenly. Gita turned the page of her guidebook and shifted her position without looking up. Karom walked gingerly over the bodies sprawled across the platform napping, through a group of children playing a hand-clapping game and knelt at the platform edge. He sat down, his legs dangling over. A group of men playing cards and puffing on strong clove-scented cigarettes eyed him from the shadows of a snack cart's canopy. Dust motes swirled in the early-afternoon sun and the slightest breeze lifted a piece of hair off Karom's forehead and swung it over his eye.

In an instant he had jumped down to the tracks. He glanced around, the walls of the platform looming up around him like a cave. He couldn't see the passengers from here, only sky and the great expanse of the tracks in the distance, far away, leading to Agra. Karom stood with both feet on one of the rails, the cool metal cutting through the inadequate rubber of his sandals and massaging the sore arches of his feet. He walked, holding his arms out balancing himself, pretending there was a book upon his head. On the seventeen-hour flight from New York to Bombay, Karom had watched a documentary on Philippe Petit, the daredevil tightrope walker who'd walked between the World Trade Towers and lived to tell the tale. Karom bent his feet to span across the track like Petit, a make-believe balancing pole in his hands as he walked forward.

He'd walked to the outskirts of the train station on the tracks like this when he heard Gita's scream. Swiveling around, he tipped off the tracks. As he righted his balance, he saw the card-playing men in the distance watching him, squatting at the edge of the platform. He saw the children hovering on the edge, holding hands tightly. And he saw Gita, looking as though she was about to launch herself over the edge but being restrained by three hefty women in Punjabi suits.

"Karom! Get off the tracks! Come back!" she shouted. Karom put his hand up in acknowledgment, but just as he did so, he felt a faint rumbling underneath the balls of his feet. He turned around and began a slow march back toward the station, putting one foot in front of the other on the metal track.

"Come back to the platform. Please!" Gita shouted. He could see her face was stained by tears, her voice strained with panic. His rubber sandals slipped against the shiny metal, and the approaching vibration tickled his feet. He was at the station and had hoisted himself up onto the platform on his own before the Punjabi women released a sobbing Gita into his arms. He held her tightly and buried his nose in her hair.

"I'm sorry. I'm sorry, baby. I'm okay. See? It was just a walk. Nothing happened. It was just the game." He let her cry in

his arms until she quieted and spread out across their backpacks to nap.

They didn't say anything further to one another until they
boarded a train two more hours later. As she climbed the stairs
into their car, Gita put her hand up and smiled at the tour
guide. "This wait is nothing," he called back. "Very short.
Very lucky."

They reached the Taj just moments before sunset, to the
sights and sounds of children screeching, parents strolling
across the manicured lawn, tourists adjusting one another's
hands for the perfect pose in front of the reflecting pool, others showing security guards how to operate elaborate cameras. The Taj was a deep aubergine, the setting sun glancing
off the Yamuna River at a distance and cloaking the grounds
and the shrine in darkness. They took a quick round, wander-
ing through the arched doorways in their bare feet, marveling
at the intricate inlaid stonework, tracing their toes over the
perfectly symmetrical marble, and stood solemnly before the
mausoleum before they realized they'd forgotten to take any
pictures. The Taj was dark by then, lit only by eight flood-
lights where moths savagely attacked the bulbs.

"No pictures," Gita said sadly. "How will we ever remember that we were here?" They were stationed directly in front
of the Taj, in front of the bench that thousands upon thousands of tourists sat on every day, with a perfectly cruel vantage
point of the structure in front of them. Karom slipped his arm
around her and squeezed her shoulder. With his other hand,
he pulled a crumpled piece of paper from his pocket. He read:

"Should guilty seek asylum here,
Like one pardoned, he becomes free from sin.
Should a sinner make his way to this mansion,

All his past sins are to be washed away.
The sight of this mansion creates sorrowing sighs,
And the sun and the moon shed tears from their eyes.
In this world this edifice has been made,
To display thereby the creator's glory!"

"It's what Shah Jahan said about the Taj," Karom said, fold-ing the paper back into his pocket. Gita closed her eyes and leaned against him. He wanted to comfort her, but he too felt let down. Nothing had *happened*. There had been no rev-elations.

Karom had been sure that he would leave the Taj Mahal with a deeper understanding of the world, of colors, of light, of love. He was sure that something magical would transform them, would transform him, the way he saw the world. He had placed too high an expectation on the Taj Mahal. After all, it was just a building. But it was a building that was homage to love, homage to the departed. He'd wondered if he would catch a glimpse of the past here, if he might tap into the spirit of the palace, the serenity of the courtyards. He'd wondered if, like a sinner, he too might be absolved, washed pure and clean, and set into the streets refreshed. He'd wondered if he might put lingering ghosts to bed and feel, for the first time, at ease with himself and finally, *finally* have the strength to put the game to rest.

Finally, Karom took her hand, pulling her back outside the gates into a world of hawkers offering prayer beads, post-cards and miniature hand-carved wooden replicas of the great shrine.

On the rickshaw ride back to the train station, they qui-etly held one another's hands. When their eyes met at a traffic light, Gita looked at Karom for a beat too long, causing him to snap, "I'm fine. I told you I'm fine," and pull his hand away from hers. Gita felt suddenly vulnerable sitting in the rickshaw as it inched along the crowded streets. On either side, beggars and street vendors thrust their hands into the open sides of the vehicle, offering open empty palms or rickety plastic toys for sale. At that moment she couldn't find solace even in the man who sat next to her; it was how she'd felt the first time she'd experienced one of his close shaves firsthand.

The previous summer, the two had been on a road trip to Maine, where they'd stopped in Portland, lingering over a breakfast of blueberry pancakes and yogurt, crawling through the Marina district in their rented convertible so Gita could hop out and use her Pantone matcher to capture the vibrant colors of the homes along the water. Her travels heavily influenced her work in her interior design studio: swaths of curtains that curled around window edges like the Caribbean Sea and mosaic patios reminiscent of the shelled precipices in Santorini. She'd once re-created a tiled wall in an open-plan bathroom based on the textures and tones of a spice display she'd seen in Essaouira.

Karom sped while Gita sat with her face directly in front of the air-conditioning vent. "I like the smell of it," she said when he looked at her quizzically. "It's the smell of cold."

They were on the way to Archer's Rock, the famous boulder that jutted out over the sea where families picnicked and sunbathed. "'This rocky edifice may be the last bastion of the unsullied natural vantage point,'" Gita read from the *National Geographic* app on her iPhone. "'Everything else has been filed down, shaved away, taking with it the history and fossilized evolutionary proof of our lives.' Oh, Kar, we *have* to go there."

By the time their car pulled up to visitors' parking, ambulances and police tape had cordoned off the graveled lot.

Scuba tanks were stacked together in a pile near one of the medical vans, and medics scurried about, stricken, possessed, mumbling into walkie-talkies.

"Park's closed, sir," a ranger said, directing their car. "Please turn around and go back the way you came." Karom couldn't believe that the ranger wore a hat just like on *Yogi Bear.* He spoke to the absurdly flat brim.

"What happened?"

"Wave."

Karom hesitantly put his hand up and looked around before he realized that the ranger wasn't instructing him to gesture to anyone. He put the car in reverse. While Karom fiddled with the AM radio to find a local channel, Gita plugged in the address of their hotel into the GPS that would lead them out of the park and back toward the highway.

"Tragedy struck at Acadia National Park today as a giant wave crashed over Archer's Rock, claiming the lives of dozens of hikers and picnickers. Body count is still unknown as medics and scuba divers continue to comb the rocky coast to recover up to 50 park visitors who are expected to have been on the rock. Accounts confirm that a rogue wave such as this one hasn't struck the area in nearly 40 years, the last similar tragedy occurring in 1971."

The trees rushed by them, faster and faster, a blur of green in ascending brightness past their windows. They flew by the distinct odor of skunk and a tiny manicured graveyard, past which Gita held her breath. The two-way road was narrow and Gita was glad that Karom was driving. She felt nervous driving in situations where the car might graze against the side of another. She panicked easily in tunnels.

Karom pressed the button to clean the windshield, the blades scraping dully against the already clean glass. Gita pressed the window down and a small spray of window cleaner struck her cheekbone. Karom pulled the car to the side of the road, though there was no shoulder there. He leaned down to the steering wheel and rested his forehead in the center of the wheel, little bleeps emitting sporadically from the horn like a suffering goat.

"Karom," Gita said, rubbing his ear. "It's not the same thing. Look at me, baby." He didn't move.

"Baby, look at me. It's a completely different situation, okay? I'm not going to let anything happen to you. You're fine. You're safe. I'm here." She grabbed his head, the hair in the back where it had grown long and scraggly, and pushed it into her shoulder. She could feel him slowly disintegrate against her body, his long sobs penetrating through her thin wind-breaker, his breath forcing muffled gasps and soggy exhala-tions. They sat there like that, allowing cars to whiz by their window, first a few at a time and then the ambulance they had seen in the parking lot, an underwater detection van and then another slew of cars. It became dark in the trees before Gita finally tapped his leg and Karom moved away, averting his face in the embarrassing dance of drying his tearstained face.

They traded places; Gita slid into the driver's seat, put the car into drive and navigated the rest of the way to their bud-get hotel while Karom leaned back in his seat, one arm swung over his eyes to shield them from the glow of the dashboard.

In the rickshaw, Gita forced herself to remember that while their trip to Agra had been uneventful, without epiphany or excitement, that was what had made it a success. She forced her hand back into his and snuggled against him, turning her back to the beggars and hawkers in the road.

★ ★ ★

"Hang on," Gita says now, as they sidestep two dogs sleeping in the middle of the lane. "When Ammama prays, is it in Hindi? English?"

"Definitely not English," Karom says. "But she says my name. Repeatedly."

"May-be," Gita singsongs, pressing her body against him, "she's praying for you to propose to me."

"Ha." Karom steps slightly away from her as they pass through the gates of Ammama's compound.

"Oh, get over it," she exclaims, grabbing his hand.

Karom stiffens. "Not here, Gita."

"Of *course* here," Gita insists. "It's the birthplace of the Kama Sutra. Romance was practically invented here."

But there is a sense of decorum in India, regardless of the historical ramifications of one dusty volume of intimate positions that sex shops like to pass off as exotic and sensual. Karom understands that the things that they take for granted back home in New York can never be accepted in this land so easily. The idea of boyfriends and girlfriends and dating, of sleeping in the same bed, even of traveling together, are all acts that had he grown up here, he himself might have frowned upon.

On their first night in Ammama's flat, Karom had reverently touched her feet as he knew she would appreciate and asked, "Where will I be sleeping?" and then "Where will Gita be sleeping?" before placing their backpacks in the appropriate rooms: Gita sharing her grandmother's double bed, Karom on the wooden pallet in the sitting room. He wondered if Gita asked her grandmother if she could sleep in the bed away from the door or away from the window, whichever it was that she was most worried about. Most women had a side of the bed, the right or left, but for Gita it was the side that she felt least vulnerable in. If they stayed in a hotel room, it was the side farthest away from the door; if they were on the ground floor in a room with garden access, it was where Gita felt intruders would be least likely to enter.

"It's because if someone were to break in, I wouldn't be the first thing they'd see," she'd explained to Karom.

"But *I* would," he'd snorted. "And I'd be the one they mauled or kidnapped or beat up. That's okay with you?"

"No...you would protect me," Gita had said. "My big strong man."

He'd shaken his head. It was a stupid argument, but still he couldn't help feeling slighted by her selfishness. He wondered if Gita was okay with her grandmother falling victim to hypothetical marauders in her second-floor flat in the suburban residential colony in East Delhi.

When they return to the flat later, after a long afternoon of shopping, Karom steps hesitantly through the door. But Ammama isn't focused on him; she tells Gita that she has something to show her. While Gita slips behind the curtain that serves as the door to Ammama's room, Karom busies himself with taking his purchases out of the bags and laying them out on the sofa: Calvin Klein shirts, a Kenneth Cole suit, all gathered at severely discounted prices. He holds up a shirt and breathes it in. It is so reassuring how much the fabric smells like India, like the mustiness of cardamom and mustard and mothballs all in one. He hears jingles and snaps and coos and sighs before Ammama slides the curtain open and beckons shyly at him. Karom follows her into the bedroom.

The bedroom is dimly lit: Ammama has drawn the curtains against prying eyes and sunlight is poking in at the corners of the windows. Gita is sitting on the bed with what appears to be a heap of gold in front of her. She sorts through it, trying on a large chandelier earring with curlicues and licks of rubies in her right ear while an enormous jade hoop perches perkily in her left nostril.

"Wow," Karom breathes. "What is all this?"

"My trousseau," Ammama says, pushing aside some of the tissues that had protectively padded the jewelry. "I want Gita to choose something. Help her decide."

Karom sits gingerly on the edge of the bed. He picks up a string of pearls and lets them slide through his fingers. Gita is wrapping a thick yellow-gold necklace with braided chains around her neck.

"Close this?" She turns around and Karom snaps the clasp at the nape of her neck. "What do you think?"

"It's beautiful," he says. "It's all so delicately elaborate."

"You have first pick and then your sisters can choose when they come next," Ammama says, taking a step toward the door. "Take your time. I'll make tea."

"Her family must have spent years collecting all this. Imagine how long it took to put it together," Karom whispers.

"Here, I need help with this headpiece." Gita aligns an emerald stone that glistens like a giant waterdrop in the center of her forehead, glancing in the mirror to make sure that the chain falls neatly into the parting of her hair. "What do you think?"

"It seems so sad to break up the set that symbolizes the start of her new life as a bride. But I guess she's passing on the legacy."

"Trust me, she doesn't want the memories. They're not happy ones. Besides, I'm *here,* Karom. She wants me to have something. What do you think of these?" Solid gold bangles cuff her wrists, glinting in the dim light.

"They're nice. I'm going to…" Karom nods toward the doorway and slides off the bed. In the kitchen, Ammama is pouring tea into the Bodum pot Karom has brought her. Her hand shakes a bit as the last drop fills the strainer. "I hope you like the teapot. Gita told me how much you like your tea. 'Once in the a.m., once in the p.m. and once before R.E.M.' Right?" Gita had also told him that Ammama would trot it out while they were there and then rewrap it in its original box and place it in the back of a cupboard until visitors came.

"It's beautiful. You shouldn't have wasted so much money," Ammama says. Karom places the pot on a tray along with the small ceramic box of sugar and a matching pitcher of milk. Gita appears at the doorway, wearing a heavy yellow-gold necklace. It droops down nearly to her midriff, rubies and emeralds twinkling brazenly. The inner strands are unpolished grayish oblong seeds rather than the now seemingly artificial perfect globes of pearls Karom has seen the ladies wear with Chanel suits on the Upper East Side. Gita doesn't look very comfortable, but she sticks her chest out and says, "I want this one."

"I wore that on my wedding day," Ammama says, smiling. "Beautiful choice. If you're sure, I'll take the rest back to the safe-deposit box at the bank."

They sit in the living room, the overhead ceiling fan making wide, useless circles as the tea cools. Karom nibbles absently on a stale biscuit.

"You've left your visits until the last minute," Ammama says. Gita looks down shiftily and traces a pattern on the stone floor with her toe. "I only hope it's convenient for your great-aunts and uncles that you come tonight."

"You'll come with us, right, Ammama?" Gita asks shyly. "It'll be fun." Gita has obligations, she's told Karom. To see

family members who remember her better than she knows
them, but these visits make them so happy and they make
Ammama happy, too.

"I'll make an early dinner and we can call a rick to take us.
I missed my nap today," Ammama says, her eyes twinkling.
"I hope I won't be too cranky."

The evening is crisper than the previous days have been.
Karom borrows a pale blue sweater from the empty closet that
once belonged to Gita's grandfather. He puts his arms through
the sweater sleeves and his nose to the fabric.

"Why do clothes in India always smell like this?" he asks.
"It's so reassuring, such a comforting scent."

"Probably because all the *dhobis* use the same detergent,"
Gita says sarcastically. "And let the clothing dry in the air to
pick up the subtle undertones of coconut trees and cow dung."

Ammama sits by the door in the sitting room. Karom
doesn't understand the name for this room; no such place exists
in Western-style homes. It is a room for receiving, for watching, for preparing, but never simply for sitting. It is the first
time he has seen anyone be still in this room since his arrival.

Ammama is wearing a dark maroon sari with a paisley
border. The previous summer, she distributed all her bright
saris and those with gold or silver thread to the twin neighbor girls upstairs. They are both in their forties, living with
their parents. One of them was married, but on her wedding
night, her husband raised his hand to her and she retaliated,
striking him on the bridge of his nose. Stunned, he told her to
pack her things and go, and she responded in kind, returning
to the flat upstairs. At least, that's what Ammama has heard.

Gita told Karom about a ritual she loved as a child, first
arriving at Ammama's flat in the summers, tearing open her

wardrobe door, running her hands across the yards and yards of silk, brocade and crepe-de-Chine saris, burying her head into the fabric to breathe in that familiar smell of India and begging Ammama to take out "this one. This one is my favorite." Gita's allegiances changed each time she visited, her tastes maturing and then reverting as trends came and went. In her tomboy years, she chose only the blues and reds, and when she finally embraced her girlhood, she lovingly pulled out more pinks and purples. Upon arriving at the flat a few days ago, Gita had flung open the wardrobe door and cried out softly as she sank back onto Ammama's bed.

"They're gone," Gita said. "What happened?"

"I'm too old. I can't wear those bright-bright things now," Ammama replied. "And the *zari* work was too fine—I couldn't iron them constantly. So I gave the whole lot to the girls upstairs. They needed some color in their lives." Gita twisted her mouth, saddened by the gaping holes between the lonely, dismal saris that remained. *But* you *need some color in* your *life,* she thought.

Ammama's apartment building is set back in the compound, and the motorized auto-rickshaws buzz about like flies only in the main road. Karom goes to fetch one while Ammama walks carefully behind, holding her cane in one hand and Gita's forearm in the other. Gita can see Karom in the distance with his arm up in the road as the little black rickshaws scurry past him.

"I like him, Gita. I really like him." Gita holds Ammama's hand as they take dainty steps together. "Do you think you'll marry?"

"I hope so, Ammama," Gita says, looking down into Ammama's eyes. "I really hope he gets things together. I really hope he can move beyond his past. Because I love him, I really do. And I think we could be happy together."

"Give it time, child," Ammama says. "Not everything happens overnight."

"It's been years, though," Gita sighs. "And he's taking such baby steps that I worry he'll never—" She stops and looks up toward him. He is standing too far into the road, extending his arm out as if he were hailing a cab on Broadway. He is getting impatient, pushing the hair out of his eyes and wiping his brow on his shoulder. He takes one more step into the road as an angry rickshaw driver shouts at him, gesticulating wildly. Panic rises and jets out of Gita's nostrils.

"Ammama, wait here." Gita props Ammama against a low-lying parapet. Gita takes off at a gallop. It seems so filmic, her hair bouncing and her shawl flying behind her, as if she is running in slow motion to catch up to the man she loves. But as she approaches him, she catches hold of his wrist and swings him back into the ditch that follows the sidewalk along Ammama's lane. Angry shouts erupt around them, rickshaws nestling close together like black beetles attacking a crumb to allow them through.

"What the hell do you think you're doing?" Gita asks, panting.

"Getting a rickshaw. What does it look like? Gita, let go. That hurts."

"You're standing in the middle of the road and you know it. This isn't Manhattan, where the cabs will actually stop. This is Delhi, Karom. People die."

"Stop being so melodramatic, Gita. No one's filming right now."

"No, *you* stop it, Karom." Tears prick the edges of Gita's eyes as their voices rise to be heard with the thrumming and honking of the vehicles that speed by. "This is neither the time nor the place. Please don't do this. Not now." A honking interrupts them. Ammama pokes her head out of a rickshaw that pulls up alongside them.

"Found one," Ammama says. "Come on, get in." Gita climbs up on the other side of her grandmother and Karom piles in the opening closest to him, his long, spidery legs nestling against the back of the driver's seat. As the rickshaw speeds by on the newly paved highway, though they are landlocked and miles from the ocean, somehow the air fills their nostrils with the tangy, briny scent of the sea.

In December 2004 his family had gathered on Poompuhar Beach: a reunion. Karom had final exams in Boston and his parents were adamant that he see the semester through. His friends had all finished their finals and started packing up for Christmas break, but Karom was enrolled in a few master's classes that ended later than the undergraduate program.

"I can take makeup exams," he'd complained. "Besides, I'm graduating next semester. All the important stuff is over. This is the first time I am going to see all my cousins together. And Naani and Nana and Ajja and Ajji will be so upset I can't come."

"They'll be upset that you are shirking your studies," his father had said. "You can join us after the exams are over."

There were games, snacks, many opportunities to get to know one another over the course of two days. Some members of the family were traveling thousands of miles to meet one another, some for the first time, some after a long time. Karom imagined them as he sat with his head against the frozen window, snow melting softly in the courtyard of the library. Now they were probably having strong hot South Indian coffee. Now they were probably telling stories of his parents as youngsters, of their sweet but short courtship when he had wooed and won her. Now they were probably singing folk songs that would only—could only—be passed down by his generation, and if he wasn't there to learn them, who would bring them to America? Now they were probably sitting on the beach, under colorful tents they'd have rented to stave off the relentless sun. Karom followed them in his mind, fabricating their activities, picturing their smiles. When he packed up his laptop case and closed the door to his dorm room, ready to jump into the cab that would take him to Logan Airport, he thought his heart might burst.

Unlike most of his friends, who would joke about the tribulations of forced holidays like Thanksgiving and Christmas, Karom enjoyed spending time with his family. This included his wise father, who had been the director on a television commercial starring his ageless, timeless, classically beautiful mother. And of course his mother, who doled out advice the way other mothers pass out homemade cookies. His cousins, whom he'd met piecemeal over the years, and their parents—his aunts and uncles whose stories his own parents had regaled him with for years and years and whose reputations spread far and wide from silly to sober—equally amused him. Both sets of grandparents, whom he saw dutifully every two years, servants his parents had grown up with, vendors who knew more about him than he would ever know about them. All of these people made up a life that was separate from the snowy, blanketed college he was leaving now, forlorn and empty, devoid of true familial love even when the campus was full.

The cabdriver was talkative, which surprised Karom. He thought he'd have to combat surliness and tip heavily for a fare on Christmas Day.

"Where you headed? Your family doesn't mind you're missing Christmas?"

"India. We're not Christian," Karom said, hugging his backpack to his chest.

"India? Is that safe? You hear about that storm?"

"You must mean the monsoons. They happen in the summer all the time. They're used to them over there."

"No, not a storm," the cabdriver said, shaking his head. He leaned over and turned on the radio. "It's this freak wave. It's biblical."

During the ride to Logan, the cab was filled with snatches of dialogue, screaming, shouting, sobbing, as various news reports filled in the current events of a rogue wave that had been triggered by underwater earthquakes, badly affecting parts of Indonesia, Sri Lanka, Thailand and India.

"That's enough," Karom said at the sight of the exit ramp to the airport. "Please turn it off." He paid the driver and stood on the sidewalk as trolleys and rolling suitcases maneuvered around him, punching buttons on his cell phone and hearing the Tamil operator prattle back hopelessly to him. There was nothing to do but stick to the plan to fly to Kanyakumari, where he would meet his parents and grandparents to witness one of the most breathtaking sunrises in the world at the very tip of the country, where the Indian Ocean met the Gulf of Mannar and the Arabian Sea. Except that all flights to India were stalled without further information of conditions there. The coastal states were in emergency: no one was going in and it was unclear who was still alive. Karom spent Christmas Day shuttling from the internet café in the airport to the gummy carpeted floor of Gate 17, where he sat slumped, tapping away at his cell phone.

Hours later he peeled himself up and took a bus and then

the T and then walked the seven long blocks back to his dorm. The brittle leaves that still hung on the trees chattered together in a ghostly whisper as the wind swept through them. There was something beautiful about the snow that had settled there in his absence. It glistened cleanly, the crystals twinkling in the crisp morning. Karom felt bad making a path to his doorway, where he let himself into his room and opened the blinds where the sun glanced off the snow mounds, blinding him momentarily. His dorm-room phone blinked red with anticipation and he dropped his bundles, even his precious laptop, in a heap on the floor and jabbed the button. A muffled, weary voice filled the room.

"Karom, I've been trying your mobile, but it doesn't seem to be connecting. This is Kishan Ramchand, your naana and naani's neighbor in Cubbon Park. We live upstairs? I think you were meant to land just now, but I'm hoping to catch you. Karom, there was this huge wave yesterday that pretty much obliterated most of the southern and western coasts of India, particularly Tamil Nadu. Obviously, you know that's where the festivities were being held, and nobody's been able to get ahold of anyone from the party. We're trying desperately, but as you can imagine, a lot of phone lines are down and it's been impossible to connect with the hotel or anyone's mobiles. Auntie and I are praying really hard here at home, but we're not sure what's happening. If by some miracle, you haven't left already, please stay put. It's a rather dangerous situation right now. Take my number and call."

His entire family. All together. On one beach.

Karom listened to the message once again before he wrote the number down shakily. Then he opened the covers on his tightly made bed and got in. It was three days before he got out again. On the third day, he reached for his cell phone and dialed Kishan's number.

"Uncle? It's Karom."

"Thank God, child. You're okay. Where have you been?"

"College. My flight was canceled. Any news?"

"It's not looking good. They're reporting that phone and power lines have been restored at this point, as well as cell networks. If we—if we haven't heard from them by now…"

"Look, you never know. What can I do? Should I come?"

"There's nothing anyone can do at this point." Karom heard Kishan slowly breaking down. A tear traveled down the bridge of Karom's nose and plopped onto the worn wooden floor-board. The room was freezing—the heat had been turned off for the break, though Karom didn't notice it at all. "And your parents were there," Kishan wailed.

"They *are* there," Karom said, wiping his face on the back of his hand. "Listen, I've got to go. Call me if you hear anything. On my cell. My mobile."

Karom sat up in bed, staring at the wall as if in a trance. Suddenly, he broke off and opened his roommate's closet. In here Lloyd kept a small pantry alongside his perfectly pressed cardigans and corduroy jackets. Karom wasn't sure why Lloyd hid the snacks, as Karom had never deigned to take anything of Lloyd's without asking—until now. There were saltines, granola bars, a large package of chocolate-covered mints and a fresh jar of peanut butter. Karom twisted the top off the pea-nut butter and pulled a gob of it onto his finger. He closed his lips over it, the sweetness making his mouth water and jerk-ing tears to his eyes. He blinked the tears back and stuck his finger in again and again. His mouth was sticky and he ran his tongue over his teeth. What was that word? The word that when he heard it pulled gently on his stomach, in his throat, at the tips of his fingernails, making him think that it would never be him. It couldn't be him.

It would be six hours before Karom logged on to his computer, searching for answers, looking up death tolls on the Indian Red Cross website, manning live streams for four different news sites at once, cross-referencing emails and then seeing his parents' names in ghostly letters upon a list of those found fatally wounded or dead. And then his grandparents. All four of them. And then a whole column, a page of his surname over and over:

Rana Seth.

Mohan Seth.

Akansha Seth.

Preeti Seth.

Madhu Seth.

Shankar Seth.

Seth.

Seth.

Seth.

Seth.

It was another two hours before he remembered the word: *orphan*. Thereafter, until Lloyd and the other students returned to campus, everything was broken up into increments of time: sixteen hours before Kishan called to confirm that everyone at the reunion was reported officially missing. Dead. Twenty-two hours before Karom dry-heaved repeatedly from hunger. Thirty-six hours before his contact lenses automatically peeled themselves away from his pupils—raw from the dry, airless room—and curled up on the desk where he sat staring at his laptop, his only beacon and companion, which rang in the New Year in front of him. Ninety-six hours before he methodically and carefully deleted all the emails from friends inquiring if his family was okay and saying that they were praying for them and was there anything anyone could do and please don't hesitate to ask. Three months before a courier rapped on his door with a delivery from Kishan wrapped in brown paper and padded with cotton wads.

A gold Rolex with a black alligator band sat nestled within the padding. The face was weathered and scratched just to the right of the crown and there were a few bits of sand wedged between the glass face and the golden hinges. A small note accompanied it.

Karom—
This was among the belongings in the safe in Naana and Naani's room. There wasn't much else—their passports and some bundles of rupees. Your parents' room held their passports and some money, as well. The passports and money are being held for administrative and tracking purposes. I'll make sure to have them sent to you as soon as possible. I wanted you to have something of meaning, and as you know, this was the watch that your naani gave your naana on their wedding night. I hope it serves as something—a memory, a wish, a light.
All my best,
Kishan Uncle

Together we learn there's nothing like time. Karom was sure that it was the first of Naani's many gestures to her new husband that everything would be okay, that even if nothing made sense in their early days as strangers to one another, the years would prove themselves stronger than unfamiliarity, that they would take this journey together, learning about one another and stumbling and catching one another and learning every step of the way. Naani was always the reassuring one; her husband would flurry about worrying if the plane would lose their luggage, or whether they would run out of vegetarian meals, or if they hadn't packed enough warm clothing for the beach.

Karom had put the watch on immediately, and unless he was bathing or sleeping or going through the security line at the airport, he never took it off. He would wear it as a constant reminder of all that he had lost, his whole family all at once, wham bam, in an instant, like the second hand that ticked on his wrist.

On the morning of their departure from Delhi, Ammama tiptoes into the sitting room, where Karom is holding his watch between his fingers, studying its slightly scarred face. Ammama stops and smiles shyly, looking down at the tray as if to show Karom what she has brought him. He motions to her to sit down next to him.

"Come," he whispers. She sits awkwardly on the bed next to him, pulling her tiny feet underneath her and adjusting her sari. The tray of bananas and cold coffee sits between them, but on this morning, there is also a thick book. Karom peels a banana and hands it to her. She shakes her head shyly. Karom urges, "Please." She nibbles at the tiny fruit and Karom peels another for himself. *So much sweeter than the huge bland ones we get back home,* Karom thinks.

"What do you say to me?" he asks. "Are you praying?" Ammama colors and looks down at the floor.

"I thought you were asleep," she says.

"I'm an early riser," Karom says. "Please tell me."

"It's nothing, really. Just an old lady's superstitions."

"Please." He takes her banana peel and places it with his

alongside the book on the tray. He turns to face her. Ammama looks at him and purses her mouth.

"You mustn't be cross with Gita for telling me. She tells me that you like to tempt fate. That you call it your game. Is that right?" Karom looks down, embarrassed. "Fate isn't an easy thing to play with. Once it decides to shift in one direction, the gusts keep on blowing, and it's out of your hands. You have to take care of one another, don't you?" He nods. "But I know there is something over you. An omen."

"An omen?"

Ammama nods solemnly.

"What kind of omen? Because I've been pretty lucky." He tells her about Acadia and the tidal wave that he and Gita narrowly missed. He tells her about 9/11, how he'd feigned illness on the morning that his class was to visit a news studio in Tower 1 because he hadn't finished a paper on *Howards End,* how instead he'd stayed home watching the news, stricken, while the first tower came crumbling down like a stale cracker.

"Do you think so? Then what is this game nonsense?"

It's Karom's turn to color. "It's just my way of feeling alive. I can't— I don't have an explanation. It's how I've conditioned myself, I suppose. To understand why I'm still...why I don't...why I can't...what's keeping me from..." He trails off and looks down at his hands sitting uselessly in his lap. "But what do you see? How can you tell?"

"I suppose the same way, I can't explain the feeling I had about you from the moment you walked through the door. But I knew it was there the moment I heard you whimpering and tossing about at night."

"I'm still doing that, huh?" Karom bites his lip. "Is this something that will hurt me? Omens don't have to be bad, you know. Are you praying to get rid of the omen?"

"I suppose I am. I am praying for you to win the game. I want you to win. Just like Gita, I want the game to end."

Karom looks down sheepishly.

She reaches for the tray and picks up the book, weighing it carefully between her two hands.

"This is mine. I want you to have it." Karom looks at the cover, his eyes wide with surprise.

"You—you wrote this?"

"It's being released this Friday. Read it, and let me know what you think. I suppose it's my form of sealing fate away in a place it can't hurt me."

Karom's eyebrows knit together.

Ammama smiles. "You'll see. I have only two copies, and I will give the other one to Gita before you leave."

"Thank you," he whispers. "I didn't even know you were a writer. Gita didn't mention…" He looks at the book again before slipping it into his backpack. "I'm honored."

Gita appears now around the corner of the living room, wearing rumpled boxer shorts and a tank top. Even in the cloistered morning air, her nipples stand at attention and Karom looks down, embarrassed. She is wearing the neckpiece Ammama has given her and she pulls her hair out from where it is tucked under her camisole strap and braids it to the side.

"What are you guys doing?" She yawns, leaning against the doorway.

"You didn't sleep with that on, did you?" Karom asks.

"Of course not. I just felt like wearing it now," Gita says, twirling one of the fat golden ropes around her finger.

"It's rather special to be wearing around the house," Karom says. "Put it away. It's delicate."

"I'll get breakfast started. You'll have to leave for the airport shortly after your baths," Ammama says, getting up.

"How much do you think this is worth?" Gita asks when Karom is alone with her in the living room.

"I have no idea. But aside from the price of the stones and the gold itself, I'm sure the antique design and the craftsmanship are worth a lot."

"I was thinking about selling it," Gita whispers, her eyes shining in the morning light. "It's gotta be worth hundreds, maybe even a thousand. And then we can go to Argentina over Christmas."

"Are you insane?" Karom nearly shouts. His anger seems to reflect off the walls of the small apartment. He feels his temple pulsing, though in the rest of his body, it feels as if his blood has actually run cold and stopped midcourse in his veins. "Gita, that's your grandmother's wedding necklace. She would never have gifted it to you if she knew you were going to sell it. It has to remain in the family."

"Well, too bad you're not in mine. 'Cause then you could save it."

"What's that supposed to mean?"

"You know what it means." Gita sticks her chin out in a manner that would normally have made Karom tackle her onto the bed and initiate hours of intimacy, had they been in his bedroom back in New York, but now it just provokes him. "Besides, Karom, we can't all hold on to the past like a narcotic. There are things that link us to our dark memories and don't let us move on. This necklace is a prime example. It's tainted."

"Tainted," Karom repeats.

Gita grits her teeth as she leans in, whispering toward him. "Yes, tainted. It's my grandmother's wedding jewelry. The groom fled this ship thirty years ago and treated her like dirt while he *was* here. Yes, let's hold on to this blissful symbol of their awful marriage forever."

Ammama sticks her head in the doorway. "Would you like Indian breakfast today or something light, like toast? Either is perfectly convenient."

"Toast," Karom says, just as Gita says, *"Dosas."*

"One of each," Ammama says, turning back toward the kitchen.

"I don't want to talk about this anymore," Gita says. "I have to finish packing." She takes the necklace off and returns to the room she has been sharing with her grandmother. Karom has already finished packing. He is a meticulous planner and has learned to pack from a flight-attendant friend who showed him how to roll T-shirts and tuck underwear into his shoes. His toiletries are stowed in the plastic compartment at the top of his bag, the tube of toothpaste curled up evenly like a scorpion's tail, ensuring that every inch of space is being utilized. His socks are balled into spheres, and his belts snaked around the perimeter, encasing all his clothes in a tight bundle. The hard shell of his maroon suitcase is streaked with dust, the way it always happens only in India. Dust gets in everywhere, no matter that Karom unzips his bag for only a few hurried minutes each day: in the morning before his bath and in the evening before bed. Dust is caked between the grooved wheels, and he wipes the plastic with a wet towel, where it spreads and nestles into the suitcase's zippered teeth. He can hear Gita's version of packing in the next room: unfolded clothes tossed into her gaping Tumi—unwashed ones stuffed into a plastic Fabindia bag—and her huffs and squats as she clambers on top to zip it. Karom sits down on what has been his bed for the past four nights. He turns his wrist upside down and examines the fine hairs that grow where the white of the underside of his arm meets the tan line that has grown deeper during their vacation. His watch ticks reassuringly away. If they leave within the hour, they will make their flight with no problems.

Karom takes the watch off now, weighing it in the center of his palm. The skin underneath his watch is white and moist and gives off a peppery odor. The spicy scents of coconut and lentils waft down the corridor. He can hear Gita as she pads into the kitchen and muffled conversation as she sets the table. The watchstrap is fraying, but in a charming antique way. He rotates the dial, watching the hands spin freely. He picks up the flat pillow and the three sheets that are folded on his pallet bed, and for an instant, he considers leaving the watch on top of the pile. Instead he slaps it back onto his wrist and pulls it tight through the loopholes before pulling his sleeve to cover the face. Karom fluffs the pillow and places it on top of the pile before picking up his suitcase and rolling it into the hallway.

(

Kamini

~

Kamini has never considered herself religious. Her nieces and lady cousins all behave as though their community spiritual leader were a cult master and they follow him about the country glassy-eyed and full of praise. She has to give the man credit, though; he is learned not only in the heavenly scriptures but is well-read, inhaling everything from *Popular Mechanics* to *New York Times* bestsellers. He recently led a lecture on "How the Ethics of *The Da Vinci Code* Apply to Our Everyday Lives as Hindus." It also doesn't hurt that he is ruggedly handsome, with his scruffy beard and soft eyes. But Kamini has never bought it.

It's not that Kamini is an atheist or even agnostic. She accepts and she believes. Just not the way the rest of the community might prefer. When those buildings were struck at the very point of New York City where the two rivers come together, she lit candles and prayed. When the terrorists attacked all the fancy Bombay hotels where the tourists, the business elite and their mistresses stayed, she did the same. With the tsunami, with her daughter's first pregnancy—and then her second and then third, all bearing the nascent fruit of long, lean girls with thick glossy black hair. When Sachin Tendulkar played the test match in South Africa. And she prayed the night before the United States announced that they had voted in that president they called "Dub-ya" for the *second* time.

It isn't religion. It is ritual. Just as writing has become her religion now in addition to her ritual. Her whole life, she's always felt as though she is on the brink of something. Nothing has felt settled or fulfilled. There has always been a longing, a waiting, desiring. Nothing has felt as though she were fully in the moment, because she has learned that there is nothing she can get comfortable with. Nothing, that is, until she began to write.

Somehow, amid all distractions of raising her daughter in a single-parent household, she'd managed to discover a talent. One that would establish some sort of living for herself and her daughter once it was clear that it would be the two of them from here on out. From the time her daughter, Savita, was born, Kamini had a full stock of stories. She'd heard hundreds over the years, from her aunts and uncles, cousins and family friends. She unearthed the round-robin story hours from her year with her cousins in the small house, where they'd lain in circles passing morsels and beginnings of a story from person to person until a fable was born. She used the foundations of these tales as the source of new ones and changed details so they were unrecognizable from those tales she told with her cousins. The stories served as a source of quiet time for herself and Savita before the door barged open invariably at some witching hour of the morning and Kamini's husband reentered their lives.

At some point, she began writing them down—those she'd created in her youth and those she spun at Savita's bedside behests, and at some point, she sent one harmlessly to a children's magazine. And they sent her back a check. So she sent another. And then suddenly, out of the woodwork, there it was: a living. It wasn't enough to keep herself and Savita in riches but it afforded their basics and allowed them a meal or two out each month.

It was a strange living, one that she couldn't admit to her family or friends, because during this time in their lives, in India it was considered uncouth for a woman—an abandoned woman especially—to go out and look for work. Never mind the strange dichotomy in this; if she didn't earn a living, she and her daughter would starve because no one was offering handouts. Somehow she was just expected to go on with their lives as if her husband, Dev, was still there, bringing in his handsome salary as head of a security unit in Breach Candy. So she wrote. She devised stories of all shapes and forms, testing them out on Savita before she dared to seal the envelope and send them in to the editor. Savita would—true to character—challenge her on several endings.

"Mama, why would the troll so easily give up his control of the land? What does he have to gain from it?"

"Mama, sometimes you write these girls as if they are so stupid. No one would make such empty-headed decisions. Why would Princess Ajanta choose a man with brute strength over a man who can outwit anyone in the kingdom? It just doesn't make sense." At this one, Kamini had bristled. *When had she ever made a decision in her life?* she'd argued. *Everything had been decided for her. From the clothes she wore to the schools she attended to the home she lived in to the man she married.*

"Maybe I am stupid," Kamini had spat back for the first time, "so you'll have to help me guide these girls."

Together they submitted hundreds of stories to children's magazines and housewives' digests, until eventually a magazine editor decided to publish an anthology of her short stories.

Kamini had been jolted into a harsh reality. "You can't print my name on the cover," she'd begged over the phone. "It has to be an alias."

The editor had sighed heavily. "These are your stories, are they not? Come, now, aren't you proud of your work? You've put years into this collection. Stand behind it. You never know what doors it will open for you."

"As long as I am getting a paycheck, that's all that matters to me. Please understand, Mr. Devindra."

And so her collection had been published, with a pale blue hard cover with gold lettering: *Tales of Girls and Animals* by Shanta Nayak. It was most difficult for Kamini, publishing a book on her own and—save Savita—not being able to tell anyone about it. The book became her friends' and family's go-to bedtime bible and she would watch as some of her younger nieces and nephews would tote it about, dog-eared and stained, everywhere they went, hugging it to their chests as they sat meekly on sofas during family visits.

"This Shanta Nayak has really done a number on us all. Now on those long train rides to see my in-laws, the kids just sit and read quietly without chewing my tongue and driving me to pieces. God bless her, truly," Kamini's second cousin said.

"She must be from our community itself," her sister responded. "Nayak is a Konkani name."

"I hadn't even thought of it," the first second cousin said. "She should do a story hour with all the children. They'd love it." For a moment Kamini's blood ran cold. She'd be found out. Luckily, the editor wrote back to her cousins that Shanta Nayak was too busy for public appearances, that she was already hard at work on the sequel. And that was how Kamini was coerced into writing a second book. This time with new stories from the crevices of her mind and without the support of Savita, who was enrolled in college in America and had little time to help her mother concoct fairytales. These stories, however, were a little more biting. They were closer to home. Kamini wrote of a man who drank too much potion and tottered around in the background of the heroine's house uselessly until the girl had to save him from the forest fire that would have otherwise consumed them all. Instead of an evil witch, there was a slave-driving auntie who would whip her young girl workers if they didn't produce enough golden flax from the magic wheat that grew in their mystical fields.

"What are these, Kaminiji?" Pinki Devindra had demanded. "These are too bitter for children. I can't print these."

"They're a bit more…realistic. We can't have our children growing up without realizing the harsh truths of life." The editor had harrumphed on the other end of the line but eventually printed them as they were, and Shanta Nayak's *True Stories of Make Believe* landed on shelves the following month. At first, mothers were shocked at their brusqueness. They didn't buy the books for their children, but *True Stories of Make Believe* became somewhat of a cult classic when children discovered it on their own, smuggling copies into their homes as though it were a trashy magazine with naked pictures of women. They read it under their covers and traded the same raggedy book among their friends. Soon parents had to admit that the stories were honest, though brutal, and began purchasing the book themselves.

Now—Kamini can hardly believe it—she has been living off her profits for the past thirty years. The books are still in high demand, and though she is still in her cramped East Delhi apartment, her books feed, clothe and keep her warm at night. She feeds Mr. Devindra—now Pinki to her—a short story from time to time, whenever she can no longer keep his ceaseless nagging for new work at bay. Savita married a man she met in college. They live in a state called Ohio—a place that Kamini thinks sounds constantly surprised to hear its own name. And though she misses her daughter, Kamini finally lives alone: with her routine, with her stories, with her ritual.

Which is why she is annoyed by Pinki's phone call this morning. He has been hounding her for a few reasons: to purchase a computer, to learn how to use it and to write a third book. He is in his early seventies now but with skin stretched as tight as a young man's and dark gray eyes that sparkle when he coaxes Kamini to write. He visits her from time to time, sometimes to drop off a packet of fan letters, other times a children's magazine he thinks she will enjoy. But today he is calling to alert her that a package is on its way to her house by special courier.

"I'm sending you a laptop computer, Kaminiji. It's one of the ones that folds, so it won't take up any more room than is necessary in your flat. I'm also sending a boy to teach you to use it. It's been fifteen years since *True Stories of Make Believe*. Leave a legacy, Kaminiji. Two books are insufficient. A trilogy is a legacy." Kamini sighs and shifts her weight as she stands hunched over the phone in the kitchen. She is roasting chilies and the smell is starting to suffocate her. She turns toward the stove, pulling the phone cord with her, and applies a few more drops of oil to the pan, where they sizzle, thin wisps of gray smoke rising from the shiny red shards. She will dry these chilies out to make a pickle, allowing them to marinate properly for six months before her granddaughter Gita visits with her boyfriend in May. *Boyfriend,* Kamini muses. What an insipid word. It is so wishy-washy, so noncommittal. She has spoken to Gita about her relationship, and while Kamini agrees that there is no need to rush into anything, the word *boyfriend* makes her grimace.

She steps back and wipes her forehead with the tail of her sari.

"Pinki, my daughter has been out of the house for thirty years, and her children only visit occasionally. I haven't been around children for such a long time. I don't know how they act, interact. I don't know their interests anymore. I've nothing to give."

"Nonsense," Pinki says, puffing on his pipe, a habit he hasn't weaned himself off of even with the recent ever-insistent warnings of cancer. "Okay, you've been languishing. Maybe you're a bit rusty. But practice on the laptop—get your fingers and your mind oiled and the words will pour out of you faster than you know it. This way you can send me stories and I can edit them as they come through. We can have a running dialogue. If you're stuck, we can chat through the computer. It'll be much better this way."

Before she knows it, the doorbell is ringing and her chilies are scalding.

"*Arey,* you sent it *now?* As we were speaking?" Kamini asks, wiping her hands on a dishrag.

"The boy only left an hour ago. He made good timing. Good luck with it. I'm sure you'll be a natural. I'll call you later with details about deadlines, content, etc."

Kamini hangs up the phone and answers the door. A young man stands behind it, clutching a rectangular satchel.

"Hi, auntie," he says. "Parcel from Mr. P. L. Devindra."

"Yes, come in," she says, glancing at the floor.

He removes his shoes dutifully.

"Where would you like it?"

"What about there?" She points to the small round dining table, vacant unless she has company. The boy kneels down and unzips the bag.

"Please sit, auntie," he says. "I'm Raj. I'm to teach you to use this."

"Just a moment." She scurries into the kitchen and puts the chilies onto a flat plate, flicking them with a few drops of vinegar. When she comes back outside, Raj is opening up the laptop like a clamshell, the black keys glittering like glass.

"Wait," she says. "You'll have to go very slowly with me. Step-by-step. How did you do that?"

Raj smiles. "There's a little catch here in the front. You push, slide, and the computer is open. Next, plug it in, like this. And finally, the most important thing—the power button." Raj pushes it, and sound reverberates throughout the sitting room. Kamini jumps back while Raj chuckles. "You'll get used to it. I'm assuming your neighbors have wireless connection, so until we hook yours up, we'll borrow theirs."

"I should take notes."

"There's really no need. It will all come to you. Just watch me and then you do it. I'm to stay here until you get the hang of things."

"I'll put on some tea," Kamini says, and sweeps into the kitchen. "Don't do anything until I return."

It quickly becomes an urban legend: Kamini Auntie, Kamini Amma, Kamini Dadima, has email. She has a Facebook page. She knows how to instant message. Everyone wants to email

her and they do; she can barely keep up with her correspondence. Her nieces and nephews, scattered about the country,
learn about her latest venture and write to her. Gita and her
sisters, Ranja and Maila, email furiously when they learn their
grandmother has learned to type and send emails, but the messages peter off when other things arise or when Kamini sends
them only three-sentence responses to their three-paragraph
notes. She just doesn't have time to respond and she doesn't
want to leave anyone out. Savita prefers calling, as she has every
Sunday morning since she moved to America, but wants to encourage her mother, so she sends a few lines off every now and
then. Kamini is exploring a whole new world, one at the very
reaches of her fingertips. Her typing is getting faster, and she
is getting increasingly curious, though Raj has warned her of
the dangers of chat rooms.

Even her morning routine has been completely altered.
She still awakes, does her ritual and has her tea. But while
the bucket is trickling to the top, she turns on the laptop and
checks her email. Raj has taught her to read the newspaper on-
line, check cricket scores, read book reviews, even find comments and fan websites about her own book. There is no end
to what one can learn. Her bucket usually spills over while she
is engrossed with family letters—she will never learn to call
them emails—and when her bath is over and her hair braided
and pinned back atop her head, she settles back to the round
table and taps away.

On her second week, Pinki rings. "Well, Kaminiji, settling
in? Raj told me you were a natural."

"It's a lot to take in, but it's very exciting. I've learned a
lot already."

"That's wonderful. But my question is—what have you
written other than emails? Any seeds of inspiration? Pearls of

wisdom? Iotas of thought? See, this is why I'm an editor and not a writer."

Kamini chuckles. "I honestly haven't given much thought to the stories. I've been rather distracted."

"Well, I don't expect them to come overnight. Take some time and think them through. Spend time with your family, around young ones. See what sorts of things they are dealing with these days. What if I gave you six months to come up with a new collection? Nine months? One year is the latest I can go, I'm afraid."

"Within the year, Pinki. I promise. I'll come see you in three months with notes and an outline. Okay?"

So Kamini works furiously. She offers to babysit for her frenzied grandnieces and grandnephews, telling her family to drop the children off at her place if they have errands to run or friends to see. She watches them interact with one another and notes how they play with her. She gently pries handheld video games out of their hands and teaches them to play cat's cradle with a piece of string, shows them the simplicity of jacks using backyard stones, introduces them to chess and checkers. She chats with them about what they fear at school or under the bed, what they want more than anything in the world, other than the next electronic game for their handheld console. She reads them stories from her past two volumes and inquires about their favorites. It is the first time she's spent time with small children since Gita, Maila and Ranja grew up, and it is difficult at first to remind herself of how to associate with these smaller creatures, but she falls into it like a rhythm.

After three months she compiles her notes and scratches of observations from her family and types them up. Then she sits at her table, ignoring the siren call of email, and writes two solid stories in preparation for the meeting with Pinki.

She takes a taxi to his office in Friends Colony and sits with him at his desk as he pores over them. At the end of the hour, he sits back, twirling his mustache and gripping his pipe between his teeth.

"I don't know, Kamini. They don't have the same fire, that grit that was so beautifully manifested in your first two. Your connection to these children seems superficial. Perhaps you can look at it from another angle. You need to keep working at it. Get some rest, and start fresh in the morning."

Despondent, she takes the notes from him and climbs back into another taxi. How will she change things? She has access to only her family's children, and if they proved uninspiring, well, then she will have to truly dig into the alcoves of her mind to find a nugget of a story. What is the matter with her? The other two books flowed like rivers, gushing out of her fingertips as her pen scratched across pages and pages. It was only after the collections had been written that she had revisited the words with Savita to make edits.

She steps back into her flat, releases the packet of notes next to her laptop and presses the power button, springing the machine to life. She puts a kettle of tea on and settles down to check her email. One from Gita, more details about her pending visit with Karom, some useless *sirdar* jokes from her nephew and one from an unknown email address. Her hand hovers over the mouse. Raj has also warned her about opening "spam" messages that can send a disease into her computer and erase everything on it, infecting all her hard work. But this email address has her own last name, Pai, so she inhales shortly and clicks on it.

Dear Kamini,
I heard that you learned how to use a computer, that you have

one at home. That is a great feat, especially at your age. My-self, I am dictating this letter to a young boy at the internet café for the cost of a beer. I wasn't sure what I was going to say to you. My first notion was that any letter to you should be filled with apologies. A complete page of apologies. But pages don't quite exist in email, so I am trying another route.

Forty-six years ago, I walked out our door. I don't know whether you keep track of this, but I do with each passing day. I am not proud of having left you, but it's also something I had to do at the time. I can get into why I did it but I want some sign from you that this is okay: Is it all right to contact you now or would you rather I stayed away? I know that you have done well for yourself; I find out bits and pieces from the guards at the gate. As you know, they work through Securicom, just as I did. We don't email, however. I call them every few months. But you are legendary with your computer skills. Your email address was easy to obtain; everyone has been talking about you. I'm very impressed with you, Kamini. I've always been im-pressed with you. It's partly why I left. But I refuse to depose the blame onto you, nor do I want to venture into those are-nas just yet. It's been forty-six years and I am an old man, as I can imagine you are an old woman, as well.

I have trouble picturing you as an old woman. It's not easy for me to fast-forward the image of you I have in my mind and lighten your raven hair or sag your skin with wrinkles. I am sure you have all your teeth, as you were fastidious about brushing each and every morning and night. I imagine you have a silver sheath of hair that you continue to braid and pin atop your head after your bath. I feel these are things that I know inherently, but the things that I don't know have been aching me. One thing I want you to know from the start: I am not dying. I haven't written this to you in an attempt to guilt you into responding to me. I am as healthy as I will ever be without disease in my body. So you can decide to respond to me of your own accord. But the curiosity is killing me.

I wonder if we have grandchildren, and where our daughter is. I wonder if you have traveled outside the perimeter of our country. Have you ever been on a plane? I wonder if you have entertained the thought of remarriage, though the guards tell me that you still live alone. And at the same time, I realize that I don't have the rights to wonder these things, because I chose to abandon them so long ago. I don't wish to reenter your life again, because I am positive that you have made a new start, and a great one, at that. I am sure that you have provided for Savita and made a home for yourself. This doesn't pardon what I did, and please try to believe me, I have spent many years trying to correct it in my head. But I can't correct it in life, nor can I erase it from memory. It happened and I have spent a great many years hoping that I can one day make it up to you. The fact remains that we don't have many days left. I'm not writing to be morbid or, again, to guilt you into responding to me. God knows that you are your own person, a strong-willed person who has made her own life. No one is going to tell you what to do now, and certainly not me, your heel of a husband who comes slinking back with his tail between his legs decades later, wanting to know what became of the life he left behind.

Here are some things about me since I left.

1. I went to college, so we are intellectual equals now. Unless, of course, you have taken another degree.

2. I live in Bangalore, where you would think I would have

learned computers ages ago, but as you know, I was always a bit of a dullard.

3. I live alone and have never remarried and had no other children.

4. I've given up drinking. I've been sober for thirty-seven years.

5. I've given up women. I am not an ascetic and don't isolate myself from society, but I don't see women anymore. I don't run about with different girls and make a spectacle of myself.

6. The impetus behind numbers four and five was your story "The Invisible Husband."

I know that you are Shanta Nayak. I knew it the moment I read the first few chapters and stories in *True Stories of Make Believe.* I kept seeing people engrossed in the book on the bus and clutching it as they walked down the street. The cover looked like a children's book, but adults were devouring it. So I went to a bookshop, sank down in a corner and read it from cover to cover. I knew it was you. The characters and style were unmistakable. It was me, and you, and Savita and my family and your family. The stories were so honest. The book was a mirror with my face reflecting back. The shopkeepers had long before given up on shooing me out, but the moment I finished the book, I went back to the small room I was renting at the time and looked at myself in the glass. I was despicable. I couldn't stand myself. And it only took some serious anger issues, an alcohol problem, womanizing, an abandoned marriage leaving behind a wife and a daughter, and a book of fairytales that illustrated our lives to show me that. But I made a change.

I want you to know that I am not telling you this because I want a piece of your success. You have worked for it and earned it. I want no part in it.

You know, for some time, I holidayed each summer, alternating between Goa and Kovalam with the same pack of useless friends who I'd see once a year when they would leave their wives for some fun. I didn't enjoy their company as much after I read your books. I didn't even enjoy my own company, for that matter.

But, for what it's worth at this point in our lives, I do want to say this: I am sorry. I feel those are futile words, but I need to say them. I am sorry. And if you'll let me hear all that I have missed over the years, I will say them again and again, each time we correspond. I will wait as long as I have to, or as long as I physically can, for your response and your blessing to learn all that has passed me by over the years.

If you have reached this stage of the letter, thank you. Thank you for listening to me. You don't owe me anything. But thank you for hearing me out and considering my plea.

Yours,

Dev

Kamini sits back and breathes for what feels like the first time since she began scrolling through the letter. She thinks about herself—getting old, as he said in his letter. She isn't sure it has happened. That is the thing about growing old with someone; they remain as a mirror for your own eyes. You can watch as their hair grows curly and wispy with loss of strength, then slowly metamorphoses to paper-thin and charcoal, stark white, sometimes even a dull, tepid brown not unlike leaves in

Northeast America, from where Savita sent her pictures from the family trip driving up the coast in the autumn. This phenomenon doesn't happen in India; the changing of the guard from lush to stark, from green to brown, from leaves to mulch. You can watch the slight smile wrinkles when they curve and peek out in the corners of eyes; at the time they are considered charming because you are considered young then. But you can watch as they pave the way for deeper grooves, etched into the face you know so well. You can watch as those grooves eventually take over to redefine the person you've known for so long without them.

You can feel the coconut-soft of someone else's skin, measure it against your own and realize that there is a richness, a fattiness within the epidermis that continuously churns out that buttery-leather feeling, unlike when you age, and the same finger that you use to check yourself is already leathery without the butter, so you can't quite differentiate what has changed and when. You can watch in that mirror as someone goes from tall, proud, confident, upright, the angles somehow shifting, like the plates beneath the earth during a quake, ever so subtly forward to humbled, tired, shoulders sagging and stooped. You can watch the bright white squares of teeth in a mouth that smile, bite, laugh, brush, before they yellow, shrink and become brittle like the former husks of themselves. And there is never a question if or when or how these things happen to you, because you see them happening right there across from you at the dining table, lying parallel to you in bed, brushing their teeth with the same movements as yours, mimicking your every move. If they are happening in that body across the way, they are happening within you. But a looking glass doesn't act as quite the same mirror; she hasn't watched these changes gradually, over time, so has she aged? She can't tell.

Twice. He has used the word *sorry* twice. This is a foreign word to Kamini, just like *please* and *thank you*. In Konkani, her familial language, these words don't exist. Gita had brought this up to Kamini when Kamini had pressed her and her sisters to try to speak it more often, lest it die out with Savita. As it is, Savita has only taught them nominal Konkani, the kind that young children want to hear in order to gossip about others in front of their faces or insult Americans without their knowledge.

"Why don't we have words for *please, thank you,* for *sorry?*" Gita had asked. "Is Konkani so impolite that we can't offer these soft words of solace?"

Kamini had clucked at her. "On the contrary, Konkani is so polite and spoken so sweetly that you never have need for these words. These are English ideals—harsh, unbecoming. So what? You insult someone with rotten words and with the same breath tell them that you are sorry? No. You ask for something nicely, so it doesn't necessitate having to use *please.* You take it from them the same way, with a smile, gently, so *thank you* becomes obsolete, too. And you don't hurt someone intentionally or insult someone intentionally or cross someone intentionally, so that your American idea becomes in our language 'my mistake'—never something we have done that we regret."

So where has Dev picked up this foreign idea of *sorry?* Has he watched American television shows where husbands and wives defy one another to do things they shouldn't and then with three minutes remaining to the episode murmur an unfeeling *sorry,* hug one another and then roll the credits? These *sorrys;* whether his boy has typed out one, two or forty, they will never penetrate into Kamini's conscience.

And the defiance of him—telling her who she was. He has no right. He has no idea who she is. He has never known who she is, and besides, if he'd had an inkling, he'd lost that privilege the moment he'd stepped out the door for the last time. Her stomach churns with these things—aging, *sorry,* his arrogant outing of her through a long-overdue email.

Suddenly, she starts as though she hears his boots in the hallway once again. She flinches as though he has raised his hand to upset the lamps and deities for her morning ritual. She can hear his rustling in the bathroom as he prepares himself for his bath, the gentle scuffing of the shaving-cream brush against his stubble, the dull scraping of the razor against his skin. She can hear the wardrobe door slamming open as he sorts through his clothes and selects a fresh shirt to wear with his uniform.

The kettle has been screaming on the stove for the past ten minutes, but she hasn't heard it. Dev's words wash over her again and again. Steam puffs out of the spout of the kettle in the kitchen, scalding water spilling over onto the stove, but Kamini doesn't shut it off. She stands up, slams the laptop shut, hurries into the bathroom and retches into the toilet.

Three days later she still doesn't feel back to normal. She has eaten toast and drunk countless cups of sugary tea, but she hasn't reopened her laptop or thought through the stories she owes Pinki. She watches mindless serials on the television, the dramatic music soaring around her, capturing her in melodrama. She focuses on fake problems, other people's lives, only changing the channel when a story line threatens to mimic her own. The writers of these serials are either the stupidest people on earth or the smartest, because they create such insipid, flimsy plots that leave you with a cliff-hanger that any intelligent person can decode before the next day's episode, but somehow you turn the television on anyway just to ensure that your hunch is right. And these actresses! They must hire only those women with the largest eyes for full dramatic effect whenever they are shocked or shamed or cuckolded. Kamini imagines the auditions, where they measure the circumference of pupils rather than dramatic talent.

She has abandoned her notes and the thoughts from the meeting with Pinki, wanting to approach the assignment with a fresh mind and new approach. It is unlike her not to respond to an email, as she has done for years to letters on ancient blue aerogram paper, so thin her pen would pierce it numerous times during her vigorous scratching to her granddaughters or a cousin abroad. Even if she is busy, she will at least begin her response within a few days. Raj has explained a little about email etiquette to her. He has told her about junk email and spam; he has shown her how to block someone's email address if they become a nuisance and he has shown her how to report someone sending impertinent messages. She isn't sure what she is going to do, considers whether her silence is a message enough, but on the fourth day, she opens her clam-shell and types: ...

The response is almost immediate. She should have held out.

Dear Kamini,
Thank you, thank you thank you thank you. This was a great sign from you, though any response would have been welcomed. Truth be told, I'm not entirely sure what it means. If you have found it in your heart not to reject me completely— even if that's the extent of it—I am grateful. The same boy is

typing my note to you, free of charge. He says that this is a great exchange, a great love story, and he wants to see how it will turn out. I told him not to hold his breath, but as you know, at our age, every rupee counts, so I haven't turned him down.

I can tell you more about myself, as that's how I interpret your ellipsis. It's absolutely fair that I show my hand before you consider telling me anything. I will go back nearly half a century to when we were still technically living under the same roof, though I was rarely home and would sleep most of the time that I was there. You prepared meals lovingly, and though we were never friends, we threaded together some loose seams of courtesy and acceptance within one another. You realized that my job kept me out all night, caring for office buildings that I could never work in, and you raised our daughter, silently and without fuss. I realize what a step down for you our marriage was. You were college educated. You could have had your choice of men, of paths, of professions. You could have been a self-made woman. My father told me your scores from university were flawless. I was impressed but also extremely humbled and scared.

My parents, my mother especially, had always impressed the importance of studies on me. It's not a revelation; I think you must have received the same from your aunts and uncles. One could never achieve their passion in life without the grades necessary to prove oneself. Praying, in my household, was part and parcel of receiving these good grades. Saraswati would smile down on me if I beseeched her before a final exam. I should bow my head in quiet contemplation before I sat down to my books. But what I failed to mention was that I was useless. I could study my whole life and it just wouldn't stick. I had tutorials, extra classes.

I wasn't built to excel on these exams. So I would invest all my attentions into prayer and of course that would never work because I hadn't put in the work required to help me learn in the first place. Nothing would come of it. Prayer became useless to me because I would pray nonstop and receive nothing in the end as benefit. So I turned my loathing from studies to prayer because it was an easier thing to hate; it was a less caustic and obvious thing to hate. You couldn't hate studies; if you hated studies and learning, it meant that you were an imbecile. If you hated prayer, you were simply a nonbeliever.

At first, I thought marrying an intelligent woman would somehow bring me up in status, but among my other doltish friends, it just lowered me in their eyes. I was the peabrain, the brute, the workhorse. You were the quietly strong woman who had been through it all—a multitude of homes, ever-changing fathers and mothers—and now you had a degree and a know-how that I would never obtain. Not to mention that you appeared street-smart on top of your scripted education. That's not why I drank. Or why I chased women—at the time believing that you were none the wiser. How could I have imagined that you wouldn't know, when my uniform would come home stinking of perfume and you were the one who did the washing, scrubbing away the evidence of lipstick and whiskey stains as though it had never occurred?

No, I take full responsibility for my actions, and my actions were wrong. I shouldn't have done that to you, Kamini, or rather, I shouldn't have married you when I knew what a wrong union it would be. I knew how desperate you were to make your own home and to start a new life away from the constantly rotating merry-go-round of your youth, tripping from one threshold to another just as one family tired of you. I knew you didn't want to become someone's charity case, so perhaps that's why you cooked and cleaned and played dumb as you did for the ten years we were married. However, having just dictated that, I don't know. Are we still married? I never put in for a divorce and my guards at the gate don't know the particulars of your life now.

Kamini stops reading. She closes the window that looks into her past with Dev and sits back in her chair. She hits the power button and the computer hums to sleep. She reaches for the notebook where she has carefully taken Pinki's notes and begins to scribble.

The first story trickles out of her at first, the words edging their way hesitantly, but gradually, they gather speed, and before she knows it, she has sheets and sheets in front of her in her tiny curly handwriting. She can never type as fast as the words appear from her brain, and the insistence with which the story tumbles forward seems no match for her computer skills. She laughs at times at her foolishness and then pities herself for her oversight. Eventually, though, once the whole thing is down on paper, she is angry.

Kamini doesn't get angry. Her family has always teased her for being levelheaded and neutral, for taking everything in stride, for accepting the world and its people as they are. But the fact is that growing up, Kamini couldn't afford to be angry. She couldn't risk a temper or a tantrum when something didn't go her way, because she was on someone else's turf, and the moment she irked them or reminded them that she really didn't have to be there, she'd be packing her few possessions and on her way to the next aunt's, uncle's or family friend's home. So even when her cousin trampled across her only school uniform with his baby feet, leaving a trail of soggy, muddy footprints across the collar, she swallowed her fury and washed it quietly in the courtyard. When her uncle jolted home thunderously drunk on the eve of her university admittance exams, she lay still and allowed him to sing loudly in the living room where she slept—even clapped for an encore when he indignantly demanded one. She didn't speak up—though her temper was flaring—to accuse him of sabotaging her chances at stepping off the roulette wheel that had become her life. In their youth, cousins and nieces and nephews had taken advantage of her, taking the ice cream bestowed to her because they knew she wouldn't yowl, leaving her with the ratty ribbon for her hair, running ahead to the school gate so she would have to dodge traffic on her own. Kamini's temper was like an eclipse: rare and always obscured by her fear of dismissal.

But she is furious now. She sets her pen down, her hands shaking at the thought. How can she still be married? Just as there are common-law marriages, aren't there common-law separations when a spouse has been absent for 75 percent of the union? She will have to look it up on Google. She wants to call someone, a cousin, a friend, to have someone reassure her and tell her that it will all be okay. But she feels shaken, unnerved. What rights does Dev still have over her? Is he justified in returning to the house—his house, really—and resuming his life from where he'd left it? Is he entitled to her royalties? To the profits from the new book that is taking shape? Is he to be granted access to her daughter and her children? Can he just pick up the relationships she has maintained with her family, with his family, even? She can feel her heart flexing rapidly against the thin skin of her chest.

All the plates are stacked on the shelf above the sink, the cups and glasses in their place. She opens the cabinet and holds a plate under her chin.

"I'm throwing a tantrum," she announces, and dashes the plate against the stone floor. It splinters into bits and she jumps at the noise. She looks down at the wreckage below her feet and picks up another plate. She shuts her eyes before she drops this one and it too crunches to the ground, a few pieces of porcelain bouncing about the room from the force. She throws five plates altogether before she stalks into her bedroom and swings open the wardrobe doors adjacent to hers. The dust cloud that springs out of the closet like a dormant genie makes her cough, but she lets it settle and grabs at the playing cards, the sweaters, the Pathani suits, the undershirts, the trousers. She stuffs them into plastic bags and knots them at the top. Each piece of clothing, each shot glass, reminds her of an outing or a wedding or a memory of Dev, and she continues packing it all away until there is nothing left but the one pale blue sweater he'd been wearing when he had first gifted her with her very own copy of *Great Expectations*. This one she shoves to a back shelf and closes the doors to the closet once again. All the bags, bursting with her husband's dregs, are placed outside her door, where the rag picker will collect them the following day. She summons the broom from the corner of the kitchen and sweeps the dish shards into a pile. Then she wipes her hands on a dishcloth, swipes the hair away from her face and settles down at the table to write.

Dev's reintroduction into her life turns out to be the antidote to her writer's block. Whether it is from anger or passion that she begins her third collection of stories, neither Pinki nor she can say. But the emotion, the rawness, the grit that had been lacking previously are all very present in the next draft that she presents to her editor three months later. Pinki sits back in his seat, puffing away at his pipe as the Delhi traffic swirls beneath them. The tea his secretary has brought Kamini is cold, and she perches at the edge of her seat, watching the changing nerves of his face as they tense and smile, relax and release.

Her new collection is just over three hundred pages, and they are filled with a new spirit: anger. These characters seek redemption and revenge; they are spiteful and boastful and cranky, but just enough so that readers won't be exasperated. She has a winning piece. This is what he tells her before he stands up from his chair, comes around his desk and shakes her hand with both of his.

"These are different, Kaminiji," he says. "They're unlike the stories in the first two books. They're for a more mature audience, I think. But I like them very much. I think we'll market this one to the scores of children that grew up with Shanta Nayak who may now have children of their own. This one will be the nostalgia edition. I'll get this into editing as soon as possible. I want to fast-track this one."

"You'd better do that, Pinki. I'm eighty-two, after all."

At home Kamini is greeted with an email from Gita.

Ammama, I am so excited! We leave tonight. Karom is over the moon, but he's nervous about returning to India after such a long time. Please don't mention any of what I've told you to him. You have always been such a good listener and I want you to understand him. I think you'll both really get along. So we depart first for Bombay and then on to Rajasthan before we come to you in Delhi. It's going to be so romantic. Send me a message ASAP if you want anything else from here. Hugs and kisses, Gita.

Kamini writes Gita back hurriedly to have a safe trip, that she doesn't want anything other than the few novels she has requested and that she is looking forward to meeting Karom. Then she opens a new email from Dev.

Kamini,
The boy has finished his business in Bangalore, so I am typing this myself very slowly. I haven't heard any news from your end, but I continue to write. I'm not sure what else to tell you. But I don't want to sit here and stew in my past and feel sorry for myself. I've done enough of that, as I'm sure you have. We've both moved forward and I just want a few nuggets from the life I left behind in order to continue. I could never take it upon myself to write you a letter, but email is a whole other thing. When I send this, I'm not sure where it goes, in the millions of pieces over my head across state lines to you. It's intangible to me, so it's as if I haven't written it. Your few responses in the form of punctuation have coaxed me to continue writing. But I'm not sure if I'm wasting my time and yours. I'm not sure what feathers I've ruffled over there. I won't continue until you tell me to, in so many words. As it is, this is taking me so long to write. Please give me some insight, something, anything to hold on to.
Yours,
Dev

That morning, she had rushed through her ritual, omitting lighting the tiny lamps that accompany her shrine. Her shrine has grown, evolved, since Dev's departure. When Gita had finished college, she and her two sisters had all back-packed through South India together, stopping in temples to collect tiny idols of Ganesh, Shiva and Lakshmi sculpted from stone, wood, shell and glass. Gita had brought them all back to Kamini, wrapped lovingly in T-shirts and tissues that she'd collected from restaurants and bathrooms. Kamini had given each one a home on her multitiered shrine. The shrine had new meaning now that her granddaughter had blessed it, fresh with new hope.

Now she shuffles into her bedroom and settles onto the low stool that has replaced her having to sink to the ground amid screaming joints. She strikes two matches before the third one allows her to light all seven of the lamps. The dais glitters with light and catches the shine of five small Ganesh figurines she has been given over the years, all from the local temple. She catches sight of herself in one of the glass frames. A shallow image of her spectacles peers back at her. Her jaw is set and she pushes a lock of hair away from her face.

He wants something to hold on to. She will act.

Back at her computer, she writes.

Dev—
Savita lives in Ohio with her husband, Haakon, who is a very good man. He is Norwegian. He has pale skin and pale hair and very light eyes. They met in college in America. Savita is beautiful. She has your build.

She and Haakon have three daughers: Gita, Ranja and Maila. They live in New York, Chicago and Ohio.

Savita is the head of a publishing company in Columbus. Her husband is a patent lawyer.

Gita is twenty-eight. She has her own interior design company.

Ranja is twenty-six. She works in politics.

Maila is twenty-four, still in university. She is studying to be a veterinarian.

-I have lived here since you left. I am single. I never remarried. I have no callers or admirers. I live alone.

-I have written two books. I am Shanta Nayak. I don't know what you wish to do with this information, but I can assure you that nothing you do to me now can hurt me. I've hidden behind that name for years now, seeking solace in a pseudonym that couldn't hurt me and my daughter, gaining income from words that no one else knew I had written. The dichotomy that I wasn't supposed to go off and be a self-made woman, yet I was still supposed to provide for the two of us—it angers me. It angers me that I have hidden behind it for all these years. When your letters came, they startled me; they forced me to question a number of things in myself that I hadn't ever questioned before. Your correspondence has done nothing but create an empty haunting in my life that with the close of this mail to you I hope to banish forever. I'm in a safe place now. I have been for years.

-You were right about one thing in your correspondence: I always felt beholden to someone—my aunts and uncles, family friends, your father for seeking me out, you for taking me in. But I'm free of this now. I don't owe anyone anything, and it's now for the first time in my life that I feel right saying this.

-I owe you nothing. I've already given you something, but I will give you nothing more. I forgave you a long, long time ago.

-Having said that, to some extent, I appreciate the gesture, of knowing that you are still alive and out there. I can't commit to more than this at this point in my life, but I know it couldn't have been easy to reach out, to write, to say sorry. I accept it. That's all I wish to say.

-I hope I have answered all of your questions. Take care of yourself and stay in good health. Please don't write to me again.

Kamini

P.S. I still pray.

P.P.S. I have ridden in a plane. Six times.

She sends the email, and before she allows herself to think about anything else, she opens a new message and composes.

After a few days of anxiously checking her email, Kamini is sure that her exorcism has worked. True to form, Dev disappears from her life for a second time. At first, Kamini is jarred. What has she done? He comes crawling back to her, and she shuns him. She is sure her friends would have scolded her for this, but they will never find out. She won't tell Savita about the email exchanges between them. Savita will be furious and demand his coordinates so that she can reconnect after all these years and give him a piece of her mind. But eventually Savita will soften; Kamini knows her daughter. Savita will imagine her father as a withered shell of the hulk he used to be when he banged about the house or brushed his teeth violently in the washroom. She will feel sorry for him in his old age, saddened that he has no family or ties to his past life. She will give in; she will cave. Kamini can't take that chance, so Dev's emails stay trapped in her computer.

Kamini busies herself with Gita's visit. She visits the shop and buys coffee. Americans drink coffee. She buys whole biscuits, not the broken ones at the bottom of the bin that

Shankar sells for half price. She has the floors cleaned and the sheets that have sat idle in the cupboards for years washed. She checks on her chili pickle, inhaling the pungent fumes that curl out from the jar. It will be at its peak in three days' time, when Gita and Karom arrive. She is tidying the table that has become her work space, with papers and pens and nubs of pencils cluttering the space around her laptop, when the doorbell rings.

Raj stands on the other side, grinning widely.

"Hi, auntie," he says. "You're a legend. You've done me proud with your computer skills. You're quite famous in the office."

"Is that right?"

"No one can believe that I've taught someone of your age how to email and use a computer. I mean—" He looks down, embarrassed.

"I know what you mean." Kamini chuckles, patting his hand. "Come, come, come inside. To what do I owe this visit?"

"I can't stay. I'm just to deliver this." He thrusts a package wrapped in brown paper forward.

"What is it?"

"Something you should open on your own. I've got to run. We'll chat on IM? It's been a while."

"My granddaughter is coming with her boyfriend."

"Ah, you've got your hands full. Okay, I'm off."

"Bye, child."

Kamini closes the door and sits down at her desk. The brown paper has been folded around the contents with twine. It reminds her of that first meeting with Dev, the paper-wrapped book, the string, *Great Expectations*. She removes the string in front of her, smoothing the paper against the table.

There is a book inside this package, too. She removes it from its wrapping and lets the paper fall to the floor. She picks up the book and caresses the cover. It is shiny and pristine, reflecting against the sun that glints into the sitting room. She opens the cover, and the crisp pages creak with newness. She puts her nose against the inner spine and inhales the fresh, inky scent. She flips the pages. It is there—the table of contents, all twenty-eight stories, the dedication page to Savita and Gita and Maila and Ranja, the About the Author page and on the back page, within the fold of the dust jacket, a grainy picture of herself that she has taken with the camera built into her laptop. She is old. She can finally see it with her own eyes, through her thick owl-like glasses, without a partner to mirror how she has aged. Wisps of gray hair have escaped her bun and halo around her head. Her skin is abrasive, like used sandpaper. Rivers of wrinkles run from her laughing eyes. Her chin dips below itself to produce its twin. But this is her face.

And this is her book. No one can take this away from her and no one can expose her now. She closes the cover and looks down on it once again, running her gnarled rootlike fingers over the raised black letters that seem to tower above the rest of the world.

Fairytales of Freedom. By Kamini Pai.

Lloyd

~

Lloyd has an affliction. He isn't sure what to call it, really, other than a terrible way to live. At inopportune moments, he imagines the worst. When he flies, he imagines the plane crashing to the ground, splintering into indecipherable bits. When he took an overnight train from Paris to Amsterdam while visiting his parents stationed abroad, he imagined the metal bars that held his bed suspended above the bottom bunk caving and crushing his cabinmate in his sleep. Sometimes when he watches his father talk, he envisions him gripping his heart and a numb but distinct pain radiating down his left arm. He can remember the first time he had it. He was twelve, on a bus, somewhere in Baltimore. He was sitting in the solitary seat that comes after a row of two seaters and there was a little black girl seated in front of him who wouldn't stop staring. He tried different tactics: eyes boring a hole into the pages of his book, pretending to sleep and then finally staring back at her unblinkingly, but she was unrelenting. He imagined the bus stopping short and her flying through the side window, glass shattering in slow motion, and the little body crunching to a halt in a tiny heap on the sidewalk.

When he was little, his eyebrows constantly scrunched together, as if he was worried all the time. His parents called him Chicken Little as he walked around clutching his stuffed animals tightly to his chest. They weren't sure where the worry came from. He too isn't sure why he imagines these scenarios. Suffice to say he's never suffered from any form of PTSD and he had a solid, strong childhood with parents and an older sister who never teased him in front of her friends in order to appear superior. The moment these visions pop into his head, he spends every conscious moment fighting and trying to rid himself of them. He thinks of the mundane—his statistics final, sewing buttons on his overcoat, devil's food cake.

Lloyd knows that Karom is haunted, too. They roomed together for four years of college, looking out for one another when one of them was stressed or anxious, bringing the other a boxed meal from the dining hall when the other had class that cut through dinner or lunch. They worked and got along, never divulging secrets to one another in an attempt to bond, but Karom and Lloyd knew enough about one another, probably more than anyone else whom either of them would call a friend did. For example, Lloyd knew that in their senior year of college, Karom began to cry out in the middle of the night, panting and bathed in sweat. Often it was garbled in another language, but one night during their last year of school when finals were over and everyone was counting down the dog days until graduation, Karom thrashed about violently in his bed just before dawn. He cried out, a single wail. It was the saddest sound Lloyd had ever heard, and he sat up, grappling with the bedsheets and groping for his glasses.

He'd become accustomed to Karom's nighttime struggles, but he'd never intervened. "Hold me, hold me, hold me," Karom cried. He had never spoken before, at least never in English. Karom continued to buck wildly in the bed, the sheets twisted about his lean frame. Lloyd crept over to him, afraid Karom would strike his arm against the wall and hurt himself in his sleep. Thick thatches of hair were plastered to his forehead and Lloyd reached out and moved one away from one eye. Karom continued his fit, now starting to weep with his words. "Hold me, please. I'm disappearing. Don't let me go."

Lloyd pulled the sheet back and carefully climbed in next to his roommate. Karom was glistening with sweat, yet his skin was icy to the touch. Lloyd put his arms around him and held him fiercely against his own body. Karom couldn't thrash about anymore, but he shuddered like a wet fish out of water, moving against Lloyd's body, whimpering softly and unintelligibly. Lloyd was as close to Karom as he'd ever been, the threadbare white shirt Karom wore to bed transparent and molded to his chest, slick with sweat. Karom sniffed a bit and burrowed his face into the warmth of Lloyd's neck. Within moments, he fell back into a deep sleep, his breath creating soft puffs of condensation against Lloyd's collarbone. Lloyd stayed there holding him tightly, and when the muscles of his arms began to ache, he loosened his grip on his roommate, slid his arms back from under Karom's body and lay silently next to him for what seemed like hours before slipping out from the bed.

It happened again and again, over the course of the reading period, into the last week when clothes and books and bicycles were packed up and dismantled for the long drives or flights home. In fact, it happened eight more times after the first one, Lloyd understanding better how to handle Karom so that he wouldn't thrash about and mistakenly cut his tongue on his teeth.

The two had never spoken of the incident; Lloyd didn't even know if Karom had been aware of what was happening. But it stirred something in Lloyd. He understood slowly what it meant to take care of someone and then to care for someone and then, before he could understand what was happening to his own body during these episodes, to crave that moist touch and the unwashed smell of Karom's sweat emanating from the sheets like a fog. Each night as they fell into their own beds, exhausted by graduation parties and awards ceremonies and packing, Lloyd found himself praying that Karom would once again need the solidity of Lloyd's body against him, his arms anchoring his chest, Lloyd's legs entwined around Karom's to prohibit the sudden jerking movements that racked his body. Now, just as much as Karom's subconscious, panic-stricken body craved Lloyd's protection, Lloyd felt himself awakening even before Karom to wait out those last few minutes before he knew the tremors would begin. And so he was by his bed, before Karom could even beseech him in the throes of his nightmare, to secure him, help him, hold him.

After graduation Lloyd hadn't allowed himself to think of those mornings. But it was like that age-old psychology experiment. *Don't think about elephants. So of course, what else are you thinking about? Elephants.* It popped into his head, much like the other pessimistic random hauntings he found entangled in his brain. But now that he is getting married—in a matter of days—to a wonderful girl who will eventually erase all of this from his mind, it doesn't matter anymore. He won't remember the sweet smell of Karom's sweat and the way his brow furrowed and then softened at Lloyd's touch. He won't have random violent thoughts amid serene moments. He won't suddenly be jerked headfirst through a taxi windshield during a routine ride to work. And he certainly won't be pulled under the river from a sudden surge of a heavy current, his fishing line entangled beneath a boulder. Lloyd reels his line in and stares at the hook dangling on the end. The bait is gone—again. He is no fisherman. What is he trying to prove? He certainly isn't fooling Malina. She'd perched on his desk watching him pack for this trip, not saying a word until he zipped up his duffel bag and leaned over to kiss her goodbye. She'd leaned backward, putting a book between their lips.

"I want you to read this on the flight. No arguments." Lloyd peered at the cover.

"*Digging Your Own Toilet: Survival Tactics for Cosmopolitan Men.* Come on, Malina."

"If you insist on going alone, then at least read up on how not to get yourself killed by a bear. I'm serious, Lloyd. I'm terrified of you going off by yourself like this."

"I'll be fine, Mal. They wouldn't let people camp out there if it wasn't safe."

"Well, I think they assume that those people have some notion of what to do if you twist your ankle during a lightning storm."

"I was in Scouts, remember? I can tie a tourniquet with the best of them. And in a lightning storm, you just stay away from the trees. Piece of cake." But he stuffed the book into his bag and leaned back in for his kiss. He knew Malina found it strange that he was going on his bachelor weekend alone. He has friends, or at least, he has people that he watches football with and drinks with and is sent Christmas cards with fat, ugly babies from. But he'd explained it to her time and again: this was the last time that he would ever be alone. "And thank goodness for that, baby, thank goodness. But there is some beauty in spending some QT getting to know myself, isn't there? Because if I'm not at peace with myself, if I don't know myself inside and out, how can I love you better?"

He ties a fly onto the hook and casts it out once again. The river gurgles gently at his toes, his socks strewn on the rock beside him, sodden with the warm mud and silt of the riverbank. Every so often a sickly sweet odor like the rotting leaves of ginkgo wafts through the breeze. Even at this early hour of the morning, the sun sparkles across the moving waters like thousands of untouchable jewels. In the middle of the river three large rocks jut out of the water, a few small roots and branches reaching out of them. On his first day Lloyd had tried to wade over to those rocks, sure that fishing from the center of the river would yield far more than from the banks. But the current had caught him by the ankles, so strong that it trapped his soles in the pebbled soil just inches into the river, and he'd hobbled, defeated, back to the shore.

This, he thinks, is what it means to be a man. Out in the open, with the fresh air and the trees and earth beneath your ass and dirt caked beneath your fingernails. It means dignity, building a fire and roasting what you catch. It means mosquito bites and sunburn and poison oak and skin rash. Well, okay, it only means all those things because in the past three days, he has acquired all of them. But that's all right. Because he is feeling them through and through. The way his skin itches so hard but he refuses to touch it. The way his face is aflame each morning before he soothes it with a thick layer of aloe.

When he'd first arrived, Lloyd had pitched his tent on the outskirts of the Upper Pine campground, taking care not to interfere with the families and hippies who had set up camp within the demarcated ropes. His eyes had been drowsy from the early flight, but he'd skimmed a yellow sign nailed on a tree trunk to stay within the allocated portion of the campsite, at *your own risk.* He hadn't read the rest of it, but he had read Malina's handbook on the flight; now he could steer clear of bears and raccoons and unwanted creatures. He could smell packaged hot dogs and s'mores but he had headed straight down to the riverbank to catch breakfast.

On this third morning, he has grown hungry and tired of fish. He has been throwing his catch onto a small grill fashioned out of an old waffle maker. He has eaten a single brown trout for the past two days, the only fish currently appropriated for camper consumption. But there is no way he will allow himself to approach the general stores that feed the steady stream of amateur campers with Pop-Tarts and hot cocoa. This is *camping,* he'd scoffed, watching them exit the stores with their arms full of unnecessary snacks. When you got tired of eating fish, well, then you learned to hunt something else. Rabbit, maybe, or the fat brown squirrels that scamper around his campsite. However, one thing nature doesn't provide is beer, and so begrudgingly, he enters the store and goes straight to the fridge section to remove two six-packs of pale brown ale. As he approaches the counter, a man wearing a red lumberjack shirt smirks at him.

"I thought you'd give in," he says.

"Excuse me?" Lloyd sets the beer on the counter and fumbles with his wallet.

"You're the only one at this campsite who hasn't been in here yet."

"Oh, well. Beer. You know. How much do I owe you?"

"Even ten." As Lloyd passes him the bill, the man catches his eye.

"Learning to hunt and gather?"

"Something like that." Lloyd swings his beer over the counter. "It's my bachelor party."

"No kidding. I didn't think you were here with buddies."

"I'm not. It's a solo thing."

"Never heard of that. Well, have fun. Watch out for bears." The man winks at Lloyd and moves to help the next customer.

The night is chilly, though it is June, and Lloyd zips up the mouth to his tent. He settles deeply into his sleeping bag wearing two pairs of socks on his feet and another on his hands. He nestles his head carefully on his bag of soiled clothes and allows his mind to wander. His wedding is in two weeks. Malina's family will arrive in one. His parents will arrive from their current posting in Prague, and his best man from New York, who is supposed to feed him shots and coaxing words of advice in the hours getting ready, roughhousing and knotting neckties. He hasn't seen Karom since last summer, when their suitemate got married in Vermont. But of all the people in Lloyd's life, Karom is the one he wants standing next to him when he takes the most important vow of his life.

Lloyd thought of those mornings in college with Karom on the first day he pitched his tent. It was the tent, in fact, that had reminded him. The tent was erected and stood straight at attention: this was Karom's picture-perfect posture, whether he studied at his desk or ate fish tacos in the dining hall. The way the canvas stretched taut against its poles, straining against the pressure of being pulled in two opposite directions, was how Karom's ropy muscles engaged under the crevice under his arm when he changed his T-shirt. The T-shirt. Lloyd dropped the pieces of the tent in a heap and scrabbled in his duffel bag, his fingers reaching through thermals and socks until they encircled capably around the piece of cloth that links him to his roommate. It is a nothing T-shirt, one that

Malina had tried to wash and convert into a rag but Lloyd had rescued from the laundry hamper just as he'd done the first time in their dorm room nine years ago.

"That thing is practically see-through. After one more wash, it's going to become Harry Potter's Invisibility Cloak," Malina had said, gently prying it out of Lloyd's hands.

"It still has some years in it," Lloyd had said defensively. "And it wasn't dirty."

"It's just an undershirt, babe. Do you even know where it was? Wedged between the mattress and the box spring."

"I know. That's where I put it." Lloyd had grabbed it back and folded it among his undershirts.

But it still has that smell: the musky, spicy, smoky smell that emanated from Karom when he returned from squash practice or squirmed in his sleep on those troubled mornings.

This night yields weakness. Lloyd is pulled in all different directions, whipping about in the clammy blackness of his tent and sleeping bag. He is visited by visions and memories, of college and childhood, but Karom is there throughout. He is there at his home as a young man, and again when Lloyd loses his first tooth. He is there when Lloyd's parents hand him the keys to his first car, before they get into a different one and drive off to the airport to a new destination that will be their home for the next two years. Somehow in his dreams, Karom ascends all levels of Lloyd's life and he is omnipresent in his past, present and future.

The next morning seems to dawn earlier than the previous ones. Lloyd is covered with a thin film of sweat and he mops himself off before stretching within the confines of his tent and poking a tentative toe outside. It is brisk, but he is starving, so he rolls his thick cabled sweater on and pulls on his boots. There is the sweet, strong sugary smell he has smelled on the previous days, like syrup bubbling over a hot stove. The sun is just beginning to peek over the mountain on the opposing side and there is that same bird he'd heard at daybreak, but there is another sound, like a gentle slapping over the water. It is rhythmic and capable and Lloyd follows it downstream, where twenty feet away the man from the general store is fly-fishing. He has on the same lumberjack shirt, along with heavy black waders and a brown sheepskin cap with earflaps pulled low over his eyes. Slap, slap. The man reels in a fish, unhooks it with ease and sends the rod sailing back over the coasting waters. Slap, slap. It is still too dark to make out the features on his face, but there is a determination to his stance and the way he holds his rod. It hangs outstretched for mere moments before he reels it back in and drops the next fish into a bucket. Lloyd walks down the bank, holding on to the branches to steady himself as he approaches the fisherman.

"Morning," the fisherman says, as though he has been expecting Lloyd all along. "You better grab your gear. They are just begging to be breakfast." Lloyd peers into his bucket. Under a foot of river water, four brown trout hang despondently together.

"Aren't you going to eat them?"

"Sure."

"But…the water?"

"Keeps 'em fresher. I nail 'em on the head when I get home. Pow. They don't know what hit 'em. If you let 'em breathe up until the last minute, their insides are fleshier." The man reels in his rod and comes up to where Lloyd is squatting, his waders squishing softly in the riverbank. He unhooks another fish and lets it splash into the bucket.

"So, what does one do on a solo bachelor party?"

"Just, you know, some quiet time with our purple mountain majesties. Live off the land. Gather my thoughts."

"Must be some slave driver, your old woman."

"Malina? No way. She's one of the easiest people I've ever
met. No fuss, no drama. I'm the woman in the relationship."

The man raises his eyebrows.

"I'm Saul."

"Lloyd."

"Another kindred spirit saddled with an old-school name.
Where'd yours come from?"

"Great-uncle."

"Holocaust Museum."

"Excuse me?"

"My parents went to Washington, D.C., on their last-hurrah
trip before I was born. Now I've heard they have this stupid
name for it: babymoon? My mom was eight months pregnant, and when you go to the museum, you get this passport
of someone's profile, to follow them throughout and connect
with the experience, and my mom got a six-year-old boy. Saul
Cohen. He had two sisters and his father was a jeweler. In the
room where they have all the shoes? That's where her water
broke. She said it was a sign."

"Forgive me, but that's kinda morbid."

Saul shrugs. "My namesake. And I'm not even Jewish." He
pulls the sheepskin cap off his head and chucks it to the ground
next to the bucket. He fluffs his hair out with his fingers, the
springy curls bouncing into an arc over his head.

The campsite is just beginning to awaken. Excited shouts
and squeals emerge from children who have ventured down to
the water's edge a few hundred feet from where Saul and Lloyd
stand, poking their toes into the rushing water and flicking
one another. The sun is just over the mountain now, casting

a shadow beneath it. It appears bruised and swollen with the potential of the arriving day.

"Look at that," Lloyd says. "The mountains really are purple."

Saul chuckles. "Ah, city boy. I knew you were going to be work. You have so much to learn."

"Is it that obvious?"

"All your gear is brand-spanking-new." Saul holds his hand out. "I gotta get these fish cleaned up and on the fire. How much longer are you out here?"

"End of the week."

"Maybe I'll teach you to tie some knots. I'll see ya." Lloyd shakes his hand before Saul grabs his bucket and hikes back up the grassy knoll.

This morning, Lloyd hikes up to the peak overlooking the canyon. It is a dry, hot day, and the lizards skitter about him as he finds crevices in the dusty rock to grip with his fingers and the toe of his boot to haul him up. He lost the trail half an hour ago, but he can see the dip between the two mountains creating a pitcher that the sun will pour into at dusk. A hawk circles lazily overhead and he stops to watch it as it coasts over the layers of wind. It'd be nice to be carried, he muses.

Somehow, between fishing and Saul and his decision to climb, an incessant pounding has taken hold in his brain. Thump, thump, thump, as though he has spent the night in an all-night discotheque where the music reverberated against his skeleton. With each level he ascends, the pounding wanes, until it is a slow, dull hum at the back of his palate. What if the thumping were to interrupt the delicate balance of inner-ear fluid and he were to lose his footing over the side of the mountain? He will fall, catching on craggy points of rock until his body is eventually claimed by the gorge and the running river below. He shakes the thought off and climbs higher.

From here he can see the entire forest spread out below him. The winding river with its elusive brown trout. The flat-faced boulders that children use as slides. The unpainted log cabin where Saul is surely peddling wares with his amused grin.

"O bee-yoo-ti-ful, for spacious skies," Lloyd sings. It seems appropriate to serenade the scene. Everything is static; no wind rustles the trees from Lloyd's vantage point and even the burbling river seems to have paused from where he sits, high above, well, everything, it seems. The landscape is awaiting homage, a sacrifice, its cheek turned up for a proffered kiss. It seems like the perfect place to let go. But can he do it? It has been fighting him but this place would be a perfect place of release. Can Lloyd overcome the soft matter that coaxed itself into his chest years ago and let it sail into the gorge below? Because that's what it is: a soft bundle of tissue, not a hard ball of resentment or bitterness. Lloyd *likes* it there. He has never tried getting rid of it in the past. But he loves Malina. And he wants her. He wants her as his partner for the next half century. He wants to make love to her and listen to her gripe about injustices and NGOs and priorities. He loves her. So he has to let go.

He remembers his first encounter with Malina. He was sitting at a bar in the Mission on a raucous Thursday evening. The thrum of the crowd was pushing closer to where he sat perched on a wooden stool. A man lurched past him, inebriated beyond control, and he leaned over, one hand on his thigh, another on the wall, as if about to vomit. Lloyd watched him as he panted softly and leaned back against the wall, as though it would suddenly grow arms and embrace him. He was careful to avoid the passersby as they careened toward the bar, laughing loudly and ordering more. Lloyd shook his head.

"Like china in a bull pen," he murmured to himself. At his ear he heard a soft tinkle, like glass being shattered. A woman had laughed at his ear, a petite woman with hair pulled back so tightly that he could clearly see every contour of her face, every pore.

"That's pretty good," she said. "I was going to go with 'like a scared rabbit in a foxhole.'" He turned and saw her face fully now. She looked bemused. "What else you got?"

Lloyd raised his eyebrows and smiled. "Well," he said, "see that couple over there?" He pointed at two men engaged in an animated though loving debate.

"Slurring as though his tongue had grown fur."

"Pitching from side to side as though caught in a squall out at sea."

Lloyd pointed at four girls standing in a circle, chattering all at once. "Henhouse at daybreak."

"Ooh, nice one."

He laughed. "I'm Lloyd."

"Malina."

"Can I get you a drink? 'He was as smooth as a baby's bottom.'"

Malina laughed. "Absolutely." And though she'd arrived with the henhouse at daybreak, Malina sat in Lloyd's proffered seat, where they analogized and spun metaphors together for the rest of the evening. It was what they did from then on, to break the silence after a particularly fierce argument or misunderstanding. It was their way to concur with one another and leave the world aside.

He leans back against a rock, propping himself up on one leg. He sees Malina's clever, patient face and her oversize horn-rimmed research glasses nestled in her curls as she turns around from her desk to smile at him. He sees her hands reach out for his, guiding them to her lips as she admonishes him for going away for a whole week without cell phone, without connection, without friends. He sees her as she laughs with her friends, piled together at a crowded sidewalk table with dogs tied to chairs, sipping wine. He'd seen her once at such a brunch. It was her "girl-time"—that was the word she'd used. But he'd gone to the restaurant where they were meeting and watched her as she interacted with her friends. It was no betrayal to how she interacted with him, but he loved seeing that side of her. It was the same side she showed Lloyd. She was the same all over, without hard angles or hidden agendas. He was filled with an even deeper love for her as he watched her trace her finger over the stem of her wineglass and heard the immediate surprising laughter that ensued as one of her friends said something that he couldn't hear. Lloyd focused on her dining partners, how they looked into her eyes when she spoke, their bodies turned toward one another in a respective acquiescence. That was friendship, Lloyd had thought. Presence.

Suddenly, the peace that has filled Lloyd up to the peak of the mountain turns to anger. It takes over his throat first, a hard lump causing tears to prick at the corners of his eyes. He is angry at Karom. Why isn't he here? He is his best man, for Christ's sake. The fact that he hasn't invited him or even told him about the plans for this camping trip doesn't factor into Lloyd's thoughts; Karom should anticipate his needs. He should know better. And he will show up only hours before the wedding. Lloyd needs him now, has needed him always. Lloyd has never asked anything of his friend.

Even that time, that one time that Lloyd had lost control at the *Midsummer Night's Dream* cast party in college, throwing up backstage behind the Grand Theater, which only hours before had been transformed into a sprawling forest, complete with real pine needles and tree trunks. Even that time, he had never asked Karom to leave his post, where he was fraternizing with the fairies—still clothed in ethereal translucent costumes—to hold him up and take him back to their dorm, where he'd coaxed three glasses of water, an Advil and two pieces of sandwich bread from Lloyd's stash in his closet into him. He didn't even know that Karom knew about his stash—his "in case of hurricane/earthquake/nuclear bomb/ terrorism" stash. He poured Lloyd into bed on his side, tossed out the few wads of crumpled-up paper in his trash can, filled it with a few fingers of water before setting it beside his bed and rubbed his back while Lloyd moaned dully. Lloyd didn't know how long Karom sat at his bedside, but he didn't go flitting back to the fairies; when he awoke a few hours later to stumble to the bathroom, Karom was curled up in his own bed a few feet away from Lloyd's, hugging a pillow and sighing in his sleep. Lloyd hadn't asked to be taken care of then, but he wants it more than ever now.

Lloyd replaces the ball in his chest and glances back down at the river. He turns back toward the way he climbed. It is time for lunch.

In the spring of the second semester of each school year, there was what was known around campus as Hiker's Hooky. The dean would ring the large Liberty-like bell in the main green, the sound clanging across the university. Just in case students lived in the upper arches of North Campus, where the ivy feathered across buildings in thicker clumps and the grass grew to knee level, emails would alert students that there would be no classes on this day. The day was chosen at random, based on whether the dean needed an extra hour of sleep or wanted to extend her vacation in Cape Cod, or simply because she'd waited too long and any longer and they'd be into the deadening days of final exams and theses that rendered students captive to desks as they pored over papers, lab rats and musical scores.

Traditionally, all the students were meant to take the college-sponsored buses to Mount Greylock, the highest point in Massachusetts, to hike from a few allotted points. The vans would disperse students at the base of the mountain, halfway up or at the summit, where they could finally stretch their legs and welcome the yolk-colored sun as it peered out over the ridged spine of the Taconic Mountains. The buses left at the crack of dawn for the three-hour drive. For the most part, the freshmen adhered to this tradition, radiating eagerness as they climbed aboard, claiming seats together according to dormitory and sports divisions, but the sophomores usually took their hooky into the city, taking over Harvard Square, walking along the Charles or shopping downtown. The juniors stayed on campus, taking advantage of the empty campus to do shots in the common rooms or on the quad, running around recklessly and jumping into the pond half-clothed, whereas the seniors mostly hung to themselves in rooms, writing theses or visiting the sanctity of the labs to finish research or finish their incomplete syllabi.

In their first three years, Lloyd and Karom had missed the opportunity to hike Mount Greylock. As freshmen they had both fallen asleep in the library studying for their first round of midterms, Karom for statistics and Lloyd for macroeconomics. The bell had resounded on campus but the two had snored, blissfully unaware, their heads on the wide wooden desks under the vaulted heavy wooden eaves of the library. The librarians had arrived in the morning to nudge them awake, but they had already missed the buses. Realizing their only other choice was to keep to their rooms for the rest of the afternoon continuing their studies, they'd timidly but courageously joined in with the juniors' festivities. Their sophomore year, they had traipsed about the city with their friends, playing pool in developed pockets of industrial Kendall and eating garlicky twirly pasta in the North End. When they were juniors, Karom had had a huge research paper due, and though Lloyd had caught up with all his work, he'd pretended to need a few hours to revise his French for the oral examination the next day in order to keep him company in the library once again.

So during their senior year, when the bell rang and awoke them—this time in their beds in a dorm in North Campus—they both decided to brave their luck with the freshmen, their keen faces straining toward the front of the bus, chattering away the whole time with the tinny sounds of Top 40 music echoing from portable CD players.

When they'd gotten to the base of the mountain, where the bus let some hikers off before it wound its way to the top for the less outdoor inclined, Lloyd and Karom decided to disembark and hike the whole way up. Lloyd had worn hiking boots expressly bought for activities like this. His parents had sent them from Switzerland. The boots were creaky and stiff; he should have at least broken them in while walking around campus or the city. Karom wore old running sneakers, which were comfortable but unsupportive. They were the only two who decided to start their hikes from the base. It might take them hours but they had the time until the buses departed again at 8:00 p.m. that night. As they started on the winding footpath up the mountain, Lloyd barely kept pace with Karom's long strides. Karom walked effortlessly, stalking up the incline like a mountain lion, his head down, determined to reach the top before sundown, while Lloyd capered in tow a few feet behind, straining with effort. When they paused at the trail break that led in three different directions, Karom turned to look at Lloyd, who was panting, small beads of sweat at his temples and slicking back his blond hair, which glinted in the sun. His T-shirt was soaked through and his sweatshirt was tied in a droopy knot at his waist.

"You okay, man? Should we slow down?"

"I'm good, I'm good. The air is so fresh. I guess I'm just not used to it," Lloyd said.

Karom sat down on a log, picking at some dirt from under his sneaker.

"Come on, let's take five."

Lloyd sat down obediently next to him, huffing the air out of his lungs and trying his best to bring his breathing back to normal.

"We didn't bring any sustenance," Lloyd said. "No water or energy bars or anything."

"I was thinking about that. But I just remembered—I went on this foraging hike once in Central Park. I learned how to dig up mushrooms and truffles and the differences between the poisonous ones and the ones best for omelets. I bet we're sitting right above a tasty snack."

"Central Park? Get out."

"Absolutely. There are over two hundred mushroom species found in the park alone." Karom told him about the unexplored parts of the park, the Ramble, where swarms of birds nested in the fall on their way down south. If you visited the gnarls of branches overhead at just the right time, it sounded as if you were in an aviary. The cheeping and tweeting was miraculous, and once, Karom had timed it so that he lay down in the underbrush in a carpet of dead leaves as the birds swelled to a symphonic peak and he'd felt as though they were lifting him by his arms and flying him overhead. He told him about the hidden upper pond that few visited, where a family of raccoons had clambered down from their nest in the crook of a tree branch while he and his parents were picnicking in the midafternoon heat one weekend afternoon, a line of masked marauders obstinately prancing past them on eerily humanlike paws. He told him about the forest in the north end of the park, far away from carousel music and carriage rides, away from balloon vendors and bicycle rickshaws. The forest in which he himself had gotten lost a few times, although the area encompassed only a few city blocks. The trails within these woods were narrow and untrodden, silent and insensate, and it was under these tall, limber oaks that Karom had discovered the trove of fungi and allium that sprouted like candy within.

"Know what a *mycophile* is?"

"Nope."

"Someone who's obsessed with mushrooms."

Karom got up and moved into the brush, carefully moving aside branches to peer under a heavy oak tree.

"Come on," he said to Lloyd. "Let's go. It's no energy bar, but it's something."

"Are you sure you know—"

"Those," Karom said, pointing to a cluster of small orange fungi growing delicately on a root creeping up from under the earth, "will kill you."

He moved around the tree and tapped at another root on the other side. Lloyd hoisted himself up and moved under the brush to join him.

"Aw, yeah. But these, these are awesome." Karom was pointing to a clutch of mushrooms that grew together like brain tissue, curling around one another in layers. "The ranger I was with had us eat them raw, because you never do. But they're rich, almost meaty. Know what these are?" Lloyd shook his head as Karom stooped to brush some dead leaves off the tops of the mushrooms and plucked the whole bunch from the earth. "Hen-of-the-woods," he said, offering them to Lloyd. "They're delicious, not to mention ridiculously expensive. Try a piece."

Lloyd hesitated. He was known in their circle as circumspect, hesitating, never the first to jump into the pond at the end of finals, not even one to jump in at all. Their friends teased him for his caution, so he constantly pushed himself to try new things: nibbling on a charred tentacle of grilled octopus at the Greek restaurant on Tasson, almost bungee jumping over spring break. He looked into the pit of his stomach for the courage—his stomach that had been emitting high-pitched squeals throughout the hike from hunger—but his stomach itself was the one that reneged on Karom's offer.

"I'm okay. Let's just wait for the concession stand at the top. Besides, Karom, those might be something else, something that grows outside of New York. I'd really rather you didn't eat them without someone identifying them for sure. It doesn't sit right with me."

Karom snorted and ripped a tender ear off the knot of mushroom.

"I know what I'm talking about," he said, stuffing it into his mouth and chewing noisily. "See?"

Lloyd closed his eyes. He saw his friend pitch forward violently, clutching at his stomach and tearing at his hair as the poison curled through his body like smoke. He wanted to grasp Karom gently about the waist and force the offending fungus from his esophagus, where it was winding down the curlicues of his insides. He could feel the weight of Karom's long limp body in his arms as he tilted his chin toward the sun, squeezed his nostrils and breathed into him.

But nothing happened. And nothing happened afterward as they continued to climb, Lloyd gasping to keep up with Karom in order to examine his face with every step, until Karom snapped at him.

"What—" his voice was staccato, as if he had sliced off the ends of his sentences "—is. The. Matter?"

"Are you…? How do you…? How are you feeling?"

"Seriously?" Karom whipped around. "I told you that I knew what I was talking about. You're such a baby. A complete worrywart. Lloyd, honestly. This is a pathetic way to live your life, always back up against the wall, never taking any risks, never accepting any challenges. It's sad. Push yourself. Move yourself to act. You're missing it. You're missing all of it."

They hiked the remaining three hours in silence, Lloyd interrupting it only to point out a shorter, steeper way that would get them to the peak just as the buses loaded up for the long drive back. At the peak nothing happened either.

On the return trip, CD players and excited chatter came to a dull drone as students dropped off to sleep, drowsy with the residue of the heat and gleam of the sun. Karom and Lloyd sat side by side, Karom's long tapered fingers resting on his thighs as he stared vacantly out the window, Lloyd leaning back with his arms crossed as he counted and recounted the diamond shapes on the roof above his head. The face of Karom's watch glinted in the passing highway lights. The watch had arrived by courier two days before. Lloyd had been sitting on his bed rereading his sociology notes when Karom accepted the package and sat on his bed to tear it open. He'd watched his face change as he read the note that accompanied it and then watched him stroke the face of the watch before he lovingly wrapped it around his wrist.

As the crunch of gravel underneath their tires changed into the hum of the highway below them, Lloyd deigned to ask, the flickering of the approaching cars in the oncoming lane defiantly casting shadows across his face, "Did you really know? What those mushrooms were?" Karom continued to watch the cars approach him. Lloyd could see them in his pupils, dancing dangerously close until they shot by in the parallel lane.

Karom cleared his throat and looked up at the ceiling. He swallowed, water catching in the creases of his eyes. His voice shook as he spoke.

"No. Not exactly. I thought so at first, but the longer I held them in my palm, I wasn't sure. They looked familiar, but I didn't recall seeing the white crests at the tip of the frond as they sprayed out. I thought I knew. I took a chance. I tested myself." He looked down at his hands and gripped his thighs with his fingers before he turned his head back toward the window and closed his eyes. Lloyd curled his hand into a fist and brushed it against Karom's. Karom's eyelids fluttered slightly, but they remained closed. Lloyd watched him carefully for the first hour as Karom twitched instinctively until finally dropping off to sleep.

Back on solid ground, Lloyd feels sickened with himself. He has carried this around for eight years. He has to shake it. The trip is partially it—one final pep talk to himself to get over it and move on. And what has he accomplished? A few measly brown trout and a hike to the top of the nearby peak. Enough is enough. There is no one else he can speak to about this. His friends back home in San Francisco would happily clap him on the back along with an invisible label across his chest and send him straight to the Castro. But it isn't like that.

He'd looked it up. Homosexuality: romantic and/or sexual attraction or behavior among members of the same sex or gender. It isn't behavior. Or romantic. It isn't even members. Lloyd is in the ideal city to be gay if he wanted to be. In fact, it might even be easier than marrying a Haitian-born woman with an accent and skin the color of coffee beans. But this is love for only one man. Karom. His Karom. It balls up in his chest like a knotted clutch of yarn, tangled among his inner organs. It has taken years to unravel a few inches of it before the ends get lost in the mess once again. And this is his final attempt to pull it out, inch by inch, before he crosses the threshold into a life with Malina, a proper one, a committed one. One where he gives himself wholly to her—without the ball in his chest, without the yearning behind his eye sockets, without the sweat-stained T-shirt that barely holds the lingering scent of his best man. Besides, Malina is a terrible knitter.

It is a start. Back in his tent, Lloyd pulls the T-shirt out from his sleeping bag and heads down to the riverbank. Squatting down on his haunches, he digs into the silt where the water laps softly at the shore, the moist dirt flecked with pebbles. He holds a ball of it in his hand and smears the shirt with it, grinding the mud into the cotton, covering the sweat stains, masking the scent. When he is satisfied, he stands abruptly. The blood rushes from his head. He sees stars. But he uses his disorientation to hurl the shirt in a straight arc over his shoulder, where it lands with a slight splash in the river. It sinks ever so slightly with the weight of the earth and immediately picks up the rapid current, sailing downstream, out of sight before Lloyd can catch his breath. And then, just like that, the start is finished.

★ ★ ★

"Explain something to me." Lloyd jumps. He has been lying on his back, watching wisps of clouds as they trail across the sky. When he stares hard, he can see the tiny molecules of the atmosphere floating miles above him. They appear like clear balloons, disappearing as soon as his eyes focus. He has been thinking about Malina, the nature of Malina, what Malina means. He fell asleep to her last night, imagining her fingers stroking the inside of his thigh, crooning her husky hum into his ear. He invoked the drag of her fingernails across his skin and his skin mottled with goose bumps almost immediately. He imagined the underside of her jaw, where the curve of her bone revealed her skin to be softer than anywhere else on her body. He kissed her fluttering eyelids. Her plump lips were tugging on his ear, urging him home. He was close. And then he was lost.

But now Saul is next to him chewing on a long piece of grass. Lloyd sits up. He is lying on a large boulder that juts into the river. The boulder vibrates with the rush of the water around it and Lloyd had been lulled into a trance.

"This whole solo-bachelor-party thing. You don't strike me as the kind of guy who doesn't have friends. What gives?"

"Why is this bothering you?"

"It's just a little different. I wanted to know your rationale. I might want to throw myself one of these one day."

"Well..." Lloyd hesitates. "It's the last time I'm going to be truly alone. For the rest of my life, there will be my wife, hopefully kids, a family. There will be obligations and necessities and joint accounts and Little League uniforms and college educations. Besides, I keep myself in good company."

"Fair enough. And very mature, I might add. I want one."

"All you have to do is get engaged." Lloyd grins.

"When's the big day?"

"Two weeks from Saturday."

"Tell me about the girl."

"Well, she's Haitian. With this flawless, luminous skin. She's all angles, her face, her arms. She has strong, sharp features that at first glance appear almost masculine, but her smile, which happens frequently, softens everything. But her eyes are piercing, as though you have to win her over before she'd simply hand those to you on a silver platter. She's... Well, here." Lloyd removes his wallet from his cargo pants and shows Saul a picture. Saul lets out a low whistle. "But that's not all. She's so smart—she started a microloan NGO that supports single mothers in Third World countries. She's fiercely loyal and insanely jealous. She's an incredible...cook."

"You were going to say lover."

Lloyd blushes. "Was it that obvious?"

"Just a smidge. But it's good. It's refreshing to see someone head over heels. It doesn't happen enough."

"Sad."

"But true."

Lloyd develops a faraway look in his eyes. "When we first started dating, I was training for the New York City Marathon. And she just happened to be in town for the weekend. We'd only been out twice, so I didn't even bother telling her how to look for me or anything. But here's the thing that got me—she looked up my number and came to Brooklyn, to Greenpoint, and she saw me and she called my name, but I had my name on my shirt, right? Like everyone does so people can cheer for you? So I probably turned my head, didn't think anything of it and just kept going.

"Shoot forward eleven miles, where I'm in the home stretch—mile twenty-four—and I hear my name. I turn around, and there's this girl, and she's holding this sign with my name and hollering at me to go, go, go. I was exhausted at the time, just holding on by an inch. But I smiled and waved at her, not really registering that this was her—second-date Malina. So I finish the race, ice my legs, have a big dinner, pass out and fly back to San Francisco the next morning, and on my way back from the airport, I'm super groggy in the cab, but it hits me. I saw Malina at the race. I dial her number and she's all sleepy sounding, but she answers the phone, 'Congratulations, champ.' And I say, 'Was that you? Did I dream it?' and she laughs and says, 'It was me. I was there in Brooklyn but you didn't see me at mile nine, so I hopped on the train and made sure you knew you had support before your big finish. How do you feel?' and I felt this warm feeling spreading through my chest, like something engulfing my insides, enmeshing my heart. I wanted to see her right then, to hold her and kiss her and tell her that I would take care of her, too. That's big. Those grand gestures, those don't happen anymore." Lloyd smiles, shaking his head.

"Wow, man."

"Sorry, I got carried away, bragging about her."

"Don't be sorry. You should never be sorry."

"What about you? You seeing anyone?"

"I was married once."

"What happened? If you don't mind—"

Saul waves him away. "Usual story. She was young. I was stupid. We thought there was a baby but it turned out to be a false alarm. And so we went our separate ways. We're still friends. I actually introduced her to her husband."

"Now, *that* is mature."

"What's the point of grudges, right? It just wastes time."

Lloyd purses his lips, thinking.

Saul taps his forehead. "What's going on in there?"

"Just that. Wasting time. I've spent so much of my life wasting time on things that will never, should never, amount to anything. I guess you could say I'm here trying to rid myself of them."

"How do you mean?"

"Excess. Anything, really. Focusing on what's important— my life, my job, my woman, my passions, eating, sleeping, waking up each morning. Everything else is beside the point. It's irrelevant."

"Like?"

"Considering other options. Temptation. Lust. It's all stupid when you know you're going home to one woman."

"Aren't all those things the very crux of a bachelor party? Besides, who is tempting you around here?" Saul looks around to the small wading area where the river has created a small current-free pool where children splash in the shallows and heavyset women stand wading in T-shirts that reach to their knees.

"Not here. Here." Lloyd taps his own forehead.

"Hmm."

Saul looks out to the river, where the waters approach the two men as they sit on the rock. If they want to, they can both hurtle forward and be embraced by the current. If they want to, they can both sit still and let the hum of the tide soothe them to sleep.

"Is it Karom?"

"Excuse me?"

"Who is tempting you? Karom. What's his—her?—presence in your life?"

"How did you know?"

"Well, I, er…" Saul looks down at his heels nervously. "Last night. I was on night patrol, checking the grounds. You're technically out of the jurisdiction, but I knew where you were

camped. You were whimpering and moving about pretty violently. I was going to unzip your tent but I thought that might
freak you out even more. So I just knelt down next to your
tent until the nightmares passed. They went on for a while.
You said the name constantly."

Lloyd looks down at his ankles. He is silent as he traces the
final line of hair that grows before the smoothness of his pale
white feet begin.

"Him. Karom is a him. He's my college roommate. He…
I… Nothing happened."

"No?"

"No."

"It's okay if it did."

"It didn't." Lloyd says this not defensively but in regret. He
still can't meet Saul's face.

"And?"

"And what?"

"Do you love him?"

Lloyd looks at Saul. His face is so calm, so soft. There isn't a
trace of judgment lodged within his questions. "I'm not sure.
I think so. But it's not like that. It's just him."

"Does he know?"

Lloyd shakes his head. "Never has. Never will."

"What's special about Karom?"

"It's inexplicable, really. We were roommates for four years
and we just…carried one another. We never talked about anything we needed or wanted. One always just filled in where
the other fell short. If I needed someone to reread my thesis
proposal, he'd print it out unbeknownst to me and leave notes
on my desk. If he took the Greyhound into New York to visit
his parents, I'd figure out the bus schedule and pick him up at
the depot when he returned. We looked out for one another

at parties and during finals. My parents were always abroad—
they're diplomats—and for the first few years of college, I'd
spend Thanksgiving and long weekends with the Seths. He
went through some personal stuff and I tried to be there for
him. I guess the personal stuff is what drew us together. It's
hokey, but it was just this bond. And I can't imagine having
it with anyone else. Not even…Malina."

Saul nods, looking over Lloyd's face. There are tears prick-
ling in the corners of his eyes and they threaten to spill.

"I've never told anyone that before. Not out loud. Not ever."

"Well, you're safe here. The bigger question is, what are
you going to do?"

"Get rid of him. From here." Lloyd taps his head again.

"How?"

Lloyd is beginning to anger. "What is this, a therapy session
in a wooded glen? Don't you think I've thought of all this?"

"Socratic method, pal. Calm down. I'm just trying to help."

Lloyd sighs and pushes the hair out of his eyes.

"I know. I'm sorry. It's just that I've tried everything, short
of getting married. And don't—" Lloyd looks directly into
Saul's eyes. "Don't think this is a Band-Aid. Malina is in a totally different category. Malina, I love, and am in love with.
She's mine. That's no question. The question is, can I live
with both of them?"

"Can you?"

"No. I don't think so. It wouldn't be fair to either of us to
start out like this."

"Either of who?"

"Malina and me."

"Ah. What about Karom? Is it fair to him?"

"I don't think he knows."

"He knows."

"How can you—"

"I just…know. Look, I don't know a lot about the guy stuff specifically. But I do know that when one person is head over heels for another, especially if they are friends, it's obvious. The other person just knows. It's clear. Regardless of how you try to mask your feelings. He may not know the extent of your feelings, but he'll know they're there. I am 99.9 percent sure of this."

"It's never affected our friendship."

"Then he's a really good friend."

"He's my best man."

"Sounds like it."

The sun is just beginning to dip down past the bend in the river and Saul lifts himself up and holds his hand out to Lloyd to pull him up. The tide is rising; the underside of the boulder, which seemed hoisted high above the water, is now soaked and the rock will soon be submerged. Flashes of fish zip by them and the leaves rustle at the very tops of the tallest trees.

"Some buddies and I are having a campfire tonight. Nothing special. Dogs and six-packs. You're welcome. Over by the trailhead for Indian Road."

"Thanks."

"See you there?"

"Sure."

The evening had been cool and relaxing. Lloyd was numbed by beer and easy conversation. Saul's friends were low maintenance and welcoming. They all wore flannel shirts over solid-color T-shirts—evening camping wear. Lloyd was glad for the company, for the distraction from the afternoon's conversation. He talked to them about easy things: movies, beer, fishing. The fire was high, and Lloyd was drawn to it. He charred his hot dog from the outside and ate it peeled, raw and blistering within a floppy bun. His mouth was tangy from ketchup and mustard.

At the end of the night, he helps Saul stamp out the dying embers of the fire and crushes the beer cans under his feet for easier transport to the recycling bin before saying his good-byes. Saul reaches for the bag.

"You'll be okay?"

Lloyd smiles. "Of course. See you."

"I'm off tomorrow. You're leaving in the afternoon?" Lloyd nods, the moonlight bright on his face. "I'll make sure to stop by." They shake hands and Lloyd turns his flashlight on for the half-mile walk back to his campsite.

As he unzips the tent and crawls inside, the beer churns in his stomach. He digs into his duffel bag to retrieve his cell phone. It is turned off, another rule of camping, but he is inside with the mouth to his tent zipped up. The tent won't tell, and neither will he. Besides, if he falls asleep tonight and doesn't wake up, he will never know if people had been trying to reach him. The air inside is warm with his breath and body heat. He pushes the power button. There are three text messages.

Baby, I hope you found the lotion I snuck in your bag. It works for poison oak, sumac and ivy. It's in the hidden inner pocket underneath the stitching. Be as careful as a tightrope walker on a greased wire. Xoxo.

He had found it on his first day there and had used copious amounts of it on his raw skin.

Don't forget to take pictures. I want to see everything that you see. I love you like a fat kid loves cake. Xoxo.

He has no camera other than the one on his cell phone, and if he uses it, she will know that he'd turned it on. There will be no pictures.

Dear Lloyd, We decided to leave a few days earlier, so we'll be there on Saturday. No need to pick us up; we'll make it to the inn. We want to be there to help you and Malina with any last-minute things you need. We love you and can't wait for your big day. Love, Mom and Dad.

Lloyd chuckles. His parents continue to write text messages like letters even though he's shown them otherwise. The tent lights up with the glow from the cell phone as he presses the voice-mail button. Karom's low murmur warms his inner ear, static-filled and tinny.

"Hey, bud, it's Karom. I'm calling you from this sort of makeshift phone booth here in Jaipur. Our train is hours delayed. Much like everything else in India, nothing works. Not to mention there's no privacy. There are three dudes staring at me right now, slowly smoking cigarettes, and the guy in charge of the booth is basically breathing down my neck as he watches the clock inch forward. Anyway. I'll try to talk. We're on our way to see the Taj Mahal and this is the worst anticipation ever, because you know I've been dying to see it practically my whole life. But we're stuck here, so I had a chance to call you. I feel like I haven't been there for you lately. You deserve a better best man, one who ignores when you say that you don't want a bachelor party and plans one anyway. One who's more involved in your life and supportive of your relationship.

Anyway, I just wanted to let you know that even though you're there and I'm here, I'm thinking about you. You should bring Malina here someday. This country is so versatile. It's the most diverse place I've ever been. After Agra we're headed to Delhi to spend our last few days here with Gita's grandmother. She says hi—Gita. Anyway, take care of yourself and I'll see you soon, bud. I can't wait for your wedding. We'll have a blast."

He had received the message last week, listened to it on his way home from work while sidestepping bums in the Tenderloin without giving it much thought. He'd saved it, savoring it in the quiet of his apartment or sometimes while he sat at his desk, staring at numbers and plans. He'd listened to it again and again during moments of weakness, of grasping, of inexactitude. Before he can think about it, he presses the delete button and everything is still.

Lloyd shuts the phone off and lies back in his sleeping bag. Little by little, the night outside washes over him: the crickets and the river and the dark and the moon. He can feel the earth underneath the tent, the small stones he wasn't able to clear away, tiny sticks that press into the small of his back. He passes his hands over them, the tent's fabric rustling against his palms. He passes his hands over his face, fluttering his eyelids shut. And he sleeps.

The morning of his departure, he awakes to rain. He'd slept hard, with dreams that chased in and out as though he were in a forest, peeking from behind trees and boulders. Just as he remembered the traces of one, it slipped away from his consciousness. Saul had been present in his dreams. Saul, Karom and Malina, but never at the same time. They existed alone, in a vacuum, and for Lloyd alone. He doesn't know the tenor of the dreams, but he awakes feeling hostile and irritable.

The air inside the tent feels moist. It smells of wet dog, sweaty and mildewed, but everything appears bone-dry. When he opens the tent cover and steps outside, it is like swimming through a glass of milk. The rain is viscous, thick, as though it has built up in the skies for a long time before being released. Lloyd secures the corners of the tent down with stones from the riverbed, thick marbled balls slick with rainwater. Pulling the wet hood of his sweatshirt over his head, he squints into the distance toward the main camping area. Some people are waterproofing their tents from the outside, stretching bright blue tarpaulins over pointy apexes. Others are herding their shrieking children into minivans and sedans to wait out the rain in comfort.

He scoops rivulets of water from his eyes and stands, hugging himself and weighing his options. He can hike, he can fish—though this defies his cardinal rule of camping of avoiding open water when it's raining—he can read by flashlight in his tent until he grows damp and more irritable. He considers calling it a day and heading to the visitors' center to catch a cab to the airport where he will wait it out until his flight that afternoon. The rain is venomous; any chance of allowing him to think any more than he already has is dangerous to his psyche and offers him the opportunity to dwell rather than act. The T-shirt had been a courageous first step. And then the voice mail. He has been behaving like a sorority sister burning the relationship residue after a breakup. So now what?

But before he allows himself to think other similar thoughts, he stoops and reenters the tent, curling up his sleeping bag and stuffing it into the bottom of his hiking backpack. It takes moments to tear down his tent and cram the rods that have held it up into a bundle. His fishing box with the tackle goes into his backpack and he uses the tent to cover the remainder of his clothes, his pack of cards and his fishing box as he settles them under a tree. He throws a cheap plastic poncho over his head and flees for the general store. The door jingles as he enters and a woman with a large curly fringe looks up.

"Can I help you?"

"Is Saul around?"

"Saul?" The woman squints at him. "There's no Saul here."

"There was the other day. Tuesday."

"I'm the manager here. I'd remember hiring a Saul."

"Maybe a friend of a friend?"

"There's only me, Lou and Jennifer. Maybe you mean Sean? He subs for us sometimes. He's Korean?"

"It's definitely Saul. Tall guy? Reddish hair?"

The woman looks at him, still squinting.

"Were you staying out near the tar pits?" she asks.

"I was staying on Campground 12. Well, not on it. To the side, closer to the river."

"The tar pits." She nods. "There's a reason they tell you to stay on the campsites. The rangers closed the tar pits off from the public a few years ago. They found them in the riverbank, and they were built over, and grass and trees and moss were replanted over them so they'd camouflage into the environment, but they still release these fumes from time to time, depending on the season. They're not dangerous, at least not to your health, but people get funny—they see things, they make things up. I wouldn't call them hallucinations, because no one ever gets out of control or sees anything they wouldn't normally see in real life. But people have created people or animals. We had a woman in here once who swore up and down that she'd seen a bull moose drinking water by the river with its calf. We've never, ever had moose in these parts. So, I wouldn't be surprised if Saul was—"

"He's real," Lloyd growls. "I had conversations with him. I was at a campfire with him and his buddies over on the Indian Head Trail."

"Last night? That rowdy party that got shut down by rangers? Open fires are illegal here. You should know that, camper." Two teenagers enter the store and are idling near the cash register. "Anyway, I've got to get back to work. Good luck finding your friend." The woman turns to the girls, and Lloyd pushes the door open with the toe of his boot and stands under the narrow, ungenerous shelter of the parapet that stretches out from the store, the rain dripping onto him from the eaves.

He considers his six days in the woods. He has thrown away a T-shirt. He has deleted a voice mail. That is all. He hasn't rid himself of the ache in his chest that doesn't cease when he remembers his first dorm room, in the corner of that old historical building. He has spent a long time remembering, summoning memories, making them dance at his fingertips. He hasn't succeeded in his exorcism; in fact, he has succeeded in creating another ghost, another presence that will continue to haunt him all the way back to San Francisco. How can Saul not be real? When they had lain on the rock warmed by the sun, Lloyd had felt Saul's flannel shirt against his own skin, washed so many times it was like silk. He'd felt Saul's fingers against his as he passed him crushed aluminum cans after the bonfire. He'd seen his smirk as he purchased beer on that third day. He knew the origin of his name, for goodness' sakes.

He swings his daypack onto his shoulders and jogs off toward the trail he'd returned from the night before. The path is washed over; bits of leaves and twigs have flooded the narrow dirt lane that had led him to the campfire the night before.

He walks for a mile before he realizes he has taken a wrong turn. Where is the opening to the circle where Saul and his friends had lolled on the ground, taking generous swigs of cheap beer? The trails in the park are set up about an enormous circle, so that everyone begins within a giant hub and chooses their trail accordingly before a spiraling path takes them to the peak of a mountain, or the mouth of where the river meets a large sparkling lake, or fields of wildflowers with petaled heads that dance in the breeze. It encourages hikers to choose their own adventures; if you don't have a trail map, you never know where a specific trail might lead you. Lloyd has already taken the one to the peak of the mountain, and on his first day, after stalking the grounds of the campsite and then pitching the tent on the outskirts, he'd found the field of wildflowers and lain down in it, weeds scratching in his ears and the hum of bees within dangerous proximity. Somehow nothing had been dangerous that day—not the bees, not the fact that he could have fallen asleep knowing nothing about the land or the animals that inhabited it. He was safe because he had chosen to take the steps that brought him here.

Lloyd chooses a path that he thinks looks familiar. The bonfire hadn't been very far into the trail; it couldn't have been if it was safe and forest-fire friendly. Saul had told him about the dangers the park had suffered the previous years, and in the visitors' center, where the taxi had dropped him and he'd embarked on his bachelor party, there were graphic photos of forest fires as flames licked up the sides of mountains, crumpling trees to the ground like abandoned sheets of drawing paper and charring everything in their way. But within a few steps into this trail, he knows it is the wrong one. He follows it anyway.

For a half hour he tramps in circles, finding the entrance

to the uphill hike he'd done the other day, when he'd peered over the ridge of the mountain, surveying the land as far as he could see. He finds a fallen tree, from under which a slim red fox darts out as he nears it. He watches the fox as it jogs suspiciously away. Its tail has deflated with the rains, and the fox holds it sheepishly between its runty legs, as a dog might after a stern admonishment. Lloyd and the fox watch one another through the streams of rain that pound down so hard that they appear white, like freshly laundered sheets. The animal is russet-red and stands out starkly against the wet verdant landscape. It watches him warily, its light brown eyes staring almost through Lloyd, its nose and whiskers twitching as rain splashes against its snout. It is majestic, though humbled in the rain, and Lloyd feels his breath catching in his throat at its beauty. They stare at one another, Lloyd careful not to move a muscle until suddenly, the fox breaks their gaze and darts up the hill.

He remembers Karom and Malina's first meeting, a showdown not unlike this one. Malina had been the one to cave. They had met over dinner in San Francisco and Karom had been aloof, tired from his flight and grumpy. He'd entered the Vietnamese restaurant overlooking the bay shifty eyed and ill-prepared for niceties.

Malina had tried, though; she had been unrelenting at that first dinner. She tried popular culture, movies—mostly obscure art-house flicks she knew Karom loved. She tried food and trucks and, when all else failed, her huge admission of her fleeting tryst with Republicanism in her junior year of college, an anecdote that incited either excited conversation or rancor. But Karom simply nodded and pushed his lower lip out, saying, "We all experimented in college, to some degree." The talk about Republicanism turned to Bush, which inevitably turned to 9/11, which easily turned to Katrina. This was something on which they all agreed: a mess, a disaster, mayhem. Lloyd excused himself to the bathroom.

"Playing devil's advocate, though, natural disaster isn't an easy thing, though, to judge. You never expect it, never prepare for it, never can be sure of how much damage it can do, even when it's there. I've seen it with my own eyes."

"Yeah?" Karom lifted his head. "What happened?"

"In 2004 there were torrential rains in Haiti that killed nearly 35,000 people. There were thousands more injured. People were homeless, displaced, missing. Babies screamed and the cries of anguished mothers filled the air. There was smoke, fires, looting. It was terrible."

"I had no idea," Karom murmured.

"When they'd cleared enough debris off the runways and the planes could finally fly again, I visited. The place looked war torn. I couldn't believe this was my home. It was this naked land, stripped of its dignity, shivering in the aftermath. It was the first time I'd been home since leaving the country at the age of four. I'd never felt so alone."

"I...I didn't know you'd lost your family. I'm so sorry."

"Oh, I didn't. They live on the east coast, which certainly felt the damage—you could see it, too, in the silt that collected in the gutters and the mold that grew all around us on garages and rooftops. But compared to the destruction done to the middle and the west of the country, it was peanuts. My family was lucky."

"So you lost no one?"

"Thank God, no."

Karom snorted and placed his hands flat on the table, placing distance between himself and Malina. "So explain to me how you experienced disaster. You don't know the meaning. Just because you read some *New York Times* articles and visited some wreckage and received some secondhand information on friends of friends of friends doesn't mean you have any idea of what this world is capable of. It's pathetic." Lloyd returned from the bathroom just in time to see his fiancée and his best friend sitting at a table in a trendy Vietnamese restaurant watching one another warily.

After dinner Malina retreated to the apartment, saying that she wanted the boys to have some one-on-one time together.

"It was very nice to meet you," Karom said stiffly. "I trust I'll see you for brunch tomorrow."

"I'm sorry we got off on the wrong foot," Malina said. "I didn't mean to overstep my boundaries." Karom shook his head with narrowed eyes, as if shaking away the evening and its memories.

As Malina got into a taxi, Lloyd grabbed his arm. "What gives? What happened back there?"

Karom snorted. "You told her, didn't you, like it was something in passing, some way to make conversation? I can't believe you, Lloyd."

"Told her what?"

"About me and my family. It's not exactly dinnertime conversation." Lloyd opened his mouth to speak. Around them, swirls of club-goers were dawdling on the sidewalk, shouting to one another, hugging and texting simultaneously. He nodded his head toward the next street, and they ducked in the alleyway to talk. "You don't just share that with anyone."

"Oh my God, Karom, she's not just anyone. She's my fiancée."

"Well, your *fiancée* just relegated my entire life into a dinnertime anecdote and made me feel about two inches tall. And to top it all off, she's acting like she's experienced the same thing. *I* am an unnatural phenomenon. Not once but twice. Twice. Did you tell your fiancée that? That I should be fucking studied for psycho-fucking-logical trauma? Go ahead. Tell her. Tell her so that she can put it in her empathetic pipe and smoke it." Karom's mouth was twitching, and his nostrils quivered and his hands shook as though stricken with palsy. At the end of his soliloquy, he stalked off toward the main road and got into a cab before Lloyd even opened his mouth to respond.

The next morning, Karom showed up at their door with flowers for Malina and a bottle of Scotch for Lloyd: amends, he said when they called down through the buzzer to ask who it was. "It's amends. I'm here to make them."

He held the offerings out to them as the door was opening, Malina standing next to Lloyd, his wiry frame supporting her gentle ballerina limbs. Her hair was pulled back in a French braid, and she smiled warmly at Karom through her lips, though her eyes remained tense. She had been crying all morning while Lloyd held her, hushing and rocking her and telling her that everything would be okay. She couldn't believe that she'd created a rift like that between herself and Karom, Lloyd's best friend. She couldn't imagine starting off on the wrong foot. Lloyd had held her and told her that he didn't like the way Karom had spoken to her, that he was going to have a strict talk with him about respect and understanding and acceptance. But Karom apologized, and then Malina apologized and then Lloyd acknowledged it all and then the rest of their weekend settled around them; Karom seemed to relax into their rhythm. They looked at pictures from college and discussed plans for the future. They talked about Gita and her assignments and Karom's marathon in the fall. They talked about wedding plans and venues and where to go to dinner that night. By evening, the previous night's venom had dissipated into the foggy San Franciscan air.

Lloyd is whorl-ing farther and farther into the woods. He has to find Saul. He has to verify his presence. He has to confront him and then let him go. That is what you do with ghosts. He will do the same with Saul, that sylvan creature who has disappeared into the night. Suddenly, Lloyd has a thought that physically jerks him upright: What if Saul has been haunting Lloyd all this time? What if Saul has been the infiltrator, the perpetrator of Lloyd's insides? What if Saul had caught Lloyd at a weak moment, possibly during those early-morning hours in Karom's bed, when he'd crawled into an orifice and had settled there, festering and implanting this idea into the fissures in Lloyd's brain? What if Lloyd is finally meeting Saul head-on now, after all these years of fighting with himself inside about who he might really be? Suddenly, Lloyd is grappling with a new opponent, of whom he hadn't even been aware. This isn't fair play, Lloyd thinks. That doesn't put us on even ground. This isn't a fair fight. But fair or not, Saul has to go. And Lloyd isn't leaving these woods with him.

Lloyd lowers himself onto a wet stump and holds his chin in his hands. Now he is haunted by two men, one real and one devised. This is the opposite of what he has come to the woods to do. Instead of exorcising one man, he has taken on another. He's succeeded in inventing a specter. He's losing his mind. The woods feel as if they are closing in on him, the damp leaves of the trees getting heavier with each drop of water that falls from the sky, the ground squelching under his heavy hiking boots that have barely been broken in. Lloyd is literally lost in the woods. He thinks about the bus that will take him back to the airport, which will arrive at the visitors' center in forty minutes. If he doesn't make that one, he will miss his flight home.

Mohan and Rana Seth

～

February 12, 1988

Dear Karom,

Your mother and I have talked, argued and deliberated over this letter for a long time. I think it's silly, writing a letter that we'll never send. But our social worker suggested a therapist—another introduction into our lives that I've been grappling with—and he suggested that we do this in order to adjust. In fact, I'm not sure how I will adjust to these New Agey exercises, but I hope it will help in the long run. The therapist has suggested that we write this letter constantly, in tandem, and without self-censorship or limitation. I'll comply, because it's easier than going to a stranger's office and spilling your guts. This, I think, is the lesser of two evils.

Your mother found a book in the library the other day and wordlessly handed it to me. I was sitting at the dining table, pondering a piece of toast as I turned it over carefully in my hand. She set it down on the table and continued on into the nursery, where you were still sleeping. I picked it up and skimmed the back. It was a copy of Nathaniel Hawthorne's diary, likely an attempt to prove that keeping a diary is no shame, when one of America's foremost writers had one. But in fact, this was no ordinary diary: it was a transcription of a marital diary kept by both Sophia and Nathaniel Hawthorne that they began together from the moment they were united in holy matrimony. These were interactive documents, intentionally designed so one could understand what the other was feeling, thinking. They read one another's contributions and built a joint narrative of their daily lives. "A rainy day—a rainy day—and I do verily believe there is no sunshine in this world, except what beams from my wife's eyes," Hawthorne wrote shortly after they wed. "We have been living in eternity, ever since we came to this old Manse....It is good to live as though this world were heaven."

No doubt Sophia read this and responded with her own joyous words: "I feel new as the Earth which is just born again—I rejoice that I am, because I am his, wholly, unreservedly his." The book was filled with glorious exultations of their love for one another, beautiful unabashed declarations describing their love as mighty and shielding against a harsh New England winter. At first, I felt embarrassed reading some of these entries, the effervescent flow of words, the saccharine showiness. I felt like an intruder in their private exchange. But it also made me regret that your mother and I hadn't kept a joint diary from the start of our lives, to document—if for nobody else but ourselves—how we began together, how we fought, how we continued together....

Reading their first words together as a naive couple made me want to tell our story from the start so that your mother can understand how I felt about her on our very first encounter. How I still feel today.

As you know, your mother and I met on a film set. Nothing fancy—an ad for Nutria face cream. I was the director of the advertisement, desperate to get into something big, even direct my own short, to break into something that might define me cinematically. I'd worked as a stagehand on commercials in the past during college as a way to make money, but it was a new thing, especially in India. I hadn't been allowed to attend film school, so all the skills I learned on set, as my first-year biology classes weren't going to afford me any insight into this foreign, enticing world. Over the years, I'll make you watch a number of Satyajit Ray and Dharma Sen movies and you won't be able to argue that you haven't become a better man for it. In fact, in this no-sending letter-writing medium, you won't even have a chance to argue back. Perhaps this therapist is onto something.

You'll see in Sen's movie *Count Your Courage,* when the platoon leader has to tell the shepherd about the land mines and he can't, that he just finds himself stumbling over the words. And he knows that the longer he waits to tell him, the harder it'll be. It's a matter of life and death, and the burden will grow greater and greater on the platoon leader's conscience. That's how I feel right now. That unless I tell you, far away from the pages of this letter, I'm going to regret it later. But it's a decision that your mother and I made and it's one we can't get away from, because we have already lied to everyone: your grandparents, our friends, our colleagues.

It was the late, great Mr. Ray who taught me something about film that no other filmmaker ever could: the importance of suspense. It isn't inherent in his movies, and Ray is no Hitchcock, but there is an element of suspense that, if you look closely, drives each and every story. If you watch

The Apu Trilogy knowing this, you'll see what I mean. So I took this lesson and walked onto the set of Nutria face cream. Suspense. I know you're wondering how I could turn an ad for face cream suspenseful. I'll tell you.

The casting director had culled down the talent pool and selected a girl who would show up at the shoot that morning. She should have been in Makeup hours before I got on the set, prepping her lines, memorizing her marks.

"Do you want to meet the talent?" I was asked moments after appearing on the set.

I told them no. I wandered around, finding fault with things—having stagehands erase scuff marks from the floor, adjusting cameras, toying with lighting. I looked through the wardrobe and vetoed half the clothes on the line, settling on the simplest sari, with no border.

"Sir, she's just finished with hair and makeup. Do you want to check her before we send her to Wardrobe?" I shook my head and kept up my time-wasting charade. All things I needed to do, but certainly I needed to meet the talent in order to determine lighting and wardrobe. In fact, I refused to meet the girl until fifteen minutes before we began rolling tape. I was thinking about everything but the focus of the scene. And that's when your mother emerged from the dressing room, poised and confident, holding out her hand to me.

The girl was completely wrong. She was dark, she was complicated; an incomplete story was written behind her face, which was more intense and bewitching than anything I'd seen before. She had fierce, inquiring eyes and a mouth that twitched before she asked a question.

She was unlike any model I'd ever worked with. There was nothing nondescript about her, which had been the casting call: "Tall, slim, pretty girl with a clear fair complexion. The face cream should be the true star."

I took one look at her and I knew I couldn't work with her. I'd be doing myself a disservice as a director if I kept her, because she wasn't what the client was looking for at all. I dialed the casting director but then regretted it immediately. How was I going to explain to him that I couldn't work with this girl because her face was "complicated"?

"Look here, Rajeet. What are you playing at?"

"How's it going, Mohan, boss? How's the talent? Rana's not bad, eh?"

"She's totally wrong. She's too dark, with intense eyes. We needed a light-skinned pretty young thing, someone a little reticent. This girl looks like she could rip my balls out from under me."

"I don't know what to tell you, boss. I thought she was pretty good. But dark is no good. Perhaps I need to change the lighting out in my office. Can you slap a few more layers of powder on her? I can't change her at this point. Your set is eating up rupees by the minute."

I hung up the phone and stalked back to the set, where your mother was standing by the sink in which she would wash her face countless times in the next few hours.

"Is there a problem?" she asked me. "Shouldn't we begin?" I rubbed my eyes and that's when it struck me. That's when I knew that I was completely taken—smitten—by this dark, charming girl with the alluring features.

There were a few girls before your mother, but I struggle with remembering even their faces as I write this. There was not one forgettable thing about your mother, though, to the point where she would leave a memento of herself on my person every time I saw her. I would return home and find a lacy handkerchief with her embroidered initials mysteriously stuffed into my pocket. She'd slip a small silver tube into my briefcase, complete with lip marks creased onto the color so that I'd realize I was in possession of something that had been so close to her mouth. I carried her lipstick around for a month before a colleague reached into my bag to borrow a pen, handed me the lipstick and cuffed me on the shoulder for being such a rascal. She certainly wanted to announce her arrival onto the scene—our scene. But there was no need for this. I was already taken by the wrong girl on the set. I didn't want her for the commercial; I wanted her for my life.

Not only is your mother a beauty, she's incredibly wily. She knew exactly what she was doing, using the Hawthornes as a point when she handed me this book. She knew that using a historical writer as a pawn would get me to tap into my feelings. It did.

But there is one thing that still plagues me: the Hawthornes' letters were written to be private, meant only for one another's eyes and hearts and emotions. This quote sums it up perfectly: "We are happier than we then knew, or perhaps than we now know, for who can tell what is to come?" They had no idea that hundreds of years later, these secret words and sentiments would be published and bound, distributed for everyone to read their private disclosures to one another. Not to mention that later, when they were blessed with children, the kids too added drawings to the pages of their parents' notebooks, transforming the marriage diary into a family affair, which is something I don't want. I don't want these diaries found by anyone—not an editor or a publisher, and certainly not by you. I don't want you adding to these pages, much less reading them. This is something I want your mother to know loud and clear. That this is my first concern in writing them.

Before your father gets all carried away with his dramatic flair, I want to interject with my motivations for this letter.

It wasn't that I ever wanted to hide anything from you. I didn't. Ever. But we wanted you to grow up naturally, normally, without hesitation or question. And that was more important than the concern we had over hiding information.

You're going through a hard time right now in your school. You aren't telling me, but I can see it in the bruised circles under your eyes. You aren't sleeping or eating properly. You smile at me and you tell me everything is okay. I've spoken to your teacher but she says that she hasn't seen any signs of bullying and that you're actually a very well-adjusted boy in class, producing drawings and learning your letters at the same speed as everyone else. I have no doubt that you're performing well in school, but that's also my concern—that you're putting on an act that's throwing Appa and me for a loop. I hope you'll confide in me soon. I hope you're all right, that these are just growing pains.

Second, I didn't mean to "trick" your father with that diary; it was meant just to show how powerful a diary can be. It can help people profess their deepest secrets, even ones they don't realize they have. I have never felt as though he hadn't shared his true feelings for me, even from the start, but sometimes without the pressure of having to speak to a face, to a live breathing person who can easily respond, writing can help break down that barrier of intimidation and truly allow people to speak their minds. I am hoping that we communicate here what might not be divulged during numerous useless sessions with a therapist, while we sit there staring at one another, listening to the torturous ticks of the clock go by, growing noisier and noisier in the echoes of our ears. I want truth, purity of truth and courage to speak our minds. That is why the forum of our therapy is on paper and not in a shrink's office.

As for the fear of having this diary found and published—

well, I can't say what happens after I leave this earth, but I will do all I can to keep it from getting into your hands, even though it is written and addressed to you. That too was done intentionally, even though only your father and I will ever be reading it. And this too is to help us cross that barrier of intimidation. Perhaps telling the truth will be easier or we can similarly trick ourselves into telling the "you" in this letter the truth instead of having to tell the real you the truth.

I find myself wondering so much about your life. I wonder about the future, what you'll be doing. What you'll look like. Who will you look like? Who will you be with? Will you love? Will you be loved? I've thought about all these things already, Karom, and you're still my little boy. I can't help it. You're my life.

I see you chuckle to yourself as you always do when you catch me eating fruit with salt, unable to abandon my "Indian ways." You also laugh when I put spicy pickle on spaghetti or massage my hair with coconut oil on the weekends. I wonder if you too will inherently pick up these habits, as they are the habits you were born with. As a bird knows how to fly or a tiger cub knows how to hunt. I wonder if one day, as your fork is traveling to your mouth holding strands of noodles covered with *achar*, you will stop to realize what you are doing, if you will remember me, if you will consider yourself truly your mother's son.

Though you'll never see this letter, I have been wondering how you might respond if you ever found it. I've never lied to you, Karom. I've always told you everything when you asked. When you asked where babies come from at the tender age of five, I sat you down and explained it all, making my own crude drawings in crayon to demonstrate anatomy. For weeks afterward you would take the drawings out from where you'd rescued them from the trash and pore over them. You'd tell everyone what you had learned—at the grocery store, at preschool… I was mortified until one day we were out having lunch at Shanghai Garden and you told Mr. Wong as we were ordering soup dumplings. Mr. Wong's almond-shaped eyes got larger and larger as you narrated your story. I tried interrupting you, but your father shook his head and said quietly to let you go on, so you did. And by the time it was over, your father was doubled over with laughter, tears leaking out from the corners of his eyes as Mr. Wong hurried to the back to put in our order and likely try to find another waiter for our table. I couldn't help but laugh then, too. And when you asked why you couldn't have a birthday at Great Adventure like your friend Joshua in the fifth grade, I never made up some cockamamy story about us not wanting to take the responsibility for ten kids in New Jersey let loose in a theme park. I calmly sat you down and told you that we just couldn't afford it right now, that things were tough at Dad's work and that I had lost an account with my office, and we would just have to make it up the following year. And you understood perfectly; in fact, you tried to return your allowance for the next three weeks, until we promised you that the five dollars you received each week wasn't hurting our finances.

But the truth is that I've never lied to you about this either; I just never told you the complete truth. I suppose the way I have justified it to myself is that I tell myself that you never really asked. But why would you ask this? As a child, you assume it, just as you assume there will be money under your pillow the morning after you lose a tooth.

There are so many reasons that we weren't forthright with you about this one. One is that I know there will be anger—your anger. It will come silently at first, simmering at the top like a pot of water for tea or spaghetti. But then it will boil over, and I won't know how to contain it. This aspect of you is something I haven't learned completely yet, partially because your anger has come so rarely yet so fairly; I have never been taken aback by your ire. You anger only when the worst has struck, when nothing else can be done, when it's a last resort. When you were a child, you would awaken in your crib and stare at the ceiling, knowing that we too would be asleep. You'd entertain yourself—I watched silently one morning from my bed when we first brought you home. You'd create patterns in the air with your finger, puff your breath out in front of you to watch the fringe of your hair dance and then finally pull yourself to a stand holding the rungs of the crib. You'd watch Dad and me carefully—I lay back with my eyes mostly closed so you couldn't see—pass your gaze over us and verify that we were asleep. You would accept this and turn back to your crib and try to sleep once again but it would fail you. I didn't understand how you had this sixth sense to you, as if you knew how to behave, like an adult. How had you somehow been taught this inherent patience, this benevolence that could barely translate to adults and the people I encountered on the streets every day? But after some time, after you felt you'd waited enough, the whimpering would begin, softly enough that at times we could barely hear it. And then you would erupt. But you had been holding back for so long that I couldn't blame you for your rage at not being picked up out of the crib or held and comforted.

I never thought I would be this person—this person whose previous life was all but erased to distant memory after a child came into my life. Your mother and I would always poke fun at our friends behind their backs when they had children. It was as if there were nothing else in their worlds anymore. Days at the beach with nothing else but a blanket, a six-pack of beer and a Frisbee didn't exist anymore. They were replaced by days at the beach with water wings and baby food and gargantuan diaper bags that eclipsed your view of the rolling waves. Everything became a world that revolved around nap times and feeding times. Spending time with our friends started to feel like constantly being at the zoo. Gradually, as you'll learn when the time comes for you and your friends to have children, you start to back away into your own personal space and become an inclusive family. Of course, you still go out and spend time with your friends but the priorities change and diaper changes really matter more than birthday parties, as we learned on my forty-fifth birthday, when we looked around the table and it was just Mom and Ravi Uncle who cheered me on as I blew out my candles. All the other parents were settling their kids in for naps or feeding them or changing them or had left before we'd served cake because their child needed to "stick to his routine." Of course, we scoffed and passed it off as "More cake for us," but it was clear what was happening in our world. So it is much to my chagrin that when I look back at our lives in New York before you entered our world, it's very difficult to remember those moments pre-Karom.

Once you were here, it was as if the memory board had been wiped clean. Everything did revolve around you: Had you eaten, had you slept, had you learned a new English word each day? Once you turned five, our goals surpassed toilet training to helping you integrate into an American world so you wouldn't feel like the odd one out in kindergarten. It happened by accident. I'd come back into the kitchen one morning from answering the phone to find you sitting there with a bowl of upturned cereal, a trail of milk dripping its way across our faulty slanted floor and a grin on your face.

"Oh, Karom," I sighed. "What a mess."

"Mess," you whispered almost under your breath. You'd gotten over your shyness for the most part by then, but it must have been the English word that made you self-conscious. You'd heard Mom and me speak in English for a few months by then, but it was when you repeated that word so softly, so hesitantly, that we realized we'd done you a disservice by not coaxing you to learn more and more each day. Then it became our mission: we bought a word-a-day calendar for kids, and although it was really made for second graders and you were only five at the time, we figured it might give you a head start into the competitive world of New York City public schools. Each morning, we sat at the kitchen table with you before kindergarten. We started basic with the numbers, the letters, and then moved on to the things we thought you'd need to know while we were at work and you were at day care: *bathroom, toilet, hungry, parents,* the subtlety between *want* and *need.* It became our one mission a day and we would test you on it as we tucked you into bed, where we learned truly what a charmer you were even as a young child who barely spoke much English.

"What do you want tonight, Karom?"

"Story."

"What do you need tonight?"

"Kiss."

In those days, those early days when we were just getting on our feet, we cut corners. We didn't always live in this beautiful brownstone in Brooklyn Heights. In the early days it was Kew Gardens, it was Middle Village, it was tiny apartments in vast nameless apartment blocks without soul, without charm. But it was what we could afford; it was the sacrifice we told ourselves we would make for the long run. When we moved to New York from Bombay, I'd struck a deal with your father that we would do it on the condition that we wouldn't settle in those ghettos of Indians I'd heard about: the ones in Edison and Jackson Heights and Flushing where people settle into communities complete with the same groceries they could have found down on Peddar Road, where they could probably have benefited from the same English lesson we gave you each morning. "I'm moving to America," I'd told Dad. "I'm not moving to some foreign form of India. If we're leaving, we're leaving. I want to live with the New Yorkers once we get on our feet. Deal?" We'd shaken on it, but it took us a little longer than expected before we headed west from the industrial-sized apartment communities and were able to put a down payment on our brownstone. Those were difficult days before Dad and Ravi got Cutting Room onto its feet. They were working late nights to make their dream of launching their own film-editing company come true, but as it was taking longer than we had expected, I was supporting our two-person family with the little I made from Tiger Translations. We ate a lot of fifty-cent meals: back then you could get a carton of cold sesame noodles from the Chinese carts on Main Street for fifty cents, two of which would feed us for an evening. We had fifty-cent pizza and fish and chips at the fast-food place on the corner on Fifty Cent Fridays. Fifty cents was the magic number. It was astounding what you could get for that amount of money back then. Fifty cents kept us alive for a long time.

It was during that time that I discovered the thrift stores. There was a row of them on Thirty-Seventh Avenue that I would walk past on my way to the 7 train. For the longest time, I avoided them. Back home in Bombay, we never bought things secondhand. Those were the things you gave to the *kabadi wala*, the junk man who came to your door to take anything deemed not biodegradable that he would try to mend or repurpose and sell again to a lower class. I hadn't ever even seen a secondhand store in Bombay, much less set foot into one. My parents would have considered themselves failures had I ever bought something "vintage." But once I overcame my nerves and my pride, it was these stores that outfitted our home so that we didn't have to sit and eat our fifty-cent pizza off the floor. Once I got over myself and passed the threshold into one that first morning, everything changed for me. These stores became more valuable than the places where you paid double to get essentially the same thing, just with a little less wear to it. But who cared, right? I could throw a slipcover on that perfectly good divan, which would give your father hours of endless joy as he reclined on it watching the evening news. I bought piles and piles of books from these shops, classics and bestsellers that I couldn't bring myself to purchase at full price from the Barnes & Noble on Fifth Avenue. Cast-iron pots and pans were actually better bought used, as they had already been treated and scratched and were perfectly poised to simmer on a stove holding a slow-cooked roast for hours. Visiting these stores became like a treasure hunt: you never knew what you were going to find. Granted, most of the stuff was junk, so you had to be truly discerning in order to find those one or two items that would be worth bringing into your home. Even once we hit it big and Dad became a partner in Cutting Room and started bringing home all those awards, even then, I realized I couldn't break my ties with the thrift stores. They were a part of me now. They had humbled me and forced me to recognize my lot in life when we'd first moved to this country. So even once we moved to our brownstone in the Heights, I'd continue to take you there so that you'd appreciate them, too.

In the beginning the concept was strange to you. Why were all these used items stored in this place? Who would buy them and take them away? And the most important question to you: Whom had they belonged to? The first time we stepped into the Goodwill on Atlantic, that was all you could grasp.

You pointed to a yellow leathery ottoman creased with age but that would clean up nicely with some polishing and asked, "Who?" At first I thought you were assigning characterizations to the furniture, like in *Beauty and the Beast*, so I just said, "Ottoman," to teach you the word and continued toward the kitchenware section. But you tugged at my dress and pointed to the ottoman again.

"Who?"

"Not who, Karom. What." But you pressed on.

"Who?"

I knelt down to you. "Baby, I don't understand you. What are you asking me?"

"Who was?"

I got it then. You wanted to know to whom that had belonged. This was the part that made me a little squeamish, I'll admit. Part of getting comfortable with the idea of buying secondhand items was pretending that they hadn't belonged to someone in the first place. I didn't want to think about what had been cooked in our cast-irons even though I had scrubbed them until they shone. I didn't want to know who had reclined on the divan before your father, who had wound the grandfather clock's hands before we had, who had eaten off our plates and sipped wine out of our goblets. In my mind, when I'd washed things upon their entry to our home, they were purified, like a child damp from

baptism and brand-new to us. But I also didn't want to con-
fuse you. I wanted you to know that these were in fact secondhand objects, that they had belonged to someone who
didn't need them anymore and therefore had brought them
here for someone else's use.

"I don't know whose this was," I'd said. "I think maybe
we can make up a story, though. Would you like to do that?"
You walked over to the ottoman and gently caressed it as
if it were a living thing. Your little fingers were so knowing, so wise. At times when you were small, I felt like you
were the incarnation of a monk, the next Dalai Lama. You
touched the wooden legs one by one and then turned to me.

"Old man with a dog," you said by way of introduction.

"Oh?" I asked, playing along. "And what's the dog's
name?"

"Buster." I laughed out loud then because I'd just started
reading you Enid Blyton's *The Five Find-Outers and Dog*. And
like that, little by little, you began walking around the rest
of the store assigning backgrounds and stories to each of
the items. You were entertaining not only to me but to the
other shoppers as you tapped a piece of furniture or a scarf
or coat and told the story of how it found itself here. Everything had a history to you; everything had a reason for belonging to someone. It was another reason that I have always
felt that you have a very old soul, that you can see deeper
into a situation than most. I wonder if this is a trait you'll
always carry with you as you grow. I wonder if you'll always create a history for everything you see and touch and
interact with. It would explain so much about who you are.

I loved those days with you. Dad doesn't love the thrift
stores like I do. He gets impatient; he's more of a "run in
and get what you want" kind of shopper, whereas I like to
browse. He and I epitomize the ideas of need and want.

Shopping is painful for him, whereas it's a release for me. So you and I had plenty of quality time together while we were shopping.

It wasn't that Dad or I ever needed a child; we have always had a solid relationship, and for many years, we were completely happy just the two of us. Of course we had times where we were easily frustrated, snapping at the slightest thing, overworked, overtired, overtaxed. But mostly, somehow we came home and fell into one another as though there was no other way. Even on those nights where the fight seeped out from us as though from a strainer, we found a bypass and circuitously made our way around the argument, watching it nervously as it became a speck on the horizon behind us. We had a good life, creating our home, making dinner, trying so hard to see into the future. We were married for only a few years before we began to think about children. We talked about it, and we both wanted them, but it was just as our careers were beginning to peak. If it happened, it happened. If not, there was always next year. I knew I could do this for only so long, but I tried my best to stay focused on my job so that we could provide for a little one, whenever that might be. But then one night, as we sat watching the news with our plates on our laps and glasses of wine on the floor next to the couch, your father and I looked at one another and we knew. The time had come to bring a child into our lives.

There's this thing that happened. It's called the Bhopal disaster. It was one of the worst industrial disasters of all time. At the Union Carbide pesticide plant in December 1984, a chemical leak killed over two thousand people immediately and the backwash continued to kill over three thousand in the ensuing days. Some reports state that as many as fifteen thousand people died altogether. The gas cloud continued out of the factory and into the town, where it consumed the lives of thousands of people. People were startled by the odor, awakened by their own vomiting, unaware of what had caught in their throats, behind their larynxes, within their esophagi. The moment they could move, they did, running away from the plant as fast as they could. Those who ran inhaled more than those who had a vehicle to ride. It resulted in illnesses, in crystallized organs that appeared frozen midbreath. Eyes burned; victims cried toxic waste for days; a river of sputum gurgled in the street. Short people and children inhaled more, as the fumes nestled closer to the ground and hung there like a shroud over the entire city.

It was a huge conspiracy theory; apparently there had been safety issues with the plant all along but foremen refused to report it or stop work in order to maintain productivity. There had been gas leaks and explosions leading up to this catastrophe that had been covered up and the work went on without fail each day, every day. Mothers were childless; husbands were wifeless; children were orphaned almost immediately.

What had happened was water. The simplest element had crept into one of the main pipes, raising the pressure in the tanks and reacting with the already toxic chemicals and imploding the tank from the inside. From there, a ripple effect occurred, as all the tanks and pipes were interconnected within the factory, and the easterly winds carried the gas swiftly into the city, where sleeping bodies lay oblivious to anything.

The factory had employed a large percentage of those who lived outside its gates. There were makeshift *chawls* and shantytowns devoted solely to the workers who tended to the chemicals, cleaned the pipes methodically, and undercut the safety measures that should have been enforced each and every day at this throbbing powder keg that erupted that night. When it was safe for workers to enter the area with insectlike gas masks, there was no point; the damage had been done, and all the health authorities, the Red Cross and the UN could do was pick the bodies off the ground like pieces of litter.

When the cameras swept across the charred gray land, it was a holocaust. Your mother and I watched the scenes on CNN in horror. I felt her break down beside me and I held her tight as she sobbed. We watched as thousands of fish bobbed on the surface of the Betwa River, killed instantly as the poison entered their gills. Over a few hours, the leaves on all the trees had turned yellow and brittle and fell off at the slightest breeze. Bloated animal carcasses from the farms and fields surrounding were cremated alongside the hundreds, thousands of dead. There was nothing; it felt surreal that a hunk of the middle of India was silenced in a few mere hours by chemicals, by oversight, by greed.

There was a huge backlash: protests and sit-ins and strikes. As soon as the area was considered safe again, the living and the ill now stormed the streets, demanding that the CEO of Union Carbide pay for the havoc he'd created and provide for the remaining affected families. And everyone was affected. Cancer, tumor necrosis, lung failure, stillborns, birth defects—no one was spared. Those lucky enough to be spared were shuttled to the very outskirts of the disaster, where tents and other makeshift shelters were erected, but there was a dearth in the number of doctors and nurses and relief workers who came to their aid.

The Indian government got involved, but everyone accused them of siding with the company, who up until this point had been employing a vast number of Indians and pumping revenue into the system. But Indians were no longer hoodwinked; they demanded justice. The case went on for years. In fact, it's still going on. UCC has nearly been exonerated and the successor and victims continue to pass down their ailments through their children and grandchildren. This is in their blood now, the chemical residue, this anathema. But it's not in yours.

Once it was official—once we'd signed all the papers and made copies for our files and pages had been stamped and signatures notarized—the staff left us in the room we'd been in for hours before they led you in. You tottered in holding the social worker's hand, wearing shabby *chappals* and exploring our faces with those huge eyes that were calm but wary. The social worker put your little hand in Mom's before stepping away and silently closing the door behind her. All that morning, we'd been aching to leave that chilled, mildewed room, but there was a force field in the room that pulled us together, that urged us to stay. I pulled up a plastic chair next to Mom's and she pulled you onto her lap and rocked you back and forth, tears spilling from her eyes into your uncombed hair, and there, for the first time since I'd laid eyes upon your mother in that screening studio years before, I felt complete.

Your mother would have been content to admire you for the rest of the day in that room, but I was firmly rational: we had to ensure that before we did anything else, you were safe. So that afternoon itself, we handed you over to masked doctors who took you into sterilized rooms and made you cough. They made you open your eyes wide, as well as your little pink mouth. They listened to your heart and let you listen, too, and you giggled with the thump of your chest resounding in your ears. They tested your reflexes; they drew blood. They counted your white blood cells and your red.

They took X-rays and bone density and scraped the inside of your cheek. In the beginning it was all a game.

"Look, look, let's see what we can find inside our mouths. Want to see it under a microscope?" Initially, the doctors co-operated with our games, but with the increasing number of tests and incoming patients, they became methodical and serious. I perfected my number of funny faces and voices and became a one-man cartoon show. Your mother crafted sock puppets to entertain you in the waiting rooms. Finally, finally, when you had been searched and searched and they had found nothing, and they told us that you were certifiably 100 percent healthy and that no chemical traces had been left on you, we took you home. We were overjoyed. I wonder, do you remember? You spoke Hindi first, chaste, beautiful Hindi, and your mother and I prattled to you non-stop in this language that we hadn't used in eight years.

We stopped for ice cream at the side of the road before the long drive back to Bombay. I was worried about sanitation, but your mother reminded me that we had long been eating these things and that you were raised on them. We bought you a Feast stick and a Thums Up and you sat there happily on a bench in the dust, with caramel across your cheek and your hands sticky with cola. There was a board on a lone table next to the snack stand, and a small pile of wooden coins, some plain and some painted black. I positioned them in a circle in the center of the board and you crept up beside me and watched as I flicked the striker into the center and all the pieces dispersed. I had even managed to get one in, and you were tickled pink. You handed me the remnants of your ice cream and strained your neck to see more closely. I shot the striker again and got another one in and you climbed up on the bench next to me. I struck and scored. You put your arm out tentatively, shyly, but almost as quickly snapped it back into your body. I reached over and put you on my lap and did it again, landing the queen nicely in a pocket, even without the gentle ricochet against the back wall.

"Now," I whispered in Hindi, "we have to follow that up." I aimed carefully, wanting so badly to please you, to win you over, but I missed. I removed the queen from the pocket and put it back in the center of the board. You looked at me quizzically.

"See," I said, "if you don't follow the queen up with an-other win, you have to put her back. She needs support. You can't just take her away—you have to sacrifice another." You nodded solemnly and I took another shot, this time sideways, using my thumb's force against my forefinger, and I got her in. And it was at that moment that I felt your tiny tensed body, constantly thrumming with nervous en-ergy from the moment we met you—even while you slept—finally relax. I felt your warm back against my chest and your small head, dusty from the side of the road, loll against my shoulder. That lean meant trust. That lean meant more to me than any hug or squeeze you have ever given me since. Up until then you could have been any child. But at that dusty rest stop, when you were healthy and leaned back into me, when you were pulsing with sugar and laughter and joy, you were our child then and there. You became our Karom.

A blind woman brought you in. You clung to her and wouldn't let go. But she couldn't have fed you even if she could have seen. The river was polluted; the livestock was dead; the fields had wilted and died. This was your only hope. They say you didn't say a word after she left. We found out later that both your mother and father worked at the plant, your mother in packaging and your father in the underbelly of the operation, scrubbing and replacing pipes. He might have even had some insight into what happened that night. We don't know what happened to them; they might have perished in the accident, or they might have survived, becoming so severely disfigured and disoriented that they couldn't remember where they came from. They could have been unrecognizable. Nevertheless, they had the foresight—and the poverty—to situate you and their home miles from the plant. They walked three miles each morning to a rattling bus that was overcrowded with livestock and people that took them another twenty miles to their jobs each morning. The blind woman looked after you while your parents worked each day. She earned her living by caring for the children in the village. She had her meal at a different home each night, and afterward, each night, someone led her home by the hand and helped her unlock her small one-roomed hut. She was blind, but she had raised you into something else. You were so well behaved, so incredibly curious but never mischievous. I wondered who this woman was and the power she had to control even those she couldn't see.

In those early days, you took to me and your dad like you had been with us all along. I'd had nightmares of having to win you over, of having to ply you with sweets and toys and do all the things they said not to do in the parenting books. I wanted you to be unequivocally ours. And you were. It was as if you understood that the situation demanded practicalities rather than emotion; your parents were gone and you couldn't take care of yourself, so we were your new parents. You were a mature grown-up in a two-year-old body. You started to call us Papa and Mama shortly after we took you home and then Mom and Dad when school began, lest you be different from any of your schoolmates. You were meant to be our son.

We hadn't wanted to hide this from you, ever. But because of the situation, because of the urgent nature of the way you came into our lives, we didn't want to have to educate you about what had happened when so many other people were trying to erase it from their memories or simply couldn't remember it because the poison had clouded their minds, rendering them incapable of thought or coherent speech. We wanted to move on. We wanted you to feel like ours. We wanted you never to feel as though you'd been abandoned or forgotten or were an outsider.

We did it to protect you, never to hurt you. We wanted you to be safe and secure with who you are and who you have always been. That day at the side of the road, the one that your dad referenced, was the first day of your life, as far as we were concerned. And from then on, we were going to stop at nothing to give you everything you needed.

I keep telling myself that if you find out, you'll understand why we didn't tell you. You'd been through so much, we wanted to keep you safe from all those ghosts. At some point, you'd forgive us and understand the power of secrets, how some secrets can keep you safe, bundled away from the raw, biting truth, from the gas leaks and deformities of Bhopal, your hometown. Maybe you'll go back there someday and see the ravages painted across the faces of those less fortunate than you. You'll see the memorial erected to commemorate the fallen, the sick, the injured and the penniless who couldn't support themselves after their households suffered losses far worse than we could ever imagine. Most of all, though, I hope you'll see the binding, unconditional

love that your mother and I have for you. You are our own,
Karom. We wanted nothing more than a normal life for you.

I won't apologize at this point, because I'm not sorry. I'm
not sorry at all that the news report we watched that night
was enough to spur us into action and call the Red Cross to
see if there was anything we could do to help. Neither of us
have ancestry in Bhopal, but this disaster was too close to
home to ignore it. We both felt the urgency like an itch, and
sending money wouldn't be enough. I thought then, as the
camera panned the scene, of those left behind, the sick, the
tortured, the abandoned. It wasn't martyrdom; it was need.
We needed to help, and people needed us. It was a symbi-
otic relationship and we scratched one another's backs. We
called multiple agencies, but no one was taking in orphans
from Bhopal, not just yet. It was too soon; mothers might
still be about, lost in the mess of bureaucracy or mayhem.
We called and called until finally a client of your father's
who had been filming in Madhya Pradesh gave him a card
with a direct contact for a woman who was running child-
support services in the area. We called her and she told us
to call back in a month's time, when everything was sorted.
A month and a week later, we were on a plane to meet you.

I'm not sorry for finding you on that bed, eyes like silver
dollars staring up at me, watching my every move, down
to the rustle of my sari, the metallic clanking of my ear-
rings. I fell in love with you then, with your dark skin that
would match mine; no one would know I hadn't birthed
you. I fell in love with the thatch of hair that fell across your
face; I knew I wouldn't ever allow a barber to cut it until it
was absolutely necessary. Your tiny fingers that held the

pen we gave you to distract you while we signed papers and papers and papers.

I'm not sorry you entered our lives with such an easy rhythm, like the entrance of an instrument to a symphony, one that harmonizes and syncopates with the surrounding elements. You fit so naturally; it was so difficult to believe you weren't ours. Initially, even, the grocers and neighbors were shocked that they hadn't seen our child up until now.

"Where have you been hiding him?"

"What a beautiful boy, such eyes like saucers."

"He looks just like you."

I was tickled pink at that one. I still think we look alike, somehow, like people who have lived together long enough that their features begin to mimic each other's. I told myself that it was our dark skin that made us fated toward one another; it was my dark skin that had fated me to your father. My dark, "complicated" skin, as he calls it, destined me for him. And so you would resemble me, if only superficially. That's truly enough for people who want to believe what you tell them.

We told anyone who asked that you are our son, that you were born here in Queens but we'd taken you back to India to your grandparents, who had been caring for you while our work schedules couldn't allow us to give you the attention you deserved. We told our friends that the pain of having you away from us was too much to bear and this was why we hadn't told anyone about you. But you soon became a favorite at the studio and I brought you to my office for the Halloween parties and the Fourth of July events they had for children and families.

You were so observant, pointing out the sparkles in the sidewalk as though they were magic. I hadn't the heart to tell you that they were part of the abrasive grit of the cement poured there so that people could see the contours of the pavement and not slip. I let you believe that the slivers were magic, and you used to wish upon the shimmering squares as though they would bring you luck. You would crane your neck up toward the buildings that spiraled up out of the ground, from where they were rooted in the underworld. You would squint to see the very tops of them and you would question why you couldn't when we were standing right underneath. I told you that we had to be standing some distance away, and you asked, in Hindi at the time, "Why do you have to be far away to see something that's right in front of you?"

"Because your eye can't take it all in. It's too big," I told you. You didn't accept this answer and you asked your father the same question even though he gave you the same answer when you saw him that evening. You were entranced somehow by the dollar-coin-sized black splotches on the pavement, your eyes flickering from one to the other as we rolled over them in your stroller. Years later you would come to learn that they were pieces of chewing gum rejected by people years before and then stomped upon until they'd lost all trace of former texture or color. You didn't understand and you continued to point at them, a strained expression on your small face. You wanted to know the names of things, in Hindi first and then in English as you grew older and understood that there was more than one way of speaking. Somewhere in your keen sense of understanding, you grew to accept the fact that there was a divide between the things that your father and I could say to you and even Ravi Uncle and the things we could say to the people on the street or in the shops we frequented, who knelt down to peer into your stroller to see eye to eye, or peered over the counter to catch a glimpse of

you and say hello. You grew shy with these English speakers, until one day you grew brazen enough to say the one
English word you had learned with gusto, *orange juice*, and
somehow that became your default greeting. When I left
you at your nursery school for the first time, I explained
to the women in charge that you were still picking up the
nuances of English and not to continually hand you juice
boxes each time you opened your mouth. This was before
Dad and I started with our vocabulary games, but within a
few weeks of interaction with the other children, you were
chattering happily away and *orange juice* was abandoned
from your repertoire, unless, of course, you truly wanted
orange juice.

Words for you became magic, just like those shimmers
in the sidewalk. When you learned a new one, you held it
in your mouth, saying it quietly to yourself and then gradually louder and louder until you somehow connected how
to properly use it. It was as if your mouth were brimming
with marbles, like Audrey Hepburn in *My Fair Lady* until
she could learn proper pronunciation and diction. Nam-
ing things was essential to you, just as it was for us when
you entered our lives.

The blind woman had called you Tej. The agency had
called you Madhav. You responded to neither, to nothing,
really, until Dad showed you how to play carom and then
suddenly, immediately, you were Karom. I was hesitant at
first to name you after a game. It seemed trivial and flip-
pant, especially after all you'd been through and all we'd
been through to find you. But Karom, well, *carom* really,
means to ricochet, to rebound. And that's what you did.
You were resilient against all the odds and you reentered
this new life with simplicity and ease. You fit. You were
natural. You were ours.

★ ★ ★

So this is our lie, or as I once told you when we were planning Mom's surprise party all those years ago, it's our half-truth. It's finally complete. It's something we'll never voluntarily tell you, in fear that it would hurt you more than it would help. You've already lost one set of parents, one family, beating hearts that once synced with yours in the tiny hut you shared with them on the outskirts of Bhopal's borderlines. What's the sense in taking them away from you again?

If the truth ever comes out to you—which I pray it won't—I hope you will have found someone to help you through this, someone you can lean on for her—or his; I don't want to be presumptuous—strength. You will love your partner unconditionally. I know this because you love us unconditionally. Those different forms of love that sprouted from you over the years, unbeknownst even to yourself, I'm sure, were my favorite parts of your childhood. Of course you had love for myself and your mother, which you gave to us almost immediately, and we wondered what we had done to deserve it. There was the love you showed when you saw a hobo huddled in a doorway or trudging through a train car. You would turn to me or Mom and beseech us with your large soulful eyes and we would pass over the snack we had in the stroller for you for after the park or the museum or the movie. There was the love you taught me when Ravi screwed up our finances and we had to eat the cost of a large percentage of films. You taught me forgiveness; you asked me what Ravi Uncle had done, and when I told you, beating my fist into the couch, you told me that I had to forgive him because that's what friends do. At first, I ignored you, but after you stepped back into your room to do your homework or sneak video games, I picked up the phone and told Ravi I'd received some sound advice from a wise man.

I think it is this love that will carry you through the rest of your life; you have so much of it to give that the person you choose to spend yours with will help you through this, this idea of having been an orphan. I cannot imagine the pain and loneliness it might bring. I've scarcely been alone for more than a few hours at a time throughout my life. But you are far stronger than me, Karom. This gift you've been given, of resiliency and strength and love, is one that many take for granted. Please don't you take it for granted, too. Please strive to allow it to take you to new heights and help others achieve it, too. We are so proud of you and we will love you forever.

I think this exercise is over. Your mother and I have both agreed. We needed these pages to harness our demons and exorcise them. I think this long eternal letter will finally come to an end. The therapist was right: this was what we needed in order to come to grips with our decision not to divulge your past to you. But I want to close with something else that I learned from one of my aforementioned heroes, Mr. Satyajit Ray. In each and every one of his films, however dark and despairing they may be, there is always a light, a glimmer of hope, a warm collaborative spark that lets the audience know there's a chance for optimism. There's the birth at the end of a crisis, a loophole at the end of a scandal. So this is my Ray ending to you, in this letter, though it's far less poetic than the master himself could make it. Everything *will* be all right, Karom, because this is your story, and we helped compose it. It will be all right because when there is love— the strong, burning love that we have for you—nothing else matters. We have taught you and coaxed you and know that above all, when all is said and done, excuse the final metaphor, but you are our Karom: striking, rebounding, resilient.

Gita

~

Newspaper mornings are sacred in our lives. For a few hours, there is nothing that can disturb us. We lie around in Karom's home—never mine, for some reason—and flip back the pages, sip coffee and read about the world happening around us. Newspaper mornings are especially lovely during the fall and winter months, when it feels appropriate to hibernate and there's no guilt to join the city for brunch or museum tours or beach days. It feels as though we're zipped away in a hidden pocket where time stands still. Especially in the winter, I feel cocooned in this compartment of the world where I can pore over ink-stained pages with nothing to disturb me.

It was during a newspaper morning that I achieved the crowning moment in my relationship with Karom. It's the moment that every girl dreams of, when it's just the two of you and the world seems as if it has stopped and your breath catches, and there's nothing anyone can do to take away those special words: "Let's go to India together."

It seemed to happen organically that day, though Karom and I had been dating for three years and I'd already broached the topic for two, only to be rebuffed each time. This time it coincided with the travel section and a spread on India's hidden art enclaves. We used these sometimes to guide our travels, heading to Maine or New York's wine country based on a well-written article. But there are a few things I would never do with Karom, like visit Niagara Falls or the Grand Canyon, go skiing or scuba diving, or take a cruise. But there was something different this time; I could sense it before we'd even scanned the articles on the front page. I opened the article up and held it up against my chest.

"Look," I said. "Have you heard of these? Small villages are becoming the tourist draw in India. Each one specializes in an art form and there's a festival where you move from town to town enjoying and buying art. There are some pretty talented people."

"We should go."

"Yeah." I sighed and folded the paper back as I reached for another section.

"No, really. We should. Next year."

I looked at him skeptically. I had asked this of him so many times that I was used to being shot down. I wasn't sure if he was teasing or feeling sorry for me. Likely the latter.

"I have to get over myself. Seriously, let's plan it."

I must have continued gaping at him in disbelief, because he kept nodding and finally came over and kissed me gently on the forehead.

"I want to go with you," he said softly.

I knew that saying those words couldn't have been easy for him. He hadn't been to India in years, not since… I couldn't imagine it. We had never suffered anything like that. My grandmother had arthritis; my great-aunt had cataracts. But there had never been anything drastic, anything so painful that robbed us of anything or anyone in an instant, something we could never get back.

But he was also no fool. He knew as well as I what going to India meant for me, for him, for us. It was the next step, the seminal step, the semifinal step before we could get married. We had to receive the blessing of his country, his earth, his past, before we could consider a life together.

"I have to start somewhere, right?" he asked. "And this month has been particularly brutal. We need to move on. Fresh start. Fresh view. Less moping." December was always the most difficult month for Karom, being the anniversary of the Bhopal disaster as well as of the tsunami. For the past few years that we'd dated, we'd each taken the day off on December 3 to spend it doing something completely removed. Our first year we had stayed in and rented five movies and drunk bottle after bottle of Chianti. Last year we'd taken the Amtrak to Boston. This year in the biting cold we hiked Bear Mountain. Despite these trips, December left Karom particularly down and the sugary cheer of the holidays seemed to further compound his misery.

I squeezed his arm as I said, "We'll do just that."

But this February morning—yet another newspaper morning—I was relentless. "Come on, Karom. This isn't going to work unless you cooperate. Write it down and pass it to me." Karom sighed and ripped out a page from his notebook. He scratched something onto it with his pen, stopping once to flick it like a thermometer to make the ink flow. He folded it and slid it across the table. I grinned excitedly and clapped my hands, bouncing up and down on my throne of floor pillows before opening it.

I like her sharp tongue. My expression fell.

"Really? This is why you love me?"

Karom sipped his coffee.

"Amongst other things, yes. But it's a big one."

"Wow, that's romantic."

"It is, actually."

I shook my head, smiling. "Explain to me why this is romantic."

"Because you're a wild card. Because you're brazen. Because you always speak your mind and I want to hear more, I want to hear the truth, because my whole life everything has been sugarcoated. No one has ever really given it to me before."

"So it's honesty."

"It's more than honesty. It's wittiness, it's gall. It's just what I said on the paper. It's your sharp tongue. Which is good for more than just the truth." Karom smiled wickedly, making me blush. His coffee table had been transformed into a café, with sections of the newspaper draped across it and Venn-diagrammed coffee rings pressed upon the wood. I had been reading an article about the tie between honesty and solidity of relationships. It was the brutally honest ones that survived, while the couples that fed one another lip service for their romantic souls were the ones that failed to last. The article asked the couple to do an exercise—a brutally honest one—where you wrote down three things you loved about your partner on a piece of paper and passed it to them, thereby removing any chance of shyness or reservation at telling them the truth.

"My turn," Karom said, resettling his spidery legs under the table. He pushed the notebook across to me. I tore a scrap of paper out and passed it to him.

"I did mine while you were in the bathroom."

You tame me.

You keep me on my toes.

Your long legs.

"Ha. Ha. Ha," Karom said. "I want the real ones. Brutal honesty, right?"

"I am being brutally honest. I think you're the first man who's ever put me in my place, whether it's been through gentle prodding or genuine honesty. I've always run so wild, and while I don't think I'll settle down, you help ground me. 'You keep me on my toes'—well, you know that one. While I can't say I love all of this particular aspect, it certainly keeps our relationship fresh and alive and it reminds me of how much I care about you, with every stunt you pull." I reached over the table and poked him. Karom grinned cheekily back.

"And the last?"

"Your legs. They're hot. They're super long and muscular and I love that you unabashedly take a step for every two of mine and don't stop to wait for me at street corners, because you know I'll be right in step with you."

Karom smiled shyly. He took a long sip of his coffee before coming around the table and nestled onto some throw pillows, leaning into me.

"Oh no, you're not off the hook so easily. Let's have them." I sat back and looked at the notebook paper.

"I can tell you what I don't love, Miss Bossy."

"Come on. *Three* things, Kar."

Even though you try to hide it, you're the most loving person I know.

"I hide my love? Really? That's not good."

"Geets, come on. You try to be this strong, sassy woman, but at the end of the day, you're just a big love bug. You can't help it—you just can't hide it. It pours out of you. It's infectious."

I smiled despite myself. "Well, that's good, I guess."

"Of course it's good. It's stellar."

"Last one, and I promise we're done. Until stage two."

Karom groaned. "What's stage two?"

"Next week."

You are my strength. This one didn't require explanation. I flicked my tongue over my lips and turned to him, carefully searching his face. His light brown eyes were calm but hungry. I could smell a rawness emanating between us. I reached back behind him and pulled his shirt over his head. He dove greedily for the cleft between my breasts and then for the soft, moist pillows of my lips. Sections of the paper were flung aside as we grasped for fingers, hair, backs of necks and hollows in clavicles.

Later, when we showered together, he traced his fingers over the newsprint etched into my skin where I'd sweat and the relationship story had imprinted onto the backs of my thighs.

The afternoon was bitingly cold; we didn't step out of the house except to dash across the street to the deli for milk when we neared the bottom of our pot of coffee. When Karom slipped his shoes on, I wrapped a scarf around his neck before closing the door behind him. I stood by the window, waiting for him to reappear on the sidewalk below. From above, he still seemed capable, not like a tiny ant scurrying about like the other pedestrians alongside him. He stood suspended on the sidewalk, hovering over the street as cars whooshed past.

"Wait, baby. Wait and look. Wait and look. Wait. Then look," I murmured.

As prompted, Karom looked one way and then the other before crossing the street, his uncovered hands stuck into his armpits. He'd read somewhere that it was the warmest part of the body, and once when we were standing outside a long line in the East Village last winter to see a performance artist, he taught me how to put my fingertips in the hollows of my underarms. I'd felt silly, standing there among the hip, well-dressed crowd, but I had to admit that it worked. I could see white clouds puffing in front of him now, cotton-candy clouds of cold. When he emerged from the store carrying the half gallon of milk, he glanced back across the street both ways again before crossing the street. Just before entering his apartment building, he looked up at the window where I stood watching and held the jug up victoriously.

These were my favorite days: just me, Karom, the newspaper and coffee, the perfect four-way relationship. With Karom in the kitchen frothing milk for another of his specialty lattes, the apartment buzzing with the warmth of the space heaters, and the features section. I have always saved the best for last. Even during meals, I selectively place the crispiest fries on the side of my plate, or the pickled radish, or the chocolate-covered almonds. A few years ago I had dated a man, a fast eater who would plow through his food and then watch me expectantly as I daintily made my way through mine. As though conversation would distract me, he would dive straight into the spoils at the side of my plate, the ones I had been reserving until the very last bite. At first, I was touched that he did this, that he was comfortable enough to eat off my plate, but gradually I grew past this and it morphed into resentment and then anger, until one day I finally slapped his hand as it reached for the fried curly parsley that had adorned my salmon-skin roll. That this was a deal breaker was one of the first things I'd told Karom upon meeting him, and Karom had never tried his hand at swiping off my plate.

He even knew to leave me to the features section. He would read it after I'd been through it once, the pages folded back and

forth and forward like origami. The features section sat crisply
in front of me, except where we had rolled and perspired on
it, some of the inky sentences leaking together into illegible
sentences. The first page mentioned the Tiger Mother, which
I rolled back in disgust. How could a woman—a mother—so
proudly state that she had done these things to her own children: kept ice cream and sleepovers at arm's length and made
them practice the piano though they had to use the bathroom,
their tights moist with pee from having to hold it for hours at
a time. This wouldn't be part of my Sunday.

There was a review of a Dharma Sen film festival at the
Modern. I'd show that to Karom when I finished with the
paper. He loved Dharma Sen.

The inside story made me suck in my breath. In fact, I
nearly forgot to breathe until Karom nudged me with the
coffee mug and I took it without looking at him, my eyes silently sipping at the words in front of me.

I read it until there was nothing more to read, and even
then I folded the paper back and looked for an addendum or a
continuation of the story. It couldn't possibly be over, could it?
Those seven hundred words weren't nearly enough to satisfy.
There had to be more. This article was, no doubt, a political
piece masked as a feature so as to garner sympathy from those
who weren't into the front page, but I knew what they were
doing. I was a newspaper scientist, a news junkie. I could see
right through this journalistic ruse.

A couple, now in their early fifties, had suddenly begun
the hunt for their son. They had lost him years ago during a
tragic event, the thirtieth anniversary of which was coming
up in a few years. The event had happened and everyone had
fled for their lives, accounting for fingers and toes, desperately searching for familiar faces in the cloud of gas. This was

no atom bomb but another human-made disaster that could have easily been diverted. This was Bhopal.

The couple had been rescued by the Red Cross not long after the plant went up in fumes and had spent days mummified in bandages. The shock rendered them barely capable of identifying themselves, let alone one another. They reunited after years; she healed and became a nurse's aide in a town outside Bhopal and he returned to the plant to help rebuild the city. The scars on both their faces rendered them impossible to identify to their remaining friends and family members lucky enough to have endured, so they'd practically lived alongside one another in adjoining hamlets until one day the woman recognized her husband's voice at a tea stall on the edge of town.

"I had given up on him," she said in translation. "In my mind, he could have been anything. He could have moved to America. He could have become a rich businessman. He could have done anything but have continued to live in this town and toil away. He could have done anything but survive this disaster."

"For days after the disaster, I saw her face everywhere," the man said, also in translation. "Even when I knew I was speaking to someone else, the face would morph into hers and I would find myself clutching at their elbow, begging her to come home with me." The couple found each other several years ago and had since attracted the attentions of a few NGOs and adoption agencies, who have committed themselves to the efforts to find their missing son, a toddler at the time, who never surfaced after the chaos of the Bhopal disaster.

"We have heard of many families reuniting after the tragedy," the man said in the article. "They found one another right afterward. Some had to wait months as they healed in the hospital. Some had to wait years because they didn't look like they used to. No one recognized them. At this point, we are old and our son must be grown. He must be married. But he must also be here somewhere. We must find him. And we must become a family once again."

The photo of the two of them entranced me for what must have seemed like hours to Karom. The man was old and wizened. The scars stretching across his face reminded me of the Joker from Batman, as if he was constantly smiling or grimacing; which was it? And his wife had turned her head from the camera at the last minute so that I could only make out her profile with her long hooked nose and the divots in her face where she'd been scarred by the chemicals. I couldn't tell if these people looked like Karom. I couldn't tell if they were looking for him.

I could sense Karom glance at me from time to time as he folded his pages back or stretched his legs out. He poked me with his toe and I smiled slightly to acknowledge him, but I couldn't give him more than that. At two-thirty I folded the page I'd read and reread for the past twenty minutes under my arm. I gathered my coffee mugs and ran water over them in the sink. In Karom's room he had allotted me a whole dresser to myself, and this was where I kept odds and ends, work clothes, exercise clothes. I even had a winter outfit here from the last blizzard, when we'd called in sick and gone sledding in Central Park. I stuck the newspaper in between a bundle of socks and buried it deep. Then I pulled on my running tights and a moisture-wicking shirt and cap.

"I'm going for a run," I announced to the living room.

"Want some company?"

"I'll just do a quick loop and be back soon."

"Okay." Karom smiled at me. "Hey. You okay?"

I nodded. "Just…antsy. Cabin fever."

He nodded and turned back to the op-ed.

On the street, I bent down to tie my shoes. Karom's neighborhood was strange. People here didn't jog, so when others went out in their sporty gear designed to absorb sweat, pedestrians watched them warily, untrusting. A couple watched as I stretched my calves against the building, weaving my hands over my head in an arc and leaning up. I was satisfied when I heard the gentle pop of my back. I slipped my headphones on and started jogging.

The northern half of the path was empty on weekend afternoons. The day was strange: it was white and bright, but the sun hadn't made an appearance all morning. Most joggers did their training in the morning, but I was fired up, and as I entered the trail, I ran faster and faster. I knew I'd hit my wind at the top of the hill, where I'd tire and have to double over at the waist to catch my breath. But when I'd sprinted up Harlem Hill, I kept on going. I caught up to the Lama, a wiry Asian man who was renowned in the park for running with bells attached to his waist and speakers droning out Tibetan chants. He ran every day in the park without fail, his long gray locks twisted into a topknot at the crown of his head and sweatbands at his temples and wrists. I smiled as I passed the Lama. Constants are reassuring.

At the bend there was another constant: Shepherdess, the woman with the two Border collies the color of sand. I'd learned they were part of a litter of eight, and they kept pace with their mistress, one always outdistancing the other by a few feet. The other was more loyal and ran alongside her mistress, whereas the other danced up to me in recognition, wanting to play. What did you call children that were separated from a larger group or litter? I wondered. Were they twins? Or still considered octuplets?

"Leave her alone, Max," the woman called, waving at me. "She's on a mission."

Who said there was no community in New York City? My breath was hard and visible, but I pushed myself past the ache in my side. I'd peter out before the 10K mark, but I held my pace. *Look at all these friendly people. Constants. More constants.*

I'd been running for a few years, but it wasn't until recently that I learned how therapeutic it really was. I could ignore a silly Karom fight or a down period at work or a dissatisfied client if I just fought through the ache in my legs and the tearing in my lungs and focused on my ability to breathe through it all. I could concentrate on the patterns of salt that traced across my face and how my eyes burned with sweat as it trickled past my lashes. In the winter, I'd be distracted by the numbness of my fingertips and my wary observation of black ice. I'd look out for park regulars, constants, and keep my eyes peeled for repeat runners that I could add to my collection.

Although my senses were alert as I traversed over steep inclines and soggy dead leaves, I kept thinking back to that article. That article could undo Karom more than it had already undone me. *What if those are his parents,* I kept wondering. I couldn't tell any resemblance by the fuzzy image and the ravage that the disaster had permanently etched across their faces, but what if, what if. And if they weren't his parents, wouldn't there—no, *couldn't* there—be many other families still out there searching for their long-lost children, their families, their lives?

There were shouts and peals of laughter and '80s pop emanating from the core of the ice-skating rink as I ran by. The ground here was slick; the hill leading up to it was a steep incline and I nearly slipped on a patch of ice cleverly hidden by a cluster of whisper-thin dry leaves. Up ahead I could see one more constant: Shirtless Wonder. Shirtless Wonder was a beautifully sculpted man with floppy, bouncing hair and lazy gray eyes. We made eye contact each time he passed me in the park. In fact, it seemed that we never ran in the same direction; he always approached and passed me, as he did now, without a shirt on. But he never acknowledged me, never bobbed his head in recognition even though we were somehow on the same running schedule, regardless of whether I ventured out on a morning or an afternoon. Once, I'd smiled as he approached me, hoping to make a connection as I had with the woman with the dogs or the hot-dog man whose cart jutted into the path at Seventy-Ninth Street, who always waved at me and pretended to pass me a bottle of Gatorade like a baton as I sprinted past him. But the man had turned his head slightly, and I'd felt wounded and never tried to engage him again.

I shivered as he sprinted toward me. He never had a shirt on, even now when the trees were sparse and the ground was cold and hard. As he passed, I inhaled his fresh sweat. Around the apex of the park again, I slowed and that was when it happened. My ankle gave and I stumbled, falling to the ground, the gloved heels of my hands striking the earth. I sat on the ground, my ankle throbbing and splayed out in front of me, dazed as I looked about. A woman who had been power walking jogged toward me.

"Are you okay?"

I squinted up at her. Even though there was no sun, the sky was bright and it hurt to look at it directly. I looked back down at my ankle.

"I think I twisted it." The woman held her hand out and

I grasped it, putting my weight on my other foot. The pain shot through it and I winced. "Yeah, it's shot."

"Do you live around here? Want me to call you a cab?"

"My boyfriend does. Do you have a cell phone I could use?"

The woman helped me to a bench on the side of the road, where I reassured her that I was fine waiting for Karom alone.

"He knows the park. Really, I'll be fine. Thank you." I sat on the bench, curling my good leg up under me, the twisted ankle dangling off the side. The wind sliced through me; my sweat was cooling and I was beginning to freeze. I peeled my gloves off and bit my fingers one by one. My fingertips were white; I couldn't feel them. I stuck them under my arms and jiggled my good leg under me. But all I could think of were the expressions of the two people in the article.

Who knew what was going through the minds of people who had lost everything in one instant, in one bad move, in one decision to work at a company that would kill thousands in an instant and then disfigure hundreds over the years? Who knew what would go through Karom's already overactive mind if he learned about this? Who knew if I'd ever be able to comfort him? Who knew if the cycle would ever end?

As the wind rustled the few remaining leaves on the tree over my head, Shirtless Wonder ran past again, this time in the opposite direction. He met my eye again as he ran off. I shook my head. I didn't get the arrogance of people sometimes. We saw one another nearly every day, yet the man didn't have the decency to nod recognition.

"Is that him?" Karom asked, jutting his chin toward the man's retreating back. He was walking toward me wheeling a bicycle. "Your park boyfriend?" I nodded. I hoped he couldn't see the guilt from the hidden article written across my face, like the telltale sign of crumbs trailing across the lips of a child who's been dipping into the cookie jar. I also hoped he hadn't gone snooping into my sock drawer after I'd left.

"He's nuts. It's below freezing. Your beautiful, stupid Adonis. So, what happened, Geets? You overdo it?" I scowled, looking at the ground. "What hurts?"

I gestured toward my dangling foot. "Ankle."

"Come on." He held the bicycle with one hand and pulled me up by the other, his arm around my waist as he hugged me to him. Sometimes his height and stature made me forget how strong he was. He turned me toward the bicycle.

"I can't ride that. It hurts...."

"Just sit on it. I'll hold it and guide you back."

I straddled the bike, holding on to his upper arm.

"Thank you." I smiled through tears.

"Does it hurt that badly?" Karom must have been surprised to see me cry. I'm pretty tough, able to withstand pain. I barely wrinkle my nose at horror movies when people are sliced and diced with chain saws and axes, as though they were paper cuts. I never get angsty during menstruation.

"I'm just mad at myself. I didn't warm up enough. I didn't watch the ground."

He rubbed the back of my head where my hair was moist from sweat. "I'm sure it's an innocent sprain. Let's get you home."

The next morning as I hobbled into my office, I threw my crutches into the corner. I've always seen people on crutches maneuvering the streets so easily before; it almost looks like fun, taking longer strides than normal, galloping down the sidewalk and receiving a wide berth. They look like they are skipping from stone to stone over a calm river, bypassing extra steps. I'm not one of those people. I just barely managed

to get myself into the door before I collapsed on my Eames
lounge chair that I bought for guests and clients. My office
is small, not at all what you would expect of an interior designer. I have dreams of opening up a large warehouse space,
high soaring ceilings, exposed brick walls, snapshots of my
past work scrolling past on plasma screens as you enter the
reception area. I want the light to come rolling in from the
outside—no curtains, no blinds, just the outside world and
maybe five or six track lights that project onto the model I'm
working on at the moment or that light up the reception area
just outside the elevator embankment. I have grand plans. But
right now I rent an old office that used to belong to a clinical
psychologist. It's in the back of an old apartment building just
off Central Park, low ceilinged and spatially challenged. It's
dark and looks out onto an air shaft, and when I work late at
night, I can see into the kitchen of an older woman who lives
alone and cooks herself elaborate meals and eats them at her
table decorated with a single flower and a single votive. We
make eye contact from time to time and I smile at her, feeling
sad about her life while I imagine she feels sad about mine.

I have a shared reception area with three other psychologists, which makes me feel awfully unprofessional, but I console myself with the fact that it's a start. I can't expect to own a
corner office in SoHo at this point in my life. I will get there,
and not a moment too soon. I did some very basic redecoration
in this space when I moved in, just enough so that potential
clients wouldn't be scared off when they came for a consul-
tation and saw the mosaic carpet with cigarette holes burned
into the border, almost as if it were a pattern. I don't want to
know what happened in this office before I took it over.

I stripped the carpet and installed hardwood floors. I
painted the walls lavender and honey, a color I created myself

one afternoon at Benjamin Moore. My Mac is the most stylish and certainly the most expensive piece in the space and so it is accented by a single spotlight that hangs above it. When I first started out, even before I had business cards printed up, my parents let me do their house, little by little. I tackled the library first, a small bedroom that none of us wanted to occupy during our time at home. It had previously been filled with IKEA bookshelves and stuffed from floor to ceiling with books. Some of the books themselves were archaic: *Backpacking in Asia in the 1980s; Learn to Swim the Salazar Method; Do Your Taxes Yourself.* With permission from my parents, I took some of these books, painted the covers, hollowed out the insides, propped them up on their sides and placed family photographs inside. Most of the rest of them, I donated to Goodwill. People don't realize that 50 percent of interior decoration is decluttering. Essentially, I got a degree in throwing things out. Their budget was meager, but I frequented thrift stores and yard sales and taught myself to reupholster. I used my father's Scandinavian background as the inspiration for the minimalistic decor; everything was a blond wood except where I'd lit a highlight with cherry or marble. The furniture was cushy and warm yet refined. I had an ironic plaster bust of my parents made that I placed at the far corner of the room, surveying the scene. I used old silk saris of my mother's that were fraying and falling apart at the golden threads to accent corners of the room, drawing attention to nooks and books and hidden treasures, like the signed first-edition copy of Shanta Nayak's *True Stories of Make Believe,* a book my mother had found in an ancient bookshop on Nineteenth Cross when we were small children. We grew up with this book and its prequel, *Tales of Girls and Animals,* and for years neither my sisters nor I could turn in to bed without a story read from its pages.

Their library became the project that lifted my business off the ground. My father's college friend came to visit and he loved it so much that he asked me to come to his corner office at Columbia, where he was a professor of political philosophy, to rethink the "drab fluorescent-lit cave" where he spent most of his time, to his wife's chagrin. Something struck me about that description. A learned man so held hostage by his work, by his desire to learn, to educate, to decipher, that he squirrels himself away in a corner of the Earth to seek the truth and think. It was such a simple thought. I remembered the bespectacled badger from *The Wind in the Willows* wearing a corduroy jacket with leather patches on the sleeves, and Professor Healdon's office transformed itself in my mind. It helped that he too looked a bit like a badger, with his pointy nose and shadows under his eyes like two black stripes that stretched to the back of his head. I created a warm, wintry space with muted wall sconces and an accountant's lamp as the only desk light by which to pore over articles and papers. I hauled in Persian carpets from the flea market in Hell's Kitchen, grasping them by their fat middles and praying that a cabdriver would take pity on me and drive me up to Morningside Heights.

One Saturday afternoon, just as I was dragging the third carpet that would complete the Professor Healdon project down Ninth Avenue, I felt a tap on my shoulder. The carpet had been wrapped in eight black trash bags and it resembled a giant sushi roll being tugged down the street. I was sure I looked ridiculous, but the generous paycheck—and the many referrals that the professor had given me—helped me swallow my pride. When I turned around, the tallest Indian man I had ever seen was looking at me quizzically.

"Can I help you?" he asked, and before I could even answer, he had hoisted one side of the carpet under his arm and started down the street. For a moment, I considered the situation: he was a tall, dark stranger who had come to my rescue on Fortieth Street. I'd always considered that conflict—that Americans, white Americans, searched for the dark man, even yearned to grow shades darker on their own, as they cooked in the sun on beaches, applied orange-tinted self-tanner and roasted themselves on indoor capsules that radiated cancerous rays. However, on the flip side, I'd seen my mother surreptitiously collect tubes of Fair & Lovely cream from her friends whenever they traveled to India, and when she herself visited, she preserved a section of her suitcase for at least seven or eight more tubes to keep and distribute among her friends, and she applied the paste lovingly each night before she went to bed. I didn't think the mixture had done much for her, but she had been using it religiously for years, so I wasn't exactly sure what her natural skin color truly was. I knew this strange ritual wasn't just my mother's quirk: it was an Indian thing, this desire to drop a few shades down the color palette, to appear lighter, brighter and fair. Both she and her mother, my *ammama,* followed this paint-chip hierarchy and would never have approved of this man based on his dark complexion. But neither of them were around to see how handsome he was.

I stood, my mouth agape, watching him take a few steps before he turned around. "I did say 'help.' There's another end to this thing and it appears to be dragging." I grinned and grabbed the other side. We marched the sushi roll to the corner, where I stopped.

"If you'd 'help' me into a cab, I can take it from here," I said.

"So you're telling me there's a gallant man with a long reach and an equally long stride on the other end of your ride?"

"Not exactly. But there is a strong gal who's been doing it

on her own all this time." But I was intrigued and attracted. I allowed him to get into the cab when one came and he got out on the other end and helped me carry the carpet up the stairs to the professor's office. I let myself in with the key and he helped me unwrap the carpet and we rolled it out, tucking it under chairs and lifting up the bookcase and the standing lamp so it could fit under, and then he looked around the room, reading the titles of books aloud and admiring the wallpaper and the lighting until ultimately I tapped him on the shoulder and told him that he deserved a drink for all his do-gooding for the day, so I took him to the nearest dive bar and we got drunk off vodka gimlets. And that was how I met Karom.

I pulled the Eames chair around to rest my foot before logging in to my computer. I brought up the Mackie file, along with some snapshots I had taken when I'd last visited their home. The Mackies lived in a two-bedroom apartment not far from my office. I knew them through a friend of a friend. She'd been trying for years to get pregnant, and finally, after numerous fertility treatments, she'd recently birthed triplets. However, at the moment, they couldn't afford to move into a larger space that could accommodate all of them, so they'd consulted me to divide the extra bedroom into the semblance of a nursery or playroom that would encourage both play and sleep. I considered sleep nooks, lofts that the children could enjoy once they outgrew their cribs, a prairie theme that could easily be converted into light, restful colors. I sketched all morning, my brow furrowed, licking my lips until they became chapped. When I took a break at noon, I allowed myself to think of anything but my work. I'm good at that—compartmentalizing.

But then it all rushed back to me—the man's scarred face,

the woman's desperate eye and their desire to be reunited with their only son. I'd dissected it over and over in my brain. What if this was a ploy to be taken care of in their old age? What if they had just created a son to take them in and nurse them until they died? I had watched too many old Bollywood movies. Karom was right—I have such an imagination. The one question I couldn't bring myself to shake was, What would this do to Karom if he found out? How would he react? As it was, we were wrestling with the game day after day. It wasn't always active, but it was omnipresent and we never knew when it would rear up. The game had control of me more than I could say. And who knew how it would change with this piece of information. Maybe it would even get better. Maybe it would finally end.

There is a small park around the corner from my office that I sit in during my self-allotted lunch hour. The park is divided into two halves—one where adults would bring their lunches to unwrap while they chatted or shouted into cell phones or tapped away at BlackBerry devices. But the other part of the park is a children's playground, and it was here that I often balanced my sandwich on my knees and watched the children slip down the well-worn slides or chase one another through the sputtery sprinkler on the muggy summer days. I always brought a book and pretended to read from it lest nannies and parents worry about a childless woman watching toddlers romp about; one could never be too careful these days.

But I watched them play, growing increasingly anxious and tensing my whole body when I predicted a fall or a shove or push that would render ear-piercing screams. I'd watch as the smallest gesture from a larger child could coax a smile to transform into a meltdown. I was more vigilant than the babysitters or the mothers because I was ready and poised for it, while the

caretakers were only hoping in the backs of their minds that
their charges might pick their feet up that extra millimeter
so they didn't trip on the rubber matting or hold their head
cocked just so under the monkey bars. I could anticipate disaster here; I could watch as it crept around me. This was one
place I was in charge, where at any moment, I could spring up
and put my hand over a head to protect it from clanking into
a metal ladder rung, or step between a fight ready to happen,
distracting the contenders with a game of tag, or mediate to
return a sand bucket to its rightful owner. I wasn't surprised
here. I wasn't taken aback or shocked. Children were so de-
lightfully easy to read. Had I been a parent here, my child
would never have returned home with bruises or scrapes or
even a dusty, tear-stained face from petty proprietary fights.

I told Karom about this place, how playgrounds were a place
to anticipate failure, and I urged him to join me one day during his lunch hour to watch the children at play.

"It's fascinating," I said. "If you just watch children, you can
figure out their every move. They really aren't that surprising. I can see danger coming whole minutes before it occurs."

Karom watched me as I spoke energetically, his eyebrows
raised in bemusement. He put his arm around my shoulders
and hugged me into him.

"My girlfriend, the playground naturalist. Just don't take
binoculars with you to the park. That's a quick way to get
arrested."

"I'm serious, Karom. I feel in control at the playground.
I can tell. I know what's going to happen, and if I had to, I
could stop it. It's so empowering." In my head, I likened it
to our situation—that I could see what was coming before a
child decided to veer out and sway over the subway platform

or play chicken with oncoming traffic. I wanted Karom to draw the parallel in his mind that I'd already drawn in mine.

But instead he said, "Geets, your child is going to be so spoiled if you do that for them. They aren't going to understand the glory of winning a playground fight or that there are consequences to not ducking when the tire swing comes their way if their skin is pristine and not covered with bruises. They're not going to learn how to be a kid. You have to let them be. It's unnatural otherwise."

Karom suffered from nightmares and night sweats. From time to time, I'd hold him at night as he shuddered, convulsing sometimes from some apparition that he claimed he couldn't remember in the morning. He never awoke during these episodes, just clung to me with sticky fingers, croons emanating from the back of his throat. We talked about them from time to time, commenting on how they would dissipate in the summer months and peak around Christmas. I'd urged him to see one of the psychologists in my office, but like a typical Indian male, he was too proud.

"I don't need one of those shrinks. I know exactly what's wrong with me, and for what I don't know, I have you to tell me," he'd joke.

I did know; he had told me one night six months after we'd first met. But he'd been taciturn at first. He'd told me he'd lost both his parents, and he'd tell me the whole thing when the right time arose. The right time was during a Pedro Almodóvar movie. We'd both been moved by it, crying silently next to one another, streams of tears forging down our faces, feeling the shudder of the other's shoulders as they trembled with emotion just before he'd collapsed, sobbing without abandon into my arms. He told me the grisly details of his story then, and I finally understood his initial reticence around me. But he was still haunted by it, had been for nearly ten years. On that same night, I'd held him and told him that I would help him, whatever it took, however it happened. I would be his strength; I would help exorcise those demons at any cost. He couldn't continue like this; it wasn't safe or healthy or normal. It wasn't right, to be constantly pursued by something that you couldn't describe when you woke up in the morning. It wasn't even physical or tangible. It didn't have a face or a texture or a smell. The closest he had come to explaining it to me was that it was a cloud, a fog, a ghostly miasma that followed him no matter where he went, under thresholds, through cracks in the ceiling, in air vents. It was very easy to tell him that I would help him, that I would be there for him to hold him in the night, to hold his hand when these visions came to life on busy thoroughfares, on subway platforms, on high buildings, and he toyed with himself when he toyed with me. But the truth was, I didn't know how I was going to help him.

But that was one of *my* strengths; I knew how to help myself, even when it wasn't easy. But now, like Karom with his nightly visions, I lived in fear. The change in the unknown, of who was out there looking for Karom, the shifting of what the earth knew as gospel. It was the fear of removing everything I knew up until now, everything that I stood for, everything that characterized him and, therefore, everything that stabilized me. It was like pulling the curtain up when the stagehands were running around placing sets and pulling down sheets of scenery; everything was exposed, raw.

The article kept me up at night, so I was prepared when Karom began his nightly ritual. It was a feeling I'd never be able to share with him, but I realized I found it interesting to watch the whole thing from beginning to end. He'd be sleeping peacefully when his upper lip would begin to twitch rhythmically. Then his fingers, and I could feel his toes flexing and releasing under the sheets. He'd begin his soft, gentle moaning and I could hear his tongue flapping about in his mouth. The twitch would follow up his legs, up his arms, until it took hold of his shoulders and hips. Finally, it would crescendo into one big aria, where it would overtake him and he would flop in the bed, writhing from his right to his left side until I'd grab him with all my strength and he'd awaken, soggy with sweat that bled Rorschach patterns into the sheets.

That evening, as I balanced on my crutches to lock my door, I looked around the vacant waiting area. It was a depressing place to wait for a psychologist. There was a white-noise machine in the corner that radiated a ghostly hum of secrecy, issues of *Sports Illustrated* and *The New Yorker* from years past on the table, their corners curling from humidity or boredom. The walls were stark white and the carpet was the same one that had previously extended into my office before I'd ripped it out. I'd felt awkward adding to the shared decor; I felt as though there was a hierarchy here and I was the newcomer. I'd wanted badly to redesign the reception area, but on my entry to the office, I'd certainly be overstepping my boundaries. These people had been here for years and I was the new kid, not to mention the entirely new profession in the back office. The psychologists had conferred upon allowing me to join them, wondering whether a nonshrink would disrupt their balance. I wondered if they liked the drabness of the reception area; it allowed patients to consider their lives, their problems, their issues, without further distraction.

I looked about the room at the nameplates on each door. There were two women and a man. The woman whose office was adjacent to mine seemed constantly harried. I'd met her only a few times as she rushed in and out, balancing bags or an umbrella or stacks of magazines that she'd brought from home. She was in her mid-fifties and she had tightly wound hair. She was always polite but never friendly. The man had a deep rumbling voice, and I could hear it over the noise machine when I stepped in and out of the office. It sounded like bowling balls being pitched down an alley, comforting and constant. I liked constants. But there was something about the other woman, the young mother who proudly displayed photos of her family in her office, unlike the other two, who pretended that they existed only as therapists and nothing more, without families or lives or interests. It made her more human somehow, and it made me gravitate toward her door, stumbling with my additional limbs, awkward as a baby giraffe. I leaned my head against the closed door but I couldn't hear any mumbling, so I knocked against it softly with the nub of my crutch. There was silence for a moment or two and then a low female voice called out for me to come in.

She was seated in an olive-green armchair next to a reading lamp. She looked up as I entered and then her eyes went wide.

"My goodness," she exclaimed. "What happened to you?"

"I got overambitious on my run in the park this weekend. It's a mild sprain, but I have to be on these for three weeks. I hope I'm not interrupting." I gestured to her book.

"Oh, not at all. It's actually—" she showed me the cover "—a novel that I can't put down. Somehow amidst all the chaos at home, I can't get through enough of it, so sometimes I have to squirrel myself away in here and pretend to have patients. I know. I'm awful." She grinned at me, her glasses slipping down her nose.

"I completely understand," I said, even though I didn't

understand what it might be like to have your life driven by children. "You need some 'you' time."

"Exactly."

"So, then, this is the worst time to ask you…"

"Not at all. Please. Sit." She gestured toward a chair.

"I just have a question. I was wondering if you were taking any additional clients? Patients? Clients. That's what I call mine."

"Patients." She smiled. "Sure. For yourself?" I nodded. "Absolutely. When would you like to come in?"

"Tomorrow?" She consulted a small gray book next to the reading lamp.

"Perfect. Shall we close out the day together? Six p.m.?"

"Please." We smiled at one another and I pivoted on my poles and negotiated my way out. I could hear the rustle of pages behind closed doors as she picked her book up where she'd left off.

When I took the train home that night, a panhandler entered and stood directly in front of me where I sat holding my crutches between my legs. He held a Greek-style paper coffee cup that jingled with coins when he moved it and a few mangy dollar bills stuck up out of its mouth, but his clothes were fresh and pressed. The train was crowded and the man couldn't move through the tight crowd of people linked together like chains.

I can't stand panhandlers—not because they're needy or make me feel guilty—they don't—but because they always invoke their age when begging for handouts. No age is ever acceptable; there's always something you can hold on to when you're asking for other people's money. You're so young; you're a child; you're with child; you have mouths to feed; you're old; you're crippled; you're a veteran; you're unemployed.

This panhandler seemed to be the lazy type, because he hadn't moved or recited his patter during the five stops it took me to reach Karom's place. We'd decided that while I was injured, I would stay with him because it would be easier to get to the office, and he could take care of me while I healed. The tracks screeched beneath my feet as the train lurched to a stop, my signal to stand. The doors burst open and the passengers spilled out onto the platform like water gushing from a pipe, people passing together in streams toward the exit.

I stood on my good foot and leaned my weight forward. Nothing happened. I tried again before I heard the peal of the "doors closing" bell, my crutches catching on the sticky floor from my panic. The panhandler grabbed me under my armpits and pulled me to my feet. At first, I flinched at being touched by the man, but I barely had time to think about it. The crowd cleared a space for him as he started to pitch backward holding me upright and I just managed to clear the doors before they slid closed behind me and the train pulled out of the station. It was going to be a long three weeks.

I decided not to tell Karom that I was seeing a shrink. In fact, I decided not to tell anyone. I couldn't get over the idea that I was seeing a therapist, not because I was embarrassed to see one but because it wasn't even my issue or problem that had driven me here. But somehow, in the safe haven behind the closed doors of Dr. Rhodes's office, it all came tumbling out.

"So tell me why you're here."

"I'm here on behalf of my boyfriend, Karom. He suffers from this condition, a traumatic condition. He had a terrible experience a few years ago. Well, two, really. He's okay, physically, I mean. But now he has these night terrors and they aren't going away and he won't see anyone about it."

"Why won't he see anyone?"

"Pride, I guess. Fear. Anger."

"Anger?"

"That he thinks these things happened to him. That he had no control over them. That he couldn't do anything to change it."

"Maybe you'd better tell me what happened."

So I did.

She jotted something down in her notepad. "That's quite a burden for someone to take on."

"I really want to help him," I said, and chewed thoughtfully on the inside of my cheek. "I think I could if I understood what he's going through and had some behavioral exercises that you think might help."

"Trauma isn't an easy thing," she said. "Especially for those not experiencing it, we can't exactly see beyond that hazy curtain to the truth."

"But he won't come here," I said. "I don't know how else to help."

"Have you ever thought about the idea that just being there for him and with him could be the best help he could ever get?"

"Sure."

"And that your support might eventually be that guiding light for where he needs to go?"

"But it's not getting any better," I said. "Nothing seems to work." I told her about the man we'd read about, the man going through grief. Some time ago, on one of our lazy Sunday lolling-abouts in Karom's apartment with coffee and the newspaper, I had read a feature of a man in Brighton Beach who had lost his mother 637 days ago. His grief was still palpable, because 637 days later he was still going through the motions of his process. Each morning, he would wake up, run six miles and then jump into the ocean and swim one mile. His mother had suffered from emphysema and was constantly gasping for oxygen, so the runs and swims were especially cathartic. "It's like I am breathing for her," the man said. December or August, he wore the same striped swimming trunks into the water and the same gray hooded sweatshirt as he ran the length of Neptune Avenue. The man wasn't sure if he was still grieving, the article said, but he went through the motions nonetheless because at this point he didn't know anything else.

He couldn't imagine his life without this ritual, having to wake up and make a cup of coffee instead of lacing up his running shoes, or turning on the morning news instead of feeling his sneakers pounding across the weathered slats of the boardwalk. In the winter months, he would run in the wake of the garbage trucks harnessed with snowplows as they carved a path in the snow. Even when the truck idled at corners, and the sanitation workers loaded trash bags and sparse-needled Christmas trees into the gaping mouth at the back, the man jogged in place, waiting patiently for the truck to guide the way. And after this run, his ice-crusted sneakers would crunch across the frozen sand until he reached the waves that crested upon the shore, peeled off his gray Everlast sweatshirt and dove into the waters that claimed him every morning. He was a neighborhood celebrity. The old Russian ladies looked out for him on their walks back from buying pickled beets and cabbage and waved at him as he clambered back onto shore, his trunks dripping with saline pollution, where he air-dried on the boardwalk, slapping and shaking hands. He blew the mucus out of his nose—snot rockets, I called them when Karom blew them during the winter months when we ran together in Central Park, our mouths puffing soft white smoke into the still air. And this ritual, crazy though it seemed, was what had grounded him for 637 days.

I'd pointed it out to Karom. "I'm not asking you to do something like this," I'd said. "This is just insane. To swim in the ocean in January and follow garbage trucks. But if you had something, anything at all to channel into."

"I ran the marathon," Karom pointed out. "Wasn't that a channel?"

"Sure, but the marathon is over. What are you doing to focus now?"

"I'm surfing."

"Since when?"

"Surfing. Flipping through channels. Channel surfing, Geets. I'm figuring it out."

I'd settled back into the sofa, sipping my coffee. The Brighton Beach man was certifiably crazy in my book, but somehow, he seemed at peace with himself, at peace with his routine. He was striking, with a shock of white hair that blew in the wind in the black-and-white snaps. His hair had turned white overnight, the article said, on the evening that his mother passed away.

Grief had been converted into activity in his mind, at least something healthy that might occupy those early-morning hours of mind-wandering and supposing. *None of this ridiculous game-playing,* I'd thought. *That needed to stop soon.*

"Tell me," Dr. Rhodes said, "what does his being an orphan mean to you? What implications does it have, not only now but in the long term?"

"Well—" I chewed again on the inside of my cheek "—it means to some extent, I have to be his family. I have to re-adopt him."

"Does he want to be adopted?"

"I don't think he has a choice. He can't go on alone like this forever. It's destructive."

"Have you had that conversation?"

"Not in words."

"And what does adopting him entail?"

"I…" I faltered. "I almost have to treat him like a baby. Start from scratch. Clean slate. Teach him my family's idiosyncracies, Konkani—that's the language my mother speaks—terms of endearment, how to eat *pinekjott* at Christmas and enough Norwegian curses to keep up with my cousins in Bergen. I have to make him our own. I have to retrain him."

"How do you mean? Doesn't he have the life skills to move forward on his own? Does he have to do everything like you and your family?"

"Of course not. He can physically survive on his own. But emotionally? He's a ticking time bomb. I don't trust him on his own. I think learned behavior is essential. And then there's the watch."

"Tell me about that."

"He wears this vintage Rolex. It used to belong to his grandfather, his mom's dad, who passed away during the tsunami. It was the only thing that they sent him after the disaster. They claimed all the passports and the money had to be kept in governmental offices for documentation, which is bullshit if you ask me. Those passports went on the black market as soon as they could and the money was swiftly pocketed into some politician's bank account. But anyway, this Rolex was a gift from his grandmother to his grandfather on their wedding night. It has an inscription on the back. It says 'Together we learn there's nothing like time.' It's just this constant reminder to Karom about what happened. I feel like every time he looks at it, it reminds him that he has to play this game. It's not allowing him to move forward. I mean, I think a lot of things aren't allowing him to move forward, but this is like some amulet that he wears to remind himself, when all I think it's doing is further compounding his game."

Dr. Rhodes paused here, scribbling furiously onto her notepad, knotting her eyebrows in concentration.

"I want to switch gears for a moment. What about you? Is there anything we can work on together to make sure you're in a good place, taking care of yourself?"

"I'm fine. Except for this bum foot." I grinned down sheepishly.

"Okay." The minutes ticked by, though I was thankful that her office didn't have one of those obnoxious clocks with a loud second hand that elevated the soar of silence. "I know that coming here, making the effort, wasn't easy. That was a big first step."

"First pivot."

"Right. We can end here today if you'd like. I won't force you to stay until you're ready to talk. This shouldn't be torture. This is for you."

"Well, there is this one thing, but it's so stupid and insignificant. It's embarrassing...."

"I should've said this from the start, but there is absolutely no judgment in this room, nor will there ever be. I will only ever make suggestions to help you, to encourage you. Okay?"

I nodded. "I read this newspaper article a few weekends ago that really destroyed me. I don't feel ready to face the day anymore. I'm not prepared for anything that comes my way. I feel lost. I always prided myself on having so much direction, so much fire it always burst forward from my insides. I always knew what to do or where to go, and even if I didn't, I was always really good at faking it or making others believe it. But I just feel empty now. And I don't know how to get it back."

"What was the article about?"

"It's about…this couple. In India. They are in their fifties now, but when the thing in Bhopal happened, they were married and had a son and somehow they got separated. And they lost one another and they lost their son in the melee and were put in hospitals and somehow got out, eked out an existence and then they recently found one another. And now they are looking for their son, because somehow they are convinced he's alive, or at least they are convinced that it wasn't Bhopal that killed him. And it's crazy, and it's a one-in-a-million shot, but all signs point to the fact that these could be Karom's parents, this could be Karom's life. And I can't stand that idea. That he might be torn away from me and all the progress we have made together. The game…"

"What about the game?"

"What if it picks up? What if he's rattled to the point of not being able to survive? What if he…?" I trailed off, unable to finish the thought. "But this will annihilate everything he has worked toward. He has just about accepted his parents' deaths. Both of them. And if one of them comes back to life, I'm just not sure he could handle it."

"Well, hang on. For one thing, you aren't even sure that these are his parents."

"No, I'm not. But the article just opened up this whole possibility."

"Let me ask you—don't you think that there are other people out there, other people that aren't his parents but that could be his family? You said that his entire family was wiped out in that disaster back in 2004. Wouldn't it be nice for Karom if he knew some of his people were still around?"

"I don't think it would be good for him. I don't think it would be good, because it would shake his world that he knows so well. He has a life and a job and friends here. He has me."

"Ah." Dr. Rhodes continued to scribble. "If I may…"

"Please," I said. "Total honesty. It's what I came for."

"I can't help but point out that you're being rather selfish with this."

"Of course I'm being selfish. I have to be. There's a chance I'll lose him in all this. There's a chance he might not need me anymore after all. That he'll escape and move back to India, that he will no longer need me as he has for all these years. I…I just feel like the whole situation is a snake, like it's this winding serpent that's escaped into my house, my life, my body, and I can't find it to take it out and put it back in the zoo. I feel…violated."

"That's a big feeling to be having. The way I see it, you have two options. You show him the newspaper article and you let him determine what this means for him or for the both of you. Or you don't, and you continue your lives and you go to India this spring as planned."

"I don't know that I could live with the guilt that there's something out there to upset the balance."

Dr. Rhodes shifted in her seat and turned toward me. "That's just something you're going to have to figure out on your own."

"But what if it's in the newspaper again? What if there's a follow-up?"

"If it upsets you that much, turn the page."

"It's that easy?"

"It can be. It can be as simple or as difficult as you like."

"Tough love," I snorted. "I get it."

"Not tough love," Dr. Rhodes said, leaning forward in her chair. "An option."

"I'd like it to be easy. I just didn't know it could be."

"Most things are." She smiled at me before leaning back in her chair and scribbling something in her pad.

"I booked the tickets," Karom said, looking up from the chopping board as I struggled to pull the key from the lock. I dropped my purse on the floor and kicked the shoe off my good foot. I leaned my crutches against the wall and walked gingerly toward him. "You're not supposed to walk on that yet. Hi." He kissed me completely and thoroughly, as he always did, though he was up to his wrists in red onion.

I vaulted myself onto the counter next to him. "Did you get the dates we wanted?"

"Everything. We fly into Bombay and out of Delhi. Trains are booked, hotels are booked. Everything. Done."

I leaned my forehead against the arm that held the onion. "You…are the best."

"Everything okay?"

"Just a little tired. Those crutches are a workout."

"Go lie down for a bit. I'll call you for dinner."

"No, it's okay." I loved watching Karom in the kitchen. I always joked that he should have given up this copywriter pretense and gone straight to cooking school. He had the technique; he could slice onions so thin you could see through them, his knife a blur as it weaved skillfully across a bamboo board. He never cried; he claimed that crying during onion chopping was a genetic thing and that he'd inherited it from his mother. I'd squeezed his shoulder after he said that. It didn't mean the same thing to him as it did to me.

"The invitation came today." He pointed his knife toward

the table near the door where mail piled up. I cantilevered myself off the marble top and reached for the cream envelope with curly writing like parsley sprigs.

"Wow, June? What's the rush?"

"I was wondering the same thing."

"He didn't tell you? While you guys were best-man planning?"

"He hasn't told me anything except to look out for an invitation and to wear black tie, a necktie, not a bow tie, and that's it."

"You boys are so low maintenance. I wish bridesmaids got off so easy. So these are their colors?"

"I guess so."

"Don't you guys talk about anything?"

"Only things of consequence."

I waited until he set the knife down before I swatted his arm.

That night, I snuggled down next to Karom in bed. For the first time in days, I suddenly felt at peace. Maybe I was comforted by my frank conversation with Dr. Rhodes or by the fact that we would be traveling to India in a few short months, where I could introduce Karom to my grandmother, one woman whose opinion I yearned for above almost all the others. My parents had raised us to be almost blasé about opinions. So long as you were happy, that was all that mattered. Of course, I was happy. I wanted Karom, but sometimes it was nice to have a familial barometer to assess your decision. I could imagine us walking around Gandhi Park, sitting on the same bench that thousands upon thousands of tourists visit each day at the Taj Mahal, striking the same poses, snapping the same photographs. I didn't care. I wanted it all, especially with him. I didn't know how we were going to work up to this trip together. Whether we would have to run emergency drills or review hypothetical situations in our minds. How did one prepare for a trip to a land where not one but two sets of your family had been killed, or now, had potentially been killed? How did one begin to face that kind of trauma and acceptance?

Karom must have felt at peace, too, because it was one of the first nights in a long time that he slept through without awakening or grappling with his internal demons. I woke up a few times to check on him, but he slept soundly, his eyebrows relaxed and his jaw loose, dreaming through the night.

There was one other thing still plaguing me, so the next Thursday, after I locked the door to my office and hobbled across the waiting room, I was poised on the edge of the threshold giving myself a pep talk. I would blurt it all out in one go as if it were poison, just rid myself of it. I needed advice.

"Come in," Dr. Rhodes said, holding the door open so that I could pitch myself into the room. I settled in the only chair that would accommodate me putting my foot up, as the doctor had suggested. I won't lie; I was milking this situation for all it was worth—on the subway, with my clients, with my parents. Dr. Rhodes didn't buy it, I could tell. This therapy business was like a ballet, and the show always went on.

"You think I'm a horrible person, don't you?" I asked.

"How so?"

"For withholding that article from Karom. For holding the fact that he might still have connections out there. For not encouraging him to seek them out."

"Gita, it would be dishonest for me to tell you that I don't have opinions or that I don't have an opinion about your situation. But the reason you came to me seems to be because *you* have an opinion about your situation, and you're trying to come to grips with it. So let's talk about that."

"I have a secret."

"The article?"

"No. I have another."

"I'm all ears." Dr. Rhodes opened her notebook, twirled her pen between her fingers and began the adagio: "So."

All at once, I felt a big rush inside me, like a wave barreling forth from the pit of my stomach. It started in my groin and pushed forward, gathering speed. For a moment I thought I was going to throw up. But it was better than that; it was release. *Go. Now. Erupt. Speak,* it said. So I did.

"So," I said. "As you know, I'm here because I want to help Karom get through whatever it is that he's dealing with. You know this much. You know that I'm committed to helping him. I have to help him. He has no family—at least I have to operate under that assumption. And he isn't exactly forthright with his friends about his feelings and emotions and how he deals with the issues that invade his head. He isn't even honest with himself. But *I* have something else to admit. Something else that no one knows, especially not Karom."

Dr. Rhodes bowed her head and let me have the floor for my big solo.

"So. I go to India every year, to visit my grandmother, Ammama. She and I are close, but she's also getting older and she lives alone—a stubborn lady who refuses to move into any assisted-living complex or have anyone stay with her. But I try to see as much of India as I can just so I am not just spending time in Delhi in the confines of her apartment. Last year was particularly bad for Karom. I keep a log of his episodes. He had seventy-three. *Seventy-three,* can you imagine? Either night sweats or 'tests' or whatever he calls them.

But seventy-three. I guess they were getting better, because the year before, there were eighty. But I don't know if that was a significant improvement or whatever. I never paid attention in statistics.

"So last year, in light of what was happening with Karom, I decided to go to Bhopal. I didn't tell Karom. I just went. I told my grandmother that I was going to Aurangabad to see the Buddhist caves and I took the overnight train to Bhopal. I knew she wouldn't understand. 'What are you going to that wretched place for?' she'd ask. Where would I stay? We have no family there. I knew she'd think it was dangerous, still dangerous, to send a girl from America who was already prone to fever and Delhi belly and malaria and Third World disease. But I knew Karom's story and I wanted to see where he was from. I wanted to understand it for myself. I felt so removed, never having met his parents or any of his family. It was like he was this tiny survivor from this host of people who I would never know, but maybe going to his homeland would help me get it.

"I arrived in the morning with a modest bag and walked from the train station into town. There was a smell in the air, something like burning rubber, that never seemed to dissipate, and once it did, I think it was only because I had gotten accustomed to it. I walked into sludge and washed my slippers in a trench whose water was only mildly cleaner than the slime that had sullied me in the first place. There were children everywhere, peering out from around corners and slapped-together porches and vestibules. Some of them smiled at me intentionally. Others had no choice but to smile, because they had cleft palates or faces contorted into what appeared to be cheerful grimaces.

"None of these children wore shoes. Had this been a New

York City street, at the intersection of Broadway and Columbus, where Lincoln Center sprouts from the crossing of these two giant avenues, and children ran about the fountain lit in the moonlight, I would have gaped. Had they bounded around the 1 train, gripping the cold steel poles as the cars lurched and rumbled, it would have been a spectacle. But in this city—in all cities in India—it's natural, normal, expected, to see dry cracked heels and bare toes white with dirt. I pretended not to see them. I pretended not to notice these small creatures' plights, their bellies distended and their legs bent with iron deficiencies. Because had I gaped, had I pointed out the discrepancy between myself and them, *I* would have been the infiltrator, the odd person standing out. *I* would have been the alien in this world, this world that to them was all they knew or was all they would ever know. I would be the one that caused alarm, the source of gossip. So I kept quiet.

"I walked around for hours, watching these children pump water—poison—from spigots into plastic tubs to take home to their families for washing clothes, for washing themselves, for pouring into their bodies. I'd read that the groundwater in Bhopal was still contaminated. The earth was toxic and it was affecting everything they did, down to the water they used and the air they breathed. I visited children's trusts and watched flies alight on the crud that leaked out of babies' eyes as they lay indifferently in beds crammed together like crackers. I watched children hobble around on feet twisted like tree roots, their arms gnarled and devoid of ability to clutch, to hold. These children can't talk. Their tongues loll about their mouths like dead weight. They make horrible moaning noises if they are hungry or sleepy or in pain. I saw children playing on corrugated metal, completely oblivious to the fact that they were walking on death itself. There were telltale signs of asbestos everywhere.

"Their mothers and fathers are dead, and those who aren't have asthma or mental problems. Young children are raising their even younger sisters and brothers. No one is fixing the situation. There has been a decades-long court case trying to bring justice to the survivors and the families who will continue living on there, but nothing has changed in years. No one is remedying the groundwater situation. No one is digging up the polluted earth. No one is facing the music. Every year, more and more children are born into that environment and nothing changes.

"I donated a large sum of money to a children's trust on that visit. It was everything I'd traveled with. I could always get more when I returned to Delhi. But I went there to learn, to understand, to try to help Karom. I want to be strong for him. I want to guide him. I know I can't be his savior, but I want to do what I can. I thought going there would help me figure out how best to support him, how to show him how to get past this. I told him I would be his strength, and I will be and I want to be, but…having gone there, to have seen the lives ravaged, the living, waking dead, whose futures will never look forward, living like zombies… I see him do these things where he's 'testing the waters.' Not suicidal, no, just brazen, cavalier, just challenging, teetering on the edge. And he does these things over and over and over and—it kills me to admit this—I want to grab him by the shoulders and shake him until his teeth rattle in his head and scream so loud that he never forgets the words, 'Wake up! Wake the *fuck* up! You ridiculous, wallowing idiot! You have no idea how lucky you are!'"

I sat back, panting. I'd started crying somewhere in the middle of my soliloquy and Dr. Rhodes handed me a box of tissues and smiled a tight little sad smile at me. She looked as if she wanted me to go on. But I was finished. I had said everything I needed to say—for now. She let the minutes tick by as I cleaned myself up and then sat back in the chair.

"So he doesn't know that you went on this trip," she said. "Will you ever tell him?"

"Probably not."

"Why is that?"

"Well, for one, he'd be furious that I did this without his knowledge and blessing, and two, I think he needs to see it for himself. I can't convey the intensity of this place to him in words—"

"You did a fine job just now."

"But that's different. You're just a listener—no offense."

"None taken."

"I mean, this is his life. This is all he knows about his heritage. He should see it firsthand. He should experience it. He should live it on his own. It shouldn't be conveyed to him in a narrative that his girlfriend tells him after visiting for a few hours. He should go."

"You'd mentioned that you two are taking a trip to India this spring. Will you go to Bhopal?"

"I won't suggest it. But if he wants to go, I am completely supportive."

"Will he suggest it?"

"Probably not. I don't know. Probably not."

"Why is that?"

"We made a deal on this trip, that we would avoid all seasides, which, if you've ever been to the coast in India, you would think was the worst deal ever. The sea is gorgeous, magical. I mean, coasts everywhere conjure romanticism. It's sad not to experience them with someone you love. So I'm loath to even suggest that we go to Bhopal. You see what I'm dealing with here—avoidance."

"Maybe the seaside, the water association, is still fresh. Maybe it's too soon to face that particular ghost. But this one might be different."

"That's the other thing. The Bhopal disaster? When it happened, it was because of water. Water flooded the pipes and caused the gas explosion. His parents, his biological ones, didn't even know it was water. They were likely suffocated slowly, this smog creeping toward them until they succumbed. And of course, you know what happened with the tsunami. So water essentially ruined Karom's life. Twice."

Dr. Rhodes sat back, her eyebrows knotted, scribbling furiously.

"Can I ask you? What do you write?"

She looked up, startled. "Just notes. About cases or things that I want to remind myself of once you leave the office, things that I want to consider or review or think about before your next visit."

"You think about your patients between visits?" I asked.

"Of course. It's my homework. These issues don't just dissipate once I step outside these walls. They're always on my mind. That's why I see a shrink of my own. Otherwise, I'd be completely burdened with other people's problems."

"So what will you tell me?"

"Well, it's not my style to tell my patients what to do. I like to guide them, gauging what it seems like they are inclined toward doing in the first place. In your situation, I think for the strength of your relationship and moving forward, because to me it seems like this is one you see lasting for a long time, I think you realize that honesty is the best policy. Now, I know that isn't an easy thing to say, much less carry out. But Karom should know not necessarily that you went to Bhopal without his blessing or even specifically about the newspaper article but that you feel this way, that as much as you want to help him, to be his strength, you have a strong opinion about the matter—that he is a lucky individual to have survived such an ordeal and that it's creating a rift in your relationship."

"But it hasn't, though. I've been really careful in that respect."

"Gita," Dr. Rhodes said gently, "it will. It's bound to. These feelings will become transparent sooner or later. So you'll have to decide how you'll want to deal with them."

I didn't go to Karom's place that night; I didn't think I could face him. There were too many unspoken things, too many secrets I was keeping from him. For the first time in our relationship, even though I'd never once been tempted by another, I felt as though I were cheating on him, that I was having a sordid affair. I texted him that I was going to spend the night at my place to get some more clothes and things I needed and that I'd call him later. When I got home, I curled up into a ball on my bed, careful to rest my ankle separately. I had a large rent-controlled apartment on an unused block in the West Village. Somehow bar, restaurant and boutique owners had overlooked this section of the trendy neighborhood with its winding streets and charming brownstones. I knew that when Karom and I were ready to get married or move in together—I had told him that one wouldn't happen without the certainty of the other—I would struggle with the idea of having to give this place up. I'd lived here ever since I moved to New York, inheriting it from a girl in my graduating class whose coloring and complexion I shared enough to pass as her sister.

With my place, I'd utilized a "Buy what you love—that

way it will all fit together" approach. So it was hodgepodge to some extent, but I am essentially hodgepodge, so it worked. There were vintage shellacked teapots that adorned the top shelves in the kitchen, in strange '70s-style colors like avocado and tangerine. I had a heavy polished-oak table with knots and wood blemishes that I'd found in a Brooklyn flea market held in a schoolyard. My dishes were all random—some white china, some bone china, some IKEA remnants from when I'd first arrived that I couldn't bear to part with. I had a fat olive-green armchair in the living room that looked as though it belonged in a smoking lounge. I had a pale lemon couch on which I'd spilled red wine on numerous occasions, so much that after a few more drunken mishaps it would look like a paisley pattern across the cushions. The walls I'd left white, mostly because my little office was so dark that I wanted a severe contrast between the two spaces. I loved my home, so it was a shame that we spent so much more time at Karom's place than mine.

I lay there remembering a trip to an art gallery we'd taken together. It was tucked into a nook of a Chinatown street where the neighboring stores held freshly gutted chickens and ducks and pork loins, all held up by thick silver meat hooks. We'd read about the exhibit in *Time Out:* it was an interactive homage to memory and the past. We were buzzed through the unmarked black door, through which we entered a long room with a high exposed ceiling. A woman who could only have been a model wordlessly pointed us at the first piece: mirrors welded together at the sides so that they formed a rectangle. In order to view the piece, you had to duck underneath so that the mirrors surrounded you like a room. You stared back at yourself from all angles: north, south, east and west, as I said. Or as Karom interpreted, past, present, future and the unknown. We made our way around the room on our own, but I noticed when Karom stopped at what appeared to be a large dining table. I stepped quietly behind him to observe this piece. At one end of the table, there was a box with a jumble of old black-and-white pictures, some faded and watermarked. There was a collection of the photos on the table itself, and next to it a shredder, fresh with curls of paper. There were three places set at the table, and if you looked carefully under all the photo and shredder paraphernalia, you could glimpse a fourth setting.

"You're supposed to interact with it," the gallery girl said. Karom picked up a photo from the top of the box and stared at the image, a large woman sitting on the steps of a brown-stone with a tiny lapdog perched on her knee. He picked up another: a family photo with generations spread across the panoramic page, their expressions frozen in time. The patri-arch of the family sat square in the middle, holding a silver-tipped cane. He was the only one smiling; the others stared straight into the camera, challengingly. "You're supposed to shred them," the girl said.

"Why?" Karom asked.

"It's supposed to represent forgetting and the past. The art-ist wanted visitors to interact with the piece, consider each photo and then banish it to memory. Go ahead."

Karom held both photos in two hands, looking from one to the other. He put them both down on the table and picked up two more, looked at them and put them down. He looked through the whole pile that way until his fingers brushed against the bottom of the box. The girl had crept back to her perch behind the desk this time and was impatiently flick-ing through Facebook. From where I stood behind Karom, I could see photos of her friends glamorously holding champagne flutes and dancing together, their makeup pristine and their dresses designer. Karom continued to sift through the photos until finally he turned around and spoke to me as though he'd known I was there all along. "I can't," he whispered, teary eyed. "I can't destroy them. They are someone's memories. I can't relegate them into the Dumpster." I nodded and he walked past me through the unmarked black door. I stood and surveyed the table, where he'd placed the photos in unintelligible piles before scooping them up and replacing them all in the box. As I walked out, I thanked the girl at the desk.

"Interesting," she said. "You can tell a lot about people when they can't shred those. Your boyfriend is sentimental."

"Something like that," I said.

Back on the street, Karom had been leaning against the metal grate of an unopened butcher shop. I'd held my hand out to him, but he'd held something else out to me. It was a photo of a small boy and his older sister. She was holding his hand as though she had been told to, and the boy was smiling sweetly at the camera.

"Look," he'd said. "I saved one."

I considered what Dr. Rhodes had said, turned it over and over in my mind. Up until now, I'd managed to keep him close to me. I'd also managed to keep my feelings toward his "fate testing" a secret. His tests rattled me; they made my blood run cold and my heart race, but as soon as I held him, it was all over. But I saw her point; even though the events had slowed down this year—there had been only seven so far and we were already in March—I knew this feeling would somehow manifest itself in me and erupt to the surface. I wondered if I could keep it inside me, at least until we traveled to India together. I wondered if I would break down and show him the article, if he would follow up on it. I wondered if he would insist on traveling to Bhopal and tracking these people or other people down. I wondered if I had the strength in me to continue to be his.

Karom

~~

Karom remembered the day he found the letters the way he remembered the fire in grade school: like a patchwork. It came in broken squares to him, whole hours of the encounter disappearing into the ether. Other moments blazed up in his memory, singeing the periphery until he forced himself to believe, to unearth the tattered pages from their hiding place in a mundane khaki folder and grip them, dog-eared and palpable. These pages were the only connection, the only evidence to support third-degree life burns and irreparable damage. He had to administer a life-saving technique to himself, searching his wan face in the surreal light of his mother's backlit makeup mirror, demanding of himself, "Karom, you are okay. *Are* you okay? Can you breathe? You can breathe."

In the third grade, his school had had to evacuate when a student had been insouciantly striking matches and throwing them into the sink with the bathroom pass shoved into the back pocket of his jeans. The red heads of the matches sizzled out demurely in the sink until the child got bored of this game and began tossing them into the wastepaper basket, slowly, tediously, until a blaze sparked once he'd returned to his seat in the third row to finish his column of sums.

Students were rushed down the narrow staircases two by two and herded onto the sidewalks, where Karom stood watching licks of orange and red poking out of the third-floor bathroom, threatening to spread. The firemen came, kitted and courageous, smiling tightly at the children before they leaped into the building and others unfurled a giant ladder from the back of the truck, stretching into the tiny window that had by then shattered, spraying slivers of glass into the branches of the trees that normally scratched at the sill during storms and gusty days.

Just like this, Karom only remembered that day in parts: the moment when he deliberated over hooking his backpack over his shoulders while his classmates filed out silently; the fireman who looked at him with his cool steely-gray eyes before clambering up the ladder with the hose thrown over his shoulder as if he were holding his towel on his way to have a shower; the screams and cries from students who realized that the class garter snake, Noname—thus christened because the students couldn't agree on a name but pronounced "No-nah-me" so as to sound Asian inspired—was trapped in her glass tank and would soon be consumed by the smoke. He remembered being shepherded into the outdoor yard, where the teacher made them line up alphabetically and then by height order and then by age order in an effort to distract them from the mayhem. He remembered returning to the classroom the next day, once the fire had been contained, but so much water had flooded the corridors, peeling the paint away from the wall, and paper towels had been bunched up, creating a papier-mâché moat leading down the hall. Noname wasn't in her cage or the class-room, nor had she been found anywhere else in the school. Karom's classmates put up posters all over, in the cafeteria, in the bathrooms, beseeching other students to thoroughly inspect all toilets before flushing, all sinks to look for that telltale sign of the small flickering tongue as it might dance forth from a faucet, to search behind bookshelves, inside desks, in arts-and-crafts closets, but the snake had never turned up.

Similarly, years later he remembered only select moments of the day he finally returned to his family's home in Brook-lyn Heights for the first time since the tsunami. He had gone on his own, eschewing the trip to Myrtle Beach with his friends in order to sort through various papers and items that needed dealing with, though they had offered to accompany him. "You shouldn't be alone when you go back for the first time," they'd said. "It's a lot to handle." But Karom hadn't wanted them to sacrifice their spring breaks, their senior year, their free time. "No, thank you," he'd said. "There's a lot to do and it will go a lot faster and efficiently if I just swoop in there, get the job done and get out." Like that fire, he re-membered back to the afternoon he discovered the sheaves of papers that outlined his life, his past, himself. Jack How-ard, his parents' lawyer, had been gently urging him to re-turn home a few weekends before so that everything didn't all crash down around him at the same time: the echoing town house, the seemingly just-made bed, the brown dried petals settled around a vase holding water as brown as pond scum, where the stems of the flowers were still submerged, smell-ing putrid and deathly. In the fridge, food had decayed for so long that a thick layer of green or pink or white fuzz grew over everything, rendering it unidentifiable and foreign. The milk in the carton was heavy with chunks. The entire kitchen smelled stale with abandonment.

He began to listen to the crowded answering machine. At first, telemarketers from December in the few days after his parents had left. Then friends who were calling concerned once they'd heard the news. And then finally, mourners called the house with their wavering voices and undulating sympathy, at which point Karom hit the delete button and the machine went silent. There was unopened mail piled in the vestibule, heaps of it together. Bills, magazines, charity letters, packages of film reels, in one a small trophy that his father had earned at a film gala for editing a fifteen-minute short of the life story of Charlie Chaplin's dog. Karom opened letters addressed to his parents from their friends across the state, Christmas cards and ultimately, on top, a layer of sympathy cards. His parents' friends didn't know his address at college, so they'd all sent reams of outreach to his home in Brooklyn. He stacked them all according to theme: Outstanding Bills, Now-Irrelevant Bills, Regular Correspondence, Sympathy Correspondence, Charity, Magazines, Junk. He dealt with it all, throwing out garbage, unplugging devices that no longer needed power, deliberating before doing three loads of laundry that lay lumped despairingly in the hamper, because it still smelled faintly of their sweat, their grime, their cells.

According to their will, it all came to him: the house, everything in it, his father's share of Cutting Room, all the accounts. Jack had traveled up to Boston to witness Karom's signature on the bottom of all the papers and had given him copies, so when Karom started searching, he wasn't sure what it was he was after. He found his mother's jewelry locked in a safe in the crawl space above their bedroom. She'd wrapped it all lovingly in pieces of tissue and tucked it carefully into an

ancient suitcase with tabbed locks like pinball-machine flip-
pers. He took each piece out and laid it across the bed, where
it looked dull and unimpressive: small pearls that dangled
precariously from yellow gold, diamonds that needed polishing, pieces of jewelry that because he'd never seen his mother
wear them before seemed foreign, which made his mother
seem even more foreign to him than ever before. He found
reels in the bottom of his father's closet, reels shot on 8 mm
film, boxed cartridges he couldn't imagine even beginning
to watch, a whole box of negatives that he began to hold up
to the pale light that streamed past the opaque curtains in his
parents' bedroom one at a time.

He considered the things he'd lost throughout his life: a
bag of marbles, disappearing one by one until the mesh sack
lay empty and forlorn; random playing cards until the deck
became useless and impossible to play with; his collection of
baseball cards, dog-eared and bent, which he'd silently written
off once a family friend told him they were only valuable if
they remained in their original form, whole, crisp and without fingerprints. Of all the things he'd lost, the one he wished
he still owned was a photograph of himself as a young adult,
holding a large tilefish from end to end as if it were a center-
fold, grinning widely. This was before the advent of digitized
film, so every photo captured was a live element and you had
to care for the negatives as much as the film roll itself.

"Your smile is as wide as the fish," Mohan had said to him
on that trip. His father had taken him to New Hampshire,
where they had fished in the ocean together, his mother packing egg sandwiches without mayonnaise lest they fester in the
sun. His favorite part of the trip was before the actual time
when they set out in the little boat with the lopsided rudder,
with Karom rowing with one oar as his father steered the

crank handle. Tide was low and he had borrowed waders from
the owner of the lodge they were staying at and bounced down
to the water's edge, where the silt and mud were layers thick,
to pull fat juicy earth crawlers from where they were poking
out of the sludge, halfway basking in the sun. He held them
up to the sun, wriggling and disturbed from their slumber,
before placing them together in the bucket that would accompany their trip. They used makeshift pulleys instead of rods,
paddles with strong fishing twine wrapped around them with
a lead weight at the bottom onto which a fat worm would be
figure-eighted and then lowered into the salty depths below.
When he felt resistance, Karom wound the wire back onto
the paddle by turning it toward himself, as you would a yo-yo
after flubbing a trick. And that feeling, of a live fresh jerky
fish thrashing about at the end of the wire, was the pure glee
that Karom felt at the end of the long day baking in the heat.
Toward the evening, as the sun dipped below the waterline,
Karom put on his father's sweater, his arms engulfed in the
sleeves, and held up his fish triumphantly on land, stretching
it like a smile. That picture of him with the sun in his eyes,
his baseball hat slung down low so that he had to tilt his head
back to see the camera, and the wet, finally still fish between
his fingers, had been one of his prized possessions. And over
the years, since it hadn't been trapped in an album or behind a
plastic frame, it had been lost forever. This was the first thing
he thought when he saw the slippery pile of negatives at the
bottom of his father's closet. Later, he would tape the box
shut with heavy silver packing tape and carry it with him to
Boston, and then back to New York to his rented apartment
above Central Park, as far away from the Brooklyn Heights
brownstone as was comfortable.

He found abandoned wallets that had never been disposed

of, creases scarred deep into the leather. He found old ID cards and passports with pictures of people he barely knew: his father with a thin mustache that barely covered his philtrum, his mother with long thick plaits like a Native American, his father with oversize square glasses that consumed his face so that Karom had to peer closely to make sure it was the same man.

He found papers, so many, many papers. He wasn't sure how important they all were so he kept them all and separated them into piles: Cutting Room Productions, Tiger Translations, House Stuff, Travel Stuff, Medical Stuff, Karom Stuff. He didn't think he'd be hungry at any point; he thought the grief might consume him instead of him wanting to consume. But by midafternoon on that very first day, he dialed the local pizza place by heart and ate a whole pie, grease fingered, gingerly picking at the pool of papers he'd created in the middle of the bedroom.

Finally, with the mouth of every drawer in the room gaping open soundlessly, Karom knew he had only his parents' bedside drawers left. Bedside drawers were sacred, not to mention that Karom didn't want to know what his parents needed just before they nodded off or just after they awakened in the early-morning hours. He braced himself for the worst: condoms, lubricant, handcuffs? But his mother's side held only a few chosen items: the mouthguard her dentist made her wear when she began grinding down her molars, the silk sleep mask Karom had bought for her birthday, a few pens and a blank notepad, and earplugs. His father's held eleven AA batteries, a small point-and-shoot camera with a blank memory card, and numerous adapters and chargers tangled together in a chaotic knot. Karom removed them and began to extricate them from one another. He needed some time to assess his next move. Since he'd arrived at home that morning, he'd been

           PIA PADUKONE

constantly moving, arranging, throwing out, cleaning, but as soon as he finished untangling the cords, he reached back into the drawer, where his hand brushed against a stack of papers that he pulled out without further thought. The papers were mismatched, held together by a binder clip. There were pages from hotel-room stationery, some torn from a spiral notebook. Others were notes on blank computer paper, on tracing paper, on Cutting Room stationery. Some were Post-it Notes, one on the back of a coloring-book page that hadn't been colored in. But it was all his parents' handwriting, first his father's, then his mother's, then his father's again. Over and over. Pages and pages. Numbered and placed in order.

"Dear Karom," it began. He sat down for the first time and began to read, and with that, the rest of the day passed out from under him. It was nightfall when he set the pages down with shaking hands and placed them a few feet away from him so he could observe them like a live animal. It was a letter, a lifelong letter to him from his parents that they'd never been meaning to send. It was a catharsis, an atoning of the sins, a bleaching of the past. It was a way for his parents to live with themselves, with each other, while Karom remained an outsider, completely ignorant of the truth. Before he felt anything, before he got angry or sad or confused, before he felt any of that, he simply could barely believe it. He couldn't believe that these words had been right under his nose for his entire life, right in his father's bedside-table drawer. It was as if his father believed that Karom would never pry into his parents' private lives, but what if he needed batteries—or a camera? It was right there, mocking him, a silent parody of his life. And he couldn't understand the connections: he looked like his mother. He had her strong aquiline nose and her dark labyrinthine coloring. He had his father's hands, long tapered fingers

at the ends of palms thick as slabs of steak. If he had discovered this while his parents were in the room, instinctively, he
would have looked at himself in their faces like in a mirror,
as if to prove this letter wrong. Immediately, he would have
aligned his hand next to his mother's like paint swatches, the
color matching perfectly so that you almost couldn't tell where
one pigment ended and the other began. He would have made
her stand straight in profile, erect as a soldier, so that he could
bring his nose in line with hers. He would have made his father raise his hand into the air and brought his own against
it, silently measuring the space between the finger segments
and taking in his father's knobby knuckles, which Karom had
resigned himself to having to inherit one day.

But now even that word lost its meaning. He could inherit
things—money, property, shares, jewelry—but never cheekbones, creativity, DNA, athletic skill. His parents couldn't pass
anything down; it ended with them. There had never been a
product of their love, an end result of their coupling, an idea
generated by the two of them, other than this other vessel of
a boy from Bhopal into which they'd poured their lives and
to which they'd dedicated themselves.

Suddenly, it all made sense. When he'd befriended Jian-
Quan, a Chinese boy who'd been adopted by a Jewish couple,
his parents had exchanged knowing glances when they walked
into the dining room to see them quizzing one another in
advanced chemistry. He should have known that look meant
"Is this too close to home? We are playing with fire, spouse."
When his parents had suggested that *Annie* wasn't an appropriate choice for the movies, and perhaps he'd like to see *E.T.*
instead. Looking back, he could even sense a flicker of un-
ease when he'd had to create a family tree in the fourth grade.
But those moments remained far away in the past and he was

alone in his familial home in Brooklyn Heights, alone with the papers with his mother's loopy words and his father's tiny scrawl, as if Mohan had been destined for medicine and the illegible prescription-pad handwriting that befell physicians. He'd read the more than fifty pages that comprised the letter over the course of the spring break week, locking himself in their home, wondering how it was that it had been kept a secret until now. Not even the emotional aspect of it, and how could his parents hide this from him, but the logistical one: how could this life be wrapped up so symmetrically, snipped of loose ends, pressed so it lay flat, and simply shoved into a drawer underneath his nose, but out of presence, out of necessity. Out of love? The way the letter looked, it certainly seemed so. And it was something he would have to reconcile himself with over the course of many, many years. Not to mention that he couldn't invoke the memory of his parents as liars but as two people who had cared so deeply and entrenched themselves so fully into his life that there was no seam where their blood ended and his began; you couldn't tell the difference. He was a Seth and he didn't want to dig or explore or make even a single phone call that might change that.

So he packed up the sheaf of papers, the unsent letter to him, the box of negatives and returned to college with them. He placed the letter in a corner of his desk along with his other research and thesis materials as though he had been extremely diligent on his latest trip to the library. Lloyd had looked at the stack every day; it was in his line of vision as he sat at his own desk and considered words or equations or philosophies. He became curious about the pile, searching it from a distance with his eyes, knowing that it was something with which Karom had returned from the hallowed house in Brooklyn but not wanting to unearth any piece of Karom that might fold under the emotional weight of what those papers signified. Once, when Karom was out at class, Lloyd finally ventured across the room and began reading the top page. He was nearly at the bottom when he heard the click of the door behind him and suddenly Karom was in the room. Lloyd pounced away from the letter as though it had come alive and were snapping its jaws in his hands. Karom walked over to the desk and put his hand on the top sheet. Lloyd had returned to his desk and propped a heavy tome in the space between them, but Karom had already seen. He picked up the stack and extended it to Lloyd.

"You should finish," Karom said, as if he were loaning out a paperback. "It's pretty compelling."

Lloyd shook his head. "I'm sorry, Karom. I didn't mean to go through your stuff. I didn't mean to violate your pri—"

"I'm not mad. Here."

"It's just that you've been so quiet about things since you got back from your house."

Karom lowered the papers. "It's not my house. It's my home."

"Right. Sorry. But we're all worried about you. We're concerned. *I'm* concerned."

"Well, this will explain some of it. I'm serious. Read it. I'll wait." Karom dropped the papers over the open book on Lloyd's desk and walked to his bed. He lay back with his arms supporting his head, listening for every rustle of a turning page or for Lloyd's breathing to change. By the time Lloyd had finished, the room was tented in darkness. The only light in the room was the circle from Lloyd's bedside lamp. Friends had knocked on the door as the dinner hour approached, but the two had ignored it. Finally, Karom heard Lloyd snap the binder clip back into place before he sat up and swung his legs onto the floor. During the Myrtle Beach trip, Lloyd had managed to sear his skin in the sun so that it had become red and raw, and it had peeled a few weeks ago. It had finally come back to his normal skin tone, but now Lloyd was again a bright red almost as riotous as his skin had been blistered on the beach. Water danced in his eyes and dribbled at his chin, and his face was snaked with vestiges of salt where the tears had dried and left behind pallid ghosts. His hands shook, nestling the papers gently as though they could be soothed by the touch. He turned to meet Karom's eyes and stood.

Karom nodded, continued nodding. "Let's just go to dinner. Come on." He opened the door and held it, waiting for his roommate.

There were times when thoughts would infiltrate Karom's mind, thoughts that he knew he shouldn't entertain but that he allowed to dance around his brain and then finally let rest like congealed soup. There was the time his Morals and Ethics class watched *Sophie's Choice* and for the rest of the semester, Karom found his mind going back and forth to the same question that the heroine in the movie was asked: What if he could have saved one of his parents? Which would he have chosen? It was a disgusting, awful question and one that he wished he hadn't ever imagined, but once it was there, he couldn't help but wonder. On the one hand, his mother had always been there for him, literally during the days when he had first arrived in New York with them, teaching him English and worrying over his own worry in his eyes. On the other, his father had raised him with as much love and affection as any mother might, kissing him constantly, breaking down the gender roles that were so steadfast in this society. His father had taught him so much about life and friendship

and love. He rejoiced in the fact that he had never made a decision about the awful choice he had set himself in his mind,
that he knew he would never be able to choose between his
parents, but still the question haunted him until he handed
in his final paper and the Morals and Ethics class was over.

But then he found himself thinking dark thoughts again
when he read shortly after the tsunami that they were con-
ducting DNA testing in Austria in order to specifically identify
the victims who hadn't been claimed. If you were a relative
of someone who had gone missing during the tragedy, you
had to call the University of Innsbruck, send them your loved
one's medical records and they would let you know once they
found a DNA match. But what would be the point? he asked
himself over and over again. So he could have official, physical proof that they were all dead? So that he could frame the
papers in his living room and be reminded every day? No,
he told himself, this was folly. That would be self-inflicted
punishment.

The *Times* had printed an article about victims' personal
effects being distributed back to their families—clothes mildewed and damp, books that had been submerged underwater
for days and then dried, so their brittle pages fell apart at the
slightest touch, decaying toiletries, waterlogged stuffed animals. Karom never bothered to inquire what had been found
from his family. He had what he needed: his watch and the
box of negatives that he'd ferreted away all those years ago
and then never touched. It had lurked in the recesses under
Karom's bed, that nebulous dark underbelly where abandoned
socks were flung unknowingly and dust bunnies grew to ex-
cessive proportions. It wasn't until six years later, to be exact,
that the box surfaced.

One morning nearly a year after they'd met, Gita sat on

the floor surrounded by soft crests of the newspaper, one leg outstretched diagonally to the side as she leaned forward on one elbow and read an article.

"Look," she'd said. "They're in the wedding section." She turned the paper around and pointed to a beatific couple, flawlessly interracial, in their professional engagement photo.

"Who's this?" Karom asked, taking the paper from her.

"My parents' friend's daughter. She's getting married today. To that guy."

"How come your parents weren't invited?"

"They were. They're here. Or not here but at the Botanic Garden. At the wedding."

"What? They're here? In the city? Why aren't we meeting them?" Karom asked. With each question, his voice had gotten increasingly higher-pitched until he crescendoed to a halt.

"Well, um, I'm meeting them tomorrow. I didn't know… I wasn't sure. If it was too early," she said, lining up her other leg parallel to the first. "I didn't know if you'd feel pressured or all 'scree-scree-scree crazy girlfriend.'" She pantomimed holding a knife and stabbing it in the air.

"Gita, it's your family. You're ridiculous. Call them now. Tell them we are meeting them for a drink. *We* are meeting them for a drink. You're crazy."

"Okay, okay. Just remember later on that you're the one who requested this." She reached for his cell phone where it was plugged in and dialed.

Gita had always made it quite clear that she would never thrust her parents upon him. Parents were a gray area, a tricky topic between them, something that Gita had initially danced around during the early stages of their relationship. In fact, she'd consistently changed the topic whenever they called; she'd pressed the ignore button on her phone and called them back later, out of Karom's earshot. But finally, he'd asked her who it was that she was avoiding.

"Is there an ex-boyfriend I should be worried about?" he'd joked.

"No, no, it's just…my family." She'd grinned, looking down at the ground. "I can always call them back."

"Why don't you answer? Speak to your parents. Please don't avoid them because of me."

She'd nodded and forgotten the matter. But Karom hadn't.

So the next evening, they met in the main bar at the Algonquin Hotel, Karom as exuberant and seraphic as the couple in the weddings section and Gita looking and feeling sheepish.

"Thought you were going to give us a miss, darling," her father said, setting his martini down on the dark-paneled bar before kissing his eldest daughter high on her temple. "Waited until the absolute last minute to hang with your mum and dad, huh?"

"Hi, baby girl." Her mother grasped her wrists in both hands and smacked her noisily on both cheeks. "Thanks for gracing us with your presence."

"Okay, enough with the third degree, guys. Near, Myma, I'd like you to meet Karom." Gita pushed the small of his back gently as she urged him forward. That morning, Gita had explained to Karom her pet names for her parents. "'Father' in Norwegian is *far,* you see," she'd explained. "And I didn't understand why I'd want my dad to be away from me. So I changed it to Near, and he couldn't very well argue with that, could he? And when Maila was born, apparently I was very jealous and unwilling to share, so Amma became My-Amma, eventually shortened into Myma."

Karom was enveloped into the perfume in the air, the light touches on his forearm from Savita and the firm handshake and the hearty slaps on the back from Haakon. Her parents didn't make a big deal about him, about his introduction. It was almost as if they had happened to run into one another at the bar moments before she met her parents, as if they were old friends from college. Except that Gita had gone to a women's college and this was the man she was sleeping with.

"How was the wedding?" Karom asked after they'd gone through formalities and first-stage niceties.

"It was lovely, though I must say I'm rather tired of the Brooklyn Botanic Garden," Savita said. "It's the third wedding we've been to in a year there." Karom looked over at Gita, his eyebrows raised. That look was incredulous. That look was an earmark for a later conversation.

"Lots of your family and friends live in New York?"

"Enough," Haakon said. "But not enough to see our Geetar as much as we'd like."

"Da-ad," Gita whined.

"Oh, right, sorry. I'm supposed to pretend that I'm okay not seeing you very often. I'm supposed to say that it's okay that my three daughters have chosen to live lives far, far away from us."

"Maila lives close by," Gita said.

"That doesn't mean we ever see her," Savita said. "So when are you two visiting us?"

After some time, Karom excused himself to the bathroom. It's important to note that the evening couldn't have been more perfect. The four of them were settled at the curve of the historic bar, casual and comfortable. A few couples loitered in ball gowns and tuxedos from earlier engagements at debutante balls or confirmations or whatever it was the white elite did on a Sunday afternoon. The drinks were strong and perfect and Karom instantly loved Gita's parents. They were warm, not overbearing; they were engaged, not insistent. They were just who he'd imagined Gita's parents would be, right down to the very manner in which they dressed, Savita in a rich red wrap dress and her husband in a tan blazer and very undadlike jeans. But in the bathroom, where he waved aside the attendant as he offered him a towel the moment he walked in, he found a stall and sat directly down on the toilet without lowering his pants. He looked at his hands and felt the sinews and veins in his palms. He could feel his blood, his parents' blood, his Bhopali blood, coursing underneath, the slight twitch of his pulse constant underneath his Rolex. His chest contracted and expanded as it should. All seemed natural and normal in this manner except that he couldn't breathe. He couldn't feel his breath, and he was gasping and gagging in an effort to regain control and then the bathroom attendant was knocking at the door, and Karom opened it but waved him off. The bathroom attendant took one look at him and raced into the bar, selecting the one person whose skin color resembled his.

"Please, miss," he implored Savita. "Your son, he's—" Gita looked at him, her eyes wide, and placed a hand on Savita's forearm, the same reassuring touch Savita had herself placed on Karom's. She raced after the attendant's receding back downstairs to the men's room, where she found Karom sunk on the floor in an open stall with his head between his hands. When he heard the click of her heels against the tile, he paused to look up and began crying all over again. Gita sank down next to him, pretzeling her arm under his leg and holding him upright. She breathed into the cavity under his arm, taking in the cleanliness of the floor and how comfortable she felt upon it. The attendant had been watching them for signs of an emergency, but the intimate gesture made him feel as though he was intruding, so he placed a Cleaning in Progress sign at the front door of the men's room and stood on guard next to it.

"Breathe, Karom, breathe. Breathe, baby." He obligingly took some large mouthfuls of air and sank into her body.

"Was it too soon?"

He nodded, his head in his arms. They sat like that together in silence, intertwined so that you could barely tell where one body started and the other ended. Gita sat with him until Karom was ready to stand up, be walked delicately to the front door of the hotel and be put in a cab. Gita returned to her parents alone.

"Is everything all right?" Savita sat up, alarmed. "Is he okay? Should we go to him?"

"He's fine, Ma. He just needs some time and to lie down. He took a cab home. We can meet another time."

"Maybe you should go to him, Geets."

"Honestly, he'll be fine. He just needs to be alone. He'll feel better if we all just stay here and have a nice time." Which they tried to do, but the Manhattans and white wines tasted sour with the heavy cloud hanging over the evening. It was the next morning that Karom called her parents once they'd flown back to Columbus, apologizing and demanding that he make it up to them.

"Nonsense," Savita said. "The important thing is that you're all right. And there will be plenty more occasions for us to spend time together. And, Karom, please let us know if there is anything we can do to help. Anything." He thanked her and promised he would.

It was also the next morning that Karom called in sick, dug under his bed and retrieved the brown cardboard box that he'd taped shut with silver packing tape years before. He used a scissor to slice it open and looked at all the shiny brown strips inside. Before he could rethink it, he scooped the whole thing up and took it down the street to the one-hour film place. The development would take more than an hour, of course, with the volume of film in the box, but Karom sat there like an anxious father pacing the steps outside a delivery room, stalking about the small space, cracking his knuckles and watching the curly-haired film man as he fed the negatives one by one into the mouth of the behemoth processor behind the counter. After three hours, there were stacks and stacks of photos. They had accumulated throughout the afternoon, piling up on the counter like a multiturreted castle. Karom hadn't looked at them as they emerged. He'd simply stood a few feet away from it all respectfully, his hands clasped behind his back as the counter boy boxed them up in a fresh cardboard box and sealed it.

"One thousand sixty-four four-by-sixes," he said. "That's $266."

Karom paid and lifted the box from the bottom. The weight was staggering—the negatives had tripled in size and area with processing—and he hailed a cab on the sidewalk as soon as he got outside.

Karom's key chain resembled that of a janitor. He had three keys for his apartment, his bike-lock key and the key to his office, and he had never been able to remove his family-home keys from the ring. They traveled with him everywhere he went—the two keys that opened the first door into the brownstone, where the mail was pushed through a slot, the one for the second door with its opaque window glass and then the last two keys for their final door, which led into the foyer. The house had stood intact after he'd finished college and moved out completely. He couldn't imagine living there with its echoing hallways and empty floorboards, nor could he stand to sell. *I'll get over it someday,* he'd told himself practically, *and by then property values will have gone up and I'll have a family and we'll redecorate and refurbish, and while the bones will be the same, it won't be the same place I grew up. It won't be the same place they lived for all those years. But at the same time, it will.* The house had been paid off gradually over the years by his parents, and when Karom had sold the share in Cutting Room, it had helped to pay off the remaining mortgage so that Karom was no longer beholden. He was a homeowner, though he hadn't been back since his final visit, when he'd spent those two lonely nights there after college removing the last of his clothes and belongings before he moved to the apartment he'd been in since in Harlem.

That afternoon the cab pulled up on the small side street where each brownstone hugged the next. At first, Karom felt disoriented and he had trouble spotting his home; they all seemed so similar. But as soon as he hauled the box onto his shoulder and jingled the keys out of his pocket, he raised the gate hinge open with his knee, slid it open with his hip, as he'd done so many times when he came home with his hands full, and closed it all in the same familiar motion. He walked up the stairs without being able to see—the box blocked his sight—counting the steps. Nine. The keys slid in noiselessly and it was only once he stood in the foyer, looking about dazedly, that he waited for himself to react. But he didn't. There was no breakdown, nor were there any tears, nor did he even find his knees wobbling so that he had to sink to the floor. He simply closed the door behind him and moved into the living room, all brisk, all business, held his breath to a cloud of dust that raised around him as he sat down, and pulled the tape off the box with one quick motion.

It seemed only fair for Karom to come here to open this

box. It was its genesis, after all. But he felt oddly at ease in this house. It made the same sounds as when he'd stayed home sick from school, though there was no gurgling of pipes behind walls or clanging of radiators, as the water and heat had been turned off years ago. There was a man who did handiwork on their street, mostly watering the sidewalk to scrape off dog poo, shoveling snow when it piled up in winter, moving cars when they needed to be parked on the alternate side of the street. Karom paid him to look in on the house from time to time, nothing serious, just make sure there were no break-ins or weather damage, no leakage from the adjoining homes, no infestations. The house was like an older relative: you checked in from time to time but it didn't need constant monitoring.

Once he'd told Gita the whole story, he could see it working through her mind: *Why doesn't he live there now? It's such a huge place. Will we ever live there together? What's to become of it?* She'd asked him the address and he knew she had gone to look from the outside, staring up at the eaves, where ivy was meandering around the shuttered windows, threatening to overtake. He could imagine the gate whining as she pulled it open, as though it had been disturbed after all these years. She'd sat there imagining Karom as he walked through the gate on his skinny preteen legs, as he'd snuck in a girl and a six-pack in high school. She'd imagined his parents, his mother with her dark complexion stepping elegantly out of a cab, his father as he came home, disheveled and excited from a new development at work. She'd imagined the hum of the house when they were all in it, talking, moving, eating, drinking. But she'd never asked to return with him, and she never would.

His mouth itched from the dust settled all around him and he sneezed three or four times before fishing out a surgical mask from under the sink and slipping the elastic over his ears.

His father would wear these while painting a wall or taking out the trash to shield his nose from noxious fumes. Karom caught sight of himself in the hall mirror. With his mouth and nose covered, he realized that his forehead and the shape of his eyes were things that didn't belong to either of his parents.

The photos were shiny, slippery between his hands, which were shaking imperceptibly. He took out a stack and held them against his chest before he flipped one down from the bottom of the pile. This was a river, a yellow-and-brown rushing river, wide as you could imagine, rushing so fast you could imagine the spray as you stood on its banks. There was a bank on the other side, but this picture was taken to convey the immensity, the vastness, of this body of water. The next image proved the previous one wrong. This was of the same body of water, but it was zoomed out so that he could see that the "river" was merely a ditch through which groundwater had surfaced. There was strength in the water, but the image had been shot in a manner that reminded him of his father's point about suspense. Why had he shot this insignificant stream as though it were a larger waterway? He put it on the couch next to him. The next was a path, a narrow pebbled path that led to a small hut on its far side, but the picture was taken from the angle of the walker approaching the hut so that you could see every stone, each spot you might place your foot along the way. The path had clearly been constructed by hand, without cement or aid of machinery to bind it; it was simply a collection of pebbles piled in a row and patted down so that it was walkable. The next was of a tree; so close was the camera lens to its leaves and branches that you couldn't see the sky or the ground behind it. Karom recognized this as a neem tree, as one grew in his grandparents' backyard in Bombay. He recognized the narrow, spiky leaves that grew like torpedoes and the tiny white flowers that he'd collected in his shirt as a child as they spiraled to the ground. The next was a yellow wooden sign that staggered the words *Hinduism, Jainism, Buddhism, Sikhism, Islam, Christianity* horizontally but highlighted one letter out of each word vertically to create the word *Indian.* He flipped through them faster and faster. Abandoned soda bottles, garbage collected by the side of the road, but Indian garbage—this much was clear. It was Indian plastic, no unnecessary packaging or waste. The soda bottles had been reused so many times that the creases in them meant that the liquid inside leaked out through plastic pores when the bottles were filled. A bald cricket ball, a crinkly potato-chip bag.

The next stack was of people, dark, angry people, shouting. His father had gotten close to their faces or used an extreme telephoto lens to click pictures that saw into their mouths. This man was missing most of his teeth but his fierce expression certainly didn't make him appear demure. There was a fire in his eyes, in his red bloodshot eyes that traveled out of the photograph and made the hair on Karom's arms stand up. The next image was of a sea of signs, homemade signs painted on posterboard and nailed to wooden poles.

We Can't Abide Union Carbide.

Warren Anderson: Clean Up Your Mess.

Meera, Age 2. On this one there was a blown-up image of a small child smiling toothlessly.

There was a tall burning effigy that looked like a scarecrow that dozens of people were milling about, throwing twigs and sticks on top of. There was a vast brown field where the remaining grass looked burned and grew in sparse patches like a prepubescent attempt at growing facial hair. There were handkerchiefs knotted together in a ring around a tree. Mothers nestled in doorways clutching their remaining children, their only valuables. Tall girders behind concrete walls, tanks with indecipherable graffiti. Piles of blankets, piles of branches, piles of ashes.

Karom retrieved a roll of masking tape from the drawer in the kitchen where it had always been kept. He taped all of the pictures up on the wall of the living room that faced him now, and when he ran out of room, he continued on the second wall and then the third, the images of Bhopal in the aftermath of the disaster spilling across corners and covering paintings already layered in a thin cover of dust. Then he stood back and took it all in, turning his body slowly at first and then faster and faster so that he could see them all; they came in a blur to him, snatches of light, meaning and film. Finally, when his balance couldn't hold him upright anymore, he collapsed in the center of the plush carpet in a cloud of dust, where he held his head up and the snapshots of what could have been spun gently around him.

Years later, as Karom and Gita board their return flight from Delhi to New York City, those photographs fill his mind. They have, in fact, filled his mind from time to time during their few weeks in India, Bhopal sitting blithely in the middle of the country like a siren. *For the past two weeks, I've been the closest I've ever physically been to my birthplace,* he thinks to himself now. *The closest I've ever been to Bhopal since I found the letter that changed everything.* But the photographs that presumably still hang on the living-room wall in his childhood home in Brooklyn Heights are the ties that Karom has to the city. He thinks of them now and tries to remember the contents of each one. They are the sole connection he feels to the place. Perhaps he will summon the strength to visit Bhopal one day in the future. But he knows it inherently through the pictures that his father took all those years ago when his parents came to Bhopal to retrieve him. He has seen Bhopal through his father's eyes. And for now, that's the closest he needs to get.

On their flight Karom and Gita are issued seats rows apart from one another on the full flight. Though they try to negotiate seat changes, no one wants either the middle or window seat when they are traveling with children, as nearly everyone besides them on the plane appears to be.

"It's okay," Karom says, squeezing her shoulder. "You're going to sleep the whole way anyway and I'll just annoy you with my fidgeting. I'll come visit you from time to time." Secretly, he is pleased to have some time to himself. For the past two weeks, it has been him and Gita constantly, and while he loves having her at his side, with their knees pressed together in the backseat of auto-rickshaws and on long pendulous train rides, he wants to reflect on his time in India, the time he has given himself to heal, to repent, to forgive. It is the first time during their trip that he will be able to consider it all: the swaying camel rides in the Thar Desert, the hot, dusty wind at the top of the Qutb Minar, the baying of doleful dogs as they settled into their beds each and every night.

He is also looking forward to opening Ammama's book and reading it solidly for the seventeen-hour flight. But when the engines rumble underneath him, humming and vibrating, he has to fight sleep, pushing it away like an obstinate child. He looks down over the land, with the slanted corrugated roofs of the shanties cresting over the expanse for miles. He sees the division of major roads and highways cleaving the earth like two halves of a sandwich. The space stretches out beneath the plane wing, and he wonders where, in all the snarls of homes, offices, cars, bullocks and carts, Ammama is below them, preparing her evening meal and shuffling about the flat, opening the cupboards to replace the sheets from Karom's makeshift bed and putting her home back in order. The plane rises into the sky, gaining miles in moments as the staticlike hum of the atmosphere increases. The weight of Ammama's book is heavy in his lap. He caresses a hand over the raised letters on the cover, opens the book and begins to read.

The Invisible Husband, Part II

From the moment Janaki was born, she was like a parcel being passed from bough to bough, just like in the age-old nursery rhyme, on the brink before it broke and she came tumbling down. Just as she learned her place in a new family, she'd be whisked off and pulled into all the discomforts of another. Just as she slid softly into her new chores and responsibilities to justify her existence there, she'd be moved and others would demand differently. There were changes in clothes, in bedding, in education. She wore saris and petticoats, skirts and blouses, school uniforms and *salwar kameez*. She wore her hair in two braids, in buns and shorn short so that she—or her guardians—didn't have to worry about lice or hairdressing.

As her own parents had passed her off to family members because they couldn't afford schooling, uniforms and the meager amounts of food she ate as a gangly girl, all elbows and knees, her relatives played a game of keep-away around her as she was tossed this way and that. Her spinster aunts in Friends Colony lived in a sprawling six-bedroom bungalow with outdoor space that overlooked a slum, while her six-year-old self had known the contours of only a cramped one-roomed flat that she'd shared with three cousins and their surly parents. She had no favorites; even those small houses held hidden gifts and surprises. Those same three cousins taught her how to make up round-robin stories and pass the sentences from mouth to mouth, whispering under their breath, the sheets tented over their heads, before their parents would shush them into sleep.

She grew up amid alcoholism that ran rampant in her family, tempers that circled the ceilings, things being smashed against the walls—Johnnie Walker bottles, denture glasses, once, a ship in a bottle that an uncle had gifted her from Ceylon. She grew up feeling walls with trembling fingers in the middle of the night, afraid to step on her uncle as he lay on a mat on the floor snuffing like a baby elephant, finally lubricated by the numerous shots of gin he'd earlier poured down his throat.

Each morning, before she went to college and before she married, she would rise and pick up her bedclothes, which were usually a makeshift pile of sheets in a room or folded into a piece of furniture in the living room that she would have to vacate before the house would begin to buzz with activity. She'd give herself a quick wash, either in the outdoor bucket or a bathroom if the home was luxurious enough to have one. Then she'd collect her few personal belongings: a stubby candle, a stainless-steel tray and a small capsule of vermilion powder that she'd been given on her cousin's wedding day. She'd light the candle, drip some wax onto the tray, plug the candle into it, dip her finger into the slightest amount of vermilion powder to caress the tiny little grooves that had been carved between her eyebrows as a little girl, face the wall and close her eyes.

She would feel her parents in her body in these early-morning hours. They would rise up into her throat, then her forehead and sit quietly at her temples as she rehashed her prayers each morning. They would sit quietly as she murmured softly, thanking her aunts or uncles or family friends for taking her in, embracing the people who had raised her to this stage. Her parents were there, still there at her temples, and when she leaned forward and pressed her forehead to the cool, dark floor, they disappeared into it, caressing her forehead once before they left.

She never knew her real parents; they were in a small village eight hundred kilometers away. Her father was sickly and his medicines were egregiously expensive. He sold half his land in order to afford them, and her mother took responsibility for the remaining fields, overseeing the tending and the culling and the tilling. During her early years, when she could just remember running barefoot through the paddies before she was sent away, Janaki remembered the sweet loamy scent of irrigation. But there was no place for her with her parents—no place and no money. Her mother had no time to care for her; all their profits from the tenuous earth went straight to the moneylender, whom they owed for years past. Her father was bedridden and could barely speak. Her only memory of him was of a ghostly, shriveled man who lay on a straw bed, his skin stretched taut across his bones like an artist's canvas.

From time to time, Janaki had a recurring, fleeting thought that she immediately felt flustered and guilty over each time it passed through her mind like smoke. If her father was so sickly and so cloistered and so seemingly useless, why couldn't he just die so that her mother could send for her and she could help her on the land and Janaki and she could live as part of a family and not constantly on the outskirts? It wasn't as though her parents were in love or her father contributed to society through poetry or philosophy. He was dead weight.

When she was seventeen, Janaki's father finally did succumb. Her mother had morphed upon her husband's death, assuming widow's garb and becoming an ascetic, praying throughout the day, eating only a few crumbs in the morning. She shrank into herself, both in body and spirit. The sale of the lands garnered enough money for Janaki to go to college, her father's dying wish. Janaki felt more regret and remorse about not feeling anything than she did about his departure from the Earth. But, she consoled herself, she scarcely knew her father; she scarcely knew her parents. She had been sent home once during the summer of her eleventh year but had been first terrified and then bored in the little hut. Her mother spent the whole day outside, seeing to finances and ensuring that the fields were earning enough profit. She would reenter her home in the evening and search Janaki's face for a few moments, as though seeing her for the first time, before brusquely turning toward their hodgepodge kitchen and preparing a hasty meal that the three of them would share in silence before bedtime. During these long days, Janaki had been unable to speak to her father, who lay outstretched in a corner of the room, the concave arches of his chest dipping up and down with each laborious breath. When he did speak, it was in a terrifying rasp that sent her cowering to the walls of the room until she gathered her wits and brought him a tumbler of water that she dribbled over his thin parched lips. The people who visited Janaki during her prayers weren't these specters, the parents she could hardly remember. She conjured up new people, smiling, supportive and present.

What should she pray for? A home, a life, somewhere she belonged, someone to whom she belonged, with whom she would never feel alone? She wasn't sure. Her prayers were jumbled, assorted. Besides, it wasn't that she believed that they would eventually achieve something tangible; it was simply some semblance of structure in her life. She could count on them each morning to bring about a sense of order.

They weren't conventional either; the words she uttered were a compilation of the prayers she'd picked up over the years: one for good health and blessings, one for wealth and happiness, even one for fertility, although she didn't even know it. Her ritual, a subconscious conglomeration of other people's dreams and desires, of their deepest secrets, wasn't even completely hers.

When she first became engaged to Arun, he would visit her at the hostel near her college, waiting for her quietly in the sitting room and then scooping her up in his arms in a bear hug like she had never experienced in her life. Arun had always been handsome. His trimmed sideburns aligned with the parallels of his earlobes while he kept his thick black curls insouciantly boyish, coiffed, styled and shining with hair oil. He was tall, broad and protective, wearing shirts half a size too small so that she could see the cut of his muscles and feel them move like coiled snakes against her body when he leaned flirtatiously against her on the couch in the sitting room. Looking back, Janaki couldn't remember how they spent her half-hour study break; they certainly didn't have philosophical conversations or engaging debates. Once, she had made the mistake of asking him what he thought of ahimsa; did he think it could succeed? He'd looked at her with such searing in his eyes and his lip curled in such loathing that she'd hurriedly changed the subject to his motorcycle. But even though their union had originally been arranged by her aunts and his father, their courtship entered a second level of tempest, fire and longing that was coaxed along by her jealous hostel mates whenever Arun visited. He was enamored with her, this smart, self-sufficient woman who had endured so much being bounced among family. And he charmed everyone around her. When her hostel mates deliberately swung by the sitting room to catch a glimpse

of the reticent Janaki sitting with her attractive male caller,
Arun always called out to them.

"Come, join us. Are you one of Janaki's classmates?" He
would beckon to other girls to sit across from them but continue to hold Janaki's hand or place his hand on her knee, a
gesture that made the other girls avoid looking either Arun
or Janaki in the eye, squirming as they made simple conversation. Later the girls would giggle together in Janaki's
room—how handsome Arun was, how genuine, how pos-
sessive of his fiancée.

Janaki's own stomach would curl with anticipation when
the girl on front-desk duty announced that she had a visi-
tor. She'd brush her hair excitedly until it would crackle with
electricity and then descend down the stairs elegantly, just as
her spinster aunts had instructed her on the afternoon they
had introduced her to him at their bungalow.

"Janaki," they'd said. "You're under no obligation, but a
young man in our community wants to meet you. He and his
father have heard of your talents at the university."

She had been the one to open the door at the bungalow
and had stepped aside as both he and his father entered,
smiling broadly at her from the soles of her feet to the parting in her hair.

"Please come," she said. "It's much cooler in the parlor."
And the two men followed her inside, where her aunts sat
expectantly on their adjoining sofas as though they were the
ones waiting to be appraised.

At once Arun offered Janaki a package from the bag that
he clutched between his fingers. "For you," he said, almost
shyly. It was a rectangular package wrapped in brown paper,
heavy and tied with twine. "Open it." Janaki looked at both
her aunts and they nodded before she slipped her fingers underneath the string. Inside was a brand-new book. The gold

lettering was intact; the corners hadn't curled from being banged about in a secondhand shop. She turned the book over so that the title was visible.

"*Great Expectations,*" she breathed. "Have you read it?"

"No," Arun said, leaning in conspiratorially toward her. "But I thought it was a good title." The conversation carried on with her aunts leading most of it with Arun's father, but Janaki held the book in her lap, turning it over and over. This would immediately become her most prized possession, a new book that was hers alone. There would be no sharing or reselling at the end of the semester. The gift immediately endeared Arun to her. If she had to get married—and she did, for she had no one else in the world to care for her—this man who seemed to understand her from the start wasn't a bad option. From time to time for the rest of that afternoon, she looked up from the book in her lap to find him staring at her, and instead of being embarrassed at being caught, he would smile at her knowingly.

Even on their wedding day, Arun remained the flirt, winking at her brazenly from her approach to the *mandap*, making her giggle and play her appropriate role as a blushing bride. He poked her foot when the priest wasn't watching and whispered a dirty joke into her ear when the family closed their eyes for prayers. But for Janaki this was going too far.

"Shh," she hissed. "Please pay attention. It's important." Arun's eyes lit up in a brief fiery rage, but he sat back and watched her quietly as she closed her eyes with the group who sat around the fire. She peeked out from under the heavy gloss of her eyelashes adorned with *kajal* and met his eyes. His chin was set hard and the round sphere of his temporomandibular joint flexed subtly under his perfectly parallel sideburns, two latent rattlesnakes poised to strike. Just after the ceremony, when they waited together silently in the antechamber to enjoy a few moments of solitude before joining their wedding reception, Arun came toward her, his eyes gleaming and his turban askew. Janaki steadied herself for a few moments of long-awaited shared passion in the crowded back room. But Arun gripped her arm with his stubby fingers, the nails peeled down to the skin, a habit he wouldn't break throughout their life together, leaving little crescents of keratin all over the house. The force pinched her, bringing tears to her eyes and causing her makeup to smudge.

"Did you pay your respects to my mother today?"

"I… She was there. In the photo on the *mandap*. We acknowledged her in the first mantra. How I wish—"

"She wasn't there. She's dead, Janaki. She's been dead for ten years. And no amount of prayer and no magical mantra will bring her back. Where were your parents today?"

Silence.

"Exactly. Your father withered away and now all your mother can do when she's summoned to attend her only daughter's wedding is turn her back on the whole affair and pray. This is what prayer does to people, Janaki. Makes them insane. Makes them think that adorning a photograph with a garland of flowers and applying some red powder to the glass will honor their soul. Makes them think that by lighting a few candles, it will bless a ceremony from afar. This isn't religion. This is obsession. And it's the worst kind."

At first, Janaki's heart had leaped. Arun understood: religion was personal and how you made it personal was what counted. But as time went on, Janaki learned that Arun wanted no part of religion, or ritual, for that matter, no matter what shape it took or how he could mold it. Religion was left at the front door of their flat. And both religion and Arun would wait one another out until one of them gave in.

At dawn a few weeks later in their new but cramped little

apartment in East Delhi, her husband had stumbled back into the house, his boots booming in the hallway. Janaki heard him but wouldn't break her concentration as she prayed, keeping one ear perked only to ensure that her daughter, a toddler at the time, continued sleeping in the adjacent room. Arun growled once or twice as he tripped over an umbrella stand, then knocked a small basil plant to the ground. He was pouring himself a tumbler of water; she could even hear as it chugged down his gravelly throat. He was in the hallway as he clicked on the light and peered at himself in the mirror, taking in his bloodshot eyes and unkempt hair. Then he was next to her, and she could feel him though her eyes were closed as he slid down to the floor, his knee pressing against hers as the stench of cheap liquor pulsed from his every pore. Janaki hesitated in her breath but continued her words quietly. *This is all I have,* she argued fiercely to herself underneath the Sanskrit words. *This is all that's mine. Even my daughter, whom I love without condition, is half his. This is all that keeps me going through each day.*

It didn't seem as though Arun was going to interrupt her. He sat quietly, even, breathing hard and rocking a bit to the rhythm of her voice. It almost appeared as though he were in a trance, that he'd been lulled to sleep sitting up. It would have been insensitive not to acknowledge him sitting there next to her, so she moved to swipe some vermilion on the seam of where his hairline met his forehead—even before she blessed herself. All at once he leaped to his feet, roaring and knocking at her arm, kicking at her tiny makeshift shrine and the candle she'd lit, grinding it into the floor. He upset the small silver capsule of red powder, and it sprayed dramatically like drops of blood across the stone floor.

"I detest religion. You know this. Why would you bring it into my house?" He towered over her, leaning over slightly with the weight of his head, heavy with an approaching hangover. Janaki didn't answer him; she couldn't. She was tightly bound within herself, her arms wrapped around her knees and her head tucked between them. She shook her head back and forth. She could hear her daughter fussing in the next room and a single peal of crying.

"Maaamaaaa!"

"Don't do this again, Janaki. You're testing me." Janaki peered out from the crevices of her arms and met his eyes. She nodded. "Go see to the girl." Arun stalked off to the bathroom, where she heard the bucket being filled before she crept into the baby's room. Maya's chubby face was tearstained and she held her fat arms toward Janaki. Janaki scooped her up and pressed her into her chest.

"Bad dream, little one? What happened?"

Maya snuffled her face into Janaki's neck as she walked them about the small apartment together. When they passed the bathroom door, Janaki could hear Arun sloughing dirt off his skin, mumbling to himself as he worked.

After this, Janaki began her ritual in her mind, from putting a one-rupee coin into the stainless-steel plate, to settling her sari around her so she could sit comfortably. If Arun was home that morning, he lay unknowingly in the bed, snoring and farting like a buffalo in heat. If Arun was still out with his buddies, Janaki would take a risk and say her prayers out loud, but not daring to get out of bed or light candles lest he walk in the door as he had that morning when he'd ground her capsule of vermilion into a flat silver disk with the heel of his boot. And when he did come home and she heard his key catch in the lock, she closed her mouth, turned over to her side, shut her eyes and finished her prayers deep within herself, imagining a chakra, a wheel spinning in the pit of her stomach that didn't slow until she finished her last words.

Arun never caught on and it was only a few weeks after his final departure, when Janaki was quite sure he would never return, that she dug out the stainless-steel plate she'd hidden deep in her wardrobe and reestablished her ritual each morning.

Arun hadn't always been a terror. But he'd always been a physical man, not an intellectual one.

At times, she would remember those moments when Arun had been gentle, when he'd been kind. She remembered his gentle proffering of the first book she'd ever owned, the time he had taken her to buy her a pair of glasses out of his own pocket money. She remembered how he would press her to him lovingly when he visited her college dormitory. She hadn't been able to believe that once they were betrothed, she would have a permanent place in life where she would finally belong. She wasn't sure she could stay in one place forever. She certainly hadn't before.

But in the end, it was Arun who turned out not to know how to stay put. Janaki could remember the day itself intimately. She remembered the sari she was wearing—deep purple with lavender flowers. She could remember the weather—bright and brisk without a cloud in the sky. She could remember what she'd prepared that morning for breakfast—watermelon *dhodak*, made from the shaved white portions of the rind, which would have been otherwise thrown out. The day had begun like any other: Janaki went through her ritual in her mind, tugged on her daughter's plait to rouse her for school, prepared tea and breakfast, and just before she fried the batter into round brown disks, she shook her daughter again because she was going to be late. Arun's shift normally lasted from 5:00 p.m. until midnight, but he was never home then. He usually cavorted with his colleagues or his friends from the cricket club until the early hours of the morning, when he would return to the house and sleep it off until he had to report for work. So it didn't surprise Janaki when he didn't show that morning or even that afternoon. He must have gone straight back to work, she thought. When he didn't show again shortly after midnight, she became concerned and called the head office. A man informed her that Arun had in fact reported for work and was out investigating an unanswered alarm somewhere in the vicinity. She hung up the phone and crept back to bed. When Maya inquired about him, Janaki said that he'd taken on another shift and would likely be late again tonight. And that happened again and again before Maya herself caught on and stopped asking where her father was.

For some time, Janaki readied herself as though Arun would return midmorning, gruff from a long night of patrolling an empty office building to slink home with his uniform crumpled and worn. She prepared his favorite foods: a cooling drink made of yogurt and fresh mango, tapioca with green chilies and lentil seeds, hard, flat pancakes of jackfruit and jaggery. She pressed his extra uniforms and his Punjabi suits for weddings they were to attend together, weddings that she would eventually attend with only Maya in tow. She cleaned the grooves of his comb, the bristles of his shaving brush, polished the extra motorcycle helmet he kept in the hall closet.

She would startle suddenly as she imagined his boots banging in the entryway, him pushing one off with the toe of the other so they lay askew in the hallway, where she had learned to push them to the side so as not to trip on her way to the kitchen. She would start from her silent prayers, certain that he had somehow crept into the bedroom unbeknownst to her and was watching her mouth form her prayers with curled nostrils and an angry little smile on his face that would

erupt without notice. Sometimes while she was cutting vege-
tables in the kitchen, she would put her knife down and peer
over her right shoulder in the event that he was standing
there watching her. She couldn't shrug off the feeling that
he hadn't simply disappeared. But after two weeks' time, it
was clear that he had.

For some time after that, she toyed with the idea of collecting all of Arun's belongings and handing them off to
the trash man, but she knew how furious he would be if he
ever came back. So she left them there: his clothes on his
side of the closet, the sweaters and shirts folded carefully on
the shelves, his bottle of aftershave, and a comb with three
of the teeth missing and thick black curls ensnared within
the remaining ones. But his absence continued to mock her;
each time she opened the wardrobe, she'd receive a whiff of
his cologne or her hand would begin to burn after she ac-
cidentally grazed one of his dress shirts or the Nehru jacket
he'd worn on their wedding day. She nostalgically cracked
open the wedding album that had been gifted to them by
her father-in-law. In it, she noticed the squared jaw of her
husband and the pose he adopted in all his photos: one hand
cradled in the other, one of them poised to peel the nails off
a finger before he surreptitiously dropped the opaque arcs
onto the ground. She began to think of Arun each time she
placed a rupee into the stainless-steel dish. It was the closest she'd ever come to praying for him. His face entered her
mind at this last gesture of her ritual, cool and steely, chis-
eled and taut, the round of his jawbone working constantly,
continuously, wherever he was.

She recalled the time when their wedding ceremony was
over and they were cemented together in the antechamber.
She'd stood with him as he gripped her forearm like a vise as
she scrolled a mental list of their similarities and differences

through her mind. And then he had strode out onto the dais to address the wedding guests with her in tow.

"Dear friends and family, can I have your attention, please?" Arun's stature and stentorian voice quickly cast a great net of silence over the room. "Thank you all for joining me and my family on my wedding day. This is a special day because I have married a very special woman." There was a polite smattering of applause here while Arun took in another breath. "She is a lovely woman, both in heart and in looks. She is kind and supportive and she's a brain. Did you all know that she stood first at her college?" There was another pause for golf claps and the buzz of conversation began again before Arun silenced it with his voice. "I have married a very smart woman, who I need by my side. I will not let her go, you can be sure of that. You can be sure that I will take care of her and she needn't lift a finger except to feed the many children we will have together." At this there was uncomfortable laughter and the tittering of the children who were sitting together in a corner. "Thank you all again. We appreciate your blessings." He'd stepped down from the dais and held his hand out to Janaki, who stepped down after him and joined the group as they moved into the next room for the reception.

After some time, when the dust had settled around Arun's side of the bed, Janaki still fleetingly thought of him from time to time. When there were elections, she wondered if he'd voted, if he'd been partially responsible for the goon they now had in office. When there were riots, she wondered if he'd been in the thick of the action, pulling hair and beating people off others, holding people back while he took their punches.

Once Arun left, Janaki let his family think that she had been provided for, that he'd left a fund in their names that would care for them both and potentially even added to it surreptitiously from time to time. But truly, all Janaki had was her massive collection of one-rupee coins that she'd ferreted away during all those morning rituals, a rapidly dwindling bank account that Arun had abandoned but certainly didn't add to, a pile of wedding jewelry that her in-laws made very clear that they didn't want leaving the family under any circumstances and the husband that would begin to appear in the early-morning hours after a long night's work.

This version of her husband was slighter and softer, and he wasn't exactly filled in completely. But not in terms of muscle: he appeared in muted, sedate black and white tones while the rest of the world was in color. He was almost ghost-like, drifting about the apartment without making the same sounds that her real husband had made, whether in the bathroom, the kitchen or even the bedroom. He looked exactly like Arun, down to the symmetrical length of his sideburns and the thick curls on his head. He was soft to the touch when she grazed against him in the bed and he never raised his voice. He stepped into the kitchen and silently began to chop the mound of onions that teetered on the countertop for that evening's dinner. He met the *kabadi wala* at the door, having rounded up all the old pieces of scrap metal and recyclables that they no longer wanted. He was part husband, part housemaid. It was the best arrangement Janaki could ever have imagined.

Except that was the problem: he didn't quite seem to be real. At least, she thought she could see him, that ghostly lingering in the early-morning hours when the spiritlike husband would actually rise a few minutes before she did in order to light her candles himself so that all Janaki had to do was place herself in front of the altar and pray. But she tested herself one afternoon as she sat in the living room darning socks and her husband sat opposite her shelling peas. Maya came in, holding *A Tale of Two Cities.*

"Mama, I don't understand this," she said, twirling her pencil between her fingers. "I have to write an essay and I just don't understand the symbolism."

"Why don't you ask your father to help you?" Janaki asked. "He loves Dickens." She looked at her shrunken husband then diligently scooping out the contents of each pea pod into a metal bowl. Maya looked at her mother and to the chair opposite and then back to her mother.

"What? Why? Has he come back?" The look in Maya's eyes was unsure; on the one hand, her eyes sparkled with the anticipation, but her mouth remained tight-lipped as though she wasn't sure that was the best thing for the two of them. Janaki looked from her daughter to her husband and back again. Maya followed her gaze and settled a quizzical look on her mother. Janaki shook her spinning head as she regarded both a suspicious Maya as well as her husband sitting quietly in his chair.

"No. He hasn't returned," Janaki said. "I'll take a look at your essay as soon as I'm finished with these socks. And the peas." That was the first and only sign Janaki needed to realize that her new husband was a figment of her imagination, but somehow his presence made her life a little easier.

It was easier to believe that he existed. Not the form of him that had actually existed, because that version was better left in the past, but a softer, quieter, more humble version who appreciated his wife as she was and made every effort to make her life easier. She liked this version and encouraged it each day. One day she had come home from the market to find that he had prepared a whole meal by himself so that all she had to do was set the table and call her daughter to dinner. She was so thrilled that she sat down in the living room and helped herself to one of Maya's film magazines, sitting indulgently in a chair flipping the pages until the darkening of the living room jolted her upright to scurry into the kitchen to make an actual dinner.

She didn't realize how much of a problem this was becoming until she caught herself responding to a wedding as a threesome: herself, Maya and this undetectable man. "This has to stop," she told herself in the mirror that evening as her husband stood behind her massaging her tense shoulders. "It's unhealthy. It's not right." She shook him off her and went to bed.

But in the morning it went right back to the way it was. Maya had a track meet that morning and had already left by the time she awoke to find a teapot on the bedside table covered with a cozy, tendrils of steam still escaping from the spout. There was a plate of her favorite biscuits covered with a napkin. She sat up in bed and poured herself some tea, leaning back against the pillows. After her first cup, she padded to the kitchen. The table was set with fresh flowers and on her plate there was a note in her husband's handwriting: "Had to run out. Check the warming box; breakfast is served!" Janaki could scarcely believe her eyes. There was a fresh omelet in a grill pan and two pieces of brown bread that had been griddled in ghee. Her favorite. She inhaled the food and sat back, tracing her finger around her teacup over and over.

When Arun returned from his errands at the market, Janaki and he had the day to themselves. They went for a long walk around the compound and then sat luxuriously on the terrace warmed by the sun, where Janaki allowed her husband to massage the tense spot in the back of her neck caused by constant hunching over the stove. As the door banged open and Maya threw her cleats onto the ground in the hallway, Janaki called out to her.

"We're in here."

Maya came charging onto the terrace, looking tired but elated.

"Hi, Ma," she said, sinking down to the ground with a slight groan. "Who's 'we'?"

"Your father and I," Janaki said. "We've been discussing how lonely the house will be when you leave for college next year."

Maya looked at Janaki carefully, as if trying to read her face.

"Ma," Maya said slowly, as if talking to a child, "Papa hasn't been here for years. Are you telling me that you're sitting here talking to him?"

"Maya, don't be impertinent. Of course he's here. He's just—" Janaki looked to the chair where not moments before Arun had been folding freshly dried sheets. "Well, he was there."

Maya looked worried. She knelt next to Janaki and took her small hand in her own. "Ma, Papa is gone. He hasn't returned. I think you're seeing things. Are you not feeling well?"

Janaki shook her head. "I don't understand it. I keep seeing him everywhere. He must be here, Maya. He made me breakfast this morning. He left tea at my bedside."

"That was *me,* Ma," Maya said sadly. "I woke up early for my race. You'd said you'd make me breakfast, but when I looked in on you, you looked so peaceful that I decided to do something nice for you instead. So I left the teapot and the biscuits and made you the omelet. Papa's gone. He's not coming back."

Janaki could feel her eyes fill with tears, but in all the years she had spent alone with her daughter, she'd never allowed herself to cry in front of her. She blinked back the water and swallowed hard, willing herself to look brave. Maya didn't let go of her hand the whole time. After what seemed like an hour, Maya spoke.

"Ma, I know things haven't been easy for you. Not ever. Not growing up. Not during your marriage; I know life with Papa certainly wasn't easy. And that it hasn't been easy since he left. But we're a team, Ma. We're going to figure this out together. We're going to make it so that we can not only survive but we're going to be happy. I don't know who you've been seeing in the house or why you've been conjuring Papa up, but I sense it's because you've been feeling so alone. And you're not. You have me. Even if I go away to college, or even if I am not here with you always, we'll make it work. I'll get a job during school and help with the bills. You'll come visit or you'll follow and stay with me. You'll always be with me. I promise."

Janaki looked away, her eyes smarting even harder now with the promise and strength of her teenage daughter, who had pledged to devote herself to her mother. That was love. That was belonging. For the first time in her life, Janaki had finally found a home where she belonged. Not this tiny cramped East Delhi apartment, where there was no end of unhappy memories and sad stories buried within the walls but with her daughter, no matter where she went. Her place was with the family she created and the family who would continue to be there for her. Home was where her heart was, and her heart was with Maya.

Amid the chatter and flurry to be the first off the plane, Karom suddenly starts as though he has forgotten something.

Sure enough, when he circles his fingers around his wrist, there is nothing. The stories in *Fairytales of Freedom* have jarred him; between them, he has dozed through lucid dreams that startle him awake so that he has to remember where he is and where he is heading. When he awakes, he isn't sure where reality lies and where the story has ended. Something has awakened in him with these stories. It is more than just the passion and the fervor. It is the way that all of Ammama's characters are underdogs, downtrodden and slated to fail, but then something or someone picks them up and carries them on their way. It isn't necessarily always skill in each instance or even luck. It is destiny. That is the lesson of each fable: that you can't control your destiny, because your destiny controls you. This is anti-everything-that-Karom-has-been-raised-with, though his parents were culturally religious, not fanatically so. But he understands the idea of karma, the idea of cause and effect and how every action causes a reaction. It is more scientific than religious. How can his life continue if he keeps toying with it, tempting, caressing it to follow his every whim? How can he continue like this, staring down traffic, popping puffer fish into his mouth, dancing with death?

He can't believe Kamini's strength. She has carried so much heartache and burden all her life in order to transform them into stories, weaving them into translucent ideas with her tiny shriveled fingers, searching down into the depths of her imagination and using the details of her own life to sketch out fables, parables and lessons that he is sure he and Gita will carry in their hearts for a long time. So this is her truth: she's spent her whole life constantly abandoned by relatives, so she's never felt a part of something.

It isn't fair to say that he has felt constantly abandoned, always alone. He had always been intensely loved as a Seth, a quintessential part of the strongest bond he thought he would ever feel, a bond that he felt tightly stretched like a rubber band before it snapped once his parents were washed away from him forever. With them went his entire family, or what he thought was his entire family until he learned about his birth parents when he ventured curiously into that bedside drawer on that fated day. He hadn't thought he could feel more alone than when he had read those words, that he had been abandoned not once but twice by parents who, it appeared, couldn't seem to hold on to him. But—and he'd had to remind himself of this daily until he'd read these pages—his form of Arun, his Gita, was not a figment of his imagination. He didn't have to conjure her up, because she was right there next to him. But he knows that like Arun in the story, his Gita will not wait around forever. How can she? Sooner or later her frustration with him will boil over and she will be forced to turn down the heat and walk away from the mess. He will have left her with no other choice, and he will have no one to blame but himself for losing her, his fiery girl.

She lopes sleepily beside him now, pulling her carry-on bag down the long hallway. Her embers have died down during the long flight. At the entrance to immigration, they part ways, Karom moving toward the international passengers/visa holders line. This line is always longer, it smells stronger and it tries his patience.

This is one of his regrets: he'd been an American citizen his entire life, but when the tragedy in Poompuhar had struck, he'd renounced his status and applied fully for allegiance to India. At the time, it had seemed like a brave, romantic move, not to mention the fact that he couldn't imagine feeling so terribly stripped away, so alienated from the horror that had happened on the beach that day. But now he carries an Indian

passport and he realizes that carrying it doesn't prove his loyalty to his family or his country of origin. It means lines, long
lines, and disdainful looks of scrutiny when he arrives back on
this end of any international trip. Gita has been urging him
to re-renounce it, to see if the American Consulate and the
country will accept him back, but like any station of bureaucracy, it is taking longer to get back than it did to be released.

A lump forms in the hollow of his throat when Gita and
he part to join separate lines at the end of an international
trip. It throbs as he watches Gita go through her own immigration gate. When they'd flown internationally for the first
time years ago, she had told him that she was a sucker for that
gate—after the stamping and peering and conjecturing was
over, and her passport was handed back and the immigration
officer told her, "Welcome home, Ms. Nilssen," tears pricked
at the corners of her eyes, and although she wasn't particularly patriotic, these were the moments when she felt for the
first time what it meant to be an American. Gita will be the
first to collect their bags from the belt, while Karom deals
with immigration officials, explaining his situation to them
and then finally swallowing the lump completely upon entering baggage claim.

As they stand in line at the taxi stand, a gray gloominess
surrounding the early morning, Karom pulls Gita close to
him and buries his nose in her hair. He wants to hold on to
her, the melancholy of immigration spilling out of him into
the sidewalk where they stand waiting. Her slim arms wrap
around his waist like vines.

The ride back into the city seems endless, even longer than
the flight from Delhi. Karom's breath catches, as it does each
time, at the sight of the New York City skyline appearing
in the distance. This is majesty, he thinks. Akin to the Taj

Mahal, his love for this city rivals that of Shah Jahan for his wife. A low fog lies over the city like gauzy cobwebs woven among the very tops of the tallest buildings. Even from this distance, a hum appears to emanate from the island, pulling him back in, as if he is in the early-morning throes of trying to escape a dream.

She is his strength; that's what Gita had told him. She would help him through this challenge of returning to the country that had over the years taken shape in his heart as a harrowing land. She would be by his side as together they traipsed the Golden Triangle, Jaisalmer, Jodhpur. It had all been dry, sand, heat: desert. It had been lizards and camels and dusty dogs in the dirt at the side of the road. That was the one condition Karom had maintained about the trip: that they stay inland and never meet the ocean.

Which is why it is ironic that they are returning to their home, an island surrounded on all sides by water, two flowing rivers and a creek to contain it. The only way to leave is to cross a bridge, tunnel under, board a boat or swim. His city holds him captive, away from the rest of the country, the rest of the world.

How could it all be over? The dust settling on everything they set down, the spiciness of lime soda, the calls to prayer that awakened them each morning in every city they visited. The sweet, pungent taste of mysterious fruit. The mangy mongrels who followed him right up until the door and then lay down on the doorstep, forgetting their allegiances to him as soon as they saw someone else emerge from a rickshaw laden with bags from the market. Is it over? Is he finally over his vow to never return, never forgive, never forget?

In a few weeks they will travel again, westward this time, to Lloyd and Malina's wedding. They will get back on a plane and lose that feeling of homecoming. But right now he feels that limbo he enters when he travels from an overseas trip in a cab, that weightlessness he feels when he can see the city from afar. You see the skyline, you see the bridges, you see the water, you see the buildings, but your head and your senses and even your speech patterns are left behind you, either on the plane, wedged forgotten between two seats, or in a hotel or at the sites from where you came. It's a strange feeling, this feeling of hanging, because you feel as if you don't belong anywhere. Not to this place or that place. You're suspended in time, hanging in this existence, and you're not sure where you're going or if you're here or there. It's as if you're watching yourself arrive. He knows the feeling won't subside until his cab fully passes onto the land on the other side of the bridge or the tunnel, when he opens and closes the doors with that gentle *chunk* and lowers his suitcase onto the sidewalk, where for a moment, for maybe the only time ever, he will trust it to rest there on its own while he pays the driver. Then it will grow fainter as he walks into his lobby wheeling his suitcase, feeling the click of his heels against the floor, and fainter still as his key slides into the lock and he stands on the threshold of his apartment, on the edge of the future with his back to the past. And it will only be when he takes that first step, when he lifts his suitcase up and over, that he'll feel a gentle popping in his ears, as if he's just descended levels in an aircraft, and that is when he will know for sure that he is home.

Lloyd

~

It is an intrepid move not having a rehearsal dinner. But skipping a rehearsal dinner means saving a couple thousand dollars.
At the very heart of it, people know what to do. You walked
down an aisle, hopefully without tripping, using whatever
rhythm you have inside you to accompany the music without looking like a complete moron. You are serious, keeping your gaze on the appropriate person; there should be no
turning of the head to smirk at friends and family, no smiling or giggling. No resurrection of inside jokes. You should
stand there, focused, serious, eye-sure of all around you, and
you will make your way to the front of the room, to the altar,
to where everyone's eyes will eventually rest and stand there
in front of everyone and take your vows. Vows are to be repeated and they are smart enough to repeat words back that a
man has just said to them moments before; they have listening and regurgitation skills. They have both been to college.

But Lloyd's parents are incensed. They berate him again and

again. "Your friends and family have flown a long way for this day. This rehearsal dinner is for them. If you wanted to cut financial corners," they say, "this isn't where to do it." Lloyd is calm, for the first time in his life, calm about this decision. He stands behind it, and Malina stands beside him, gripping the inside of his wrist, that soft, vulnerable part, as though to protect it from his father, whose own large blue vein pulses at the side of his neck, incredulous at his son's poor planning.

Karom and Gita arrive at the vineyard inn at that moment, just as Lloyd's father is getting warmed up. Lloyd takes this opportunity to excuse himself from the fracas and hug Karom tightly, whispering, "Get me out of here."

Gita hands him a chilled bottle of wine she has purchased for herself and Karom to enjoy on their second-story veranda, along with two frosted glasses she has swiped from the adjoining bar, and whispers, "Go. Quickly."

Lloyd grips the bottle of wine by the neck, beads of sweat already perspiring on the green glass, and Karom steers him by the elbow out to the gazebo on the far part of the grassy knoll where the wedding will take place the next afternoon. They will sit there for the better part of the afternoon, chatting as fat bumblebees hover at their knees and the sun casts long shadows across the neatly trimmed lawn.

Gita moves in to introduce herself to Lloyd's parents and Malina, talking rapidly about the weather and the serene surroundings and whether there is anything she could do to help—she knows how to fold napkins into swans and tie intricate bows, and her calligraphy, though a bit rusty, has been prominently displayed on the outside of several wedding-invitation envelopes. Malina looks at her gratefully as she speaks, nodding her head, her eyes large with gratitude.

"Please," she breathes. "You can absolutely help. We have

gift bags to distribute." And the two walk off, leaving Lloyd's stunned parents on the porch of the inn.

Later, Gita watches Lloyd and Karom from the terrace of their room, warmed inside by the thought of Karom taking care of another who needs him so much right now. She feels flushed, delighted by that need, the urgency that someone else other than herself might need Karom and that Karom might be able to provide.

But now they are gone, both Lloyd and his bride. They have escaped in the early-morning hours, after the girls fell asleep in various parts of the bridal suite and Lloyd slipped away from his college buddies, who were already tottering backward on their heels, numbed by alcohol.

They have left a note, or Malina has, in her carefully slanted letters, that they have decided to get married on their own, where they are honeymooning, that they are sorry, and that everyone should go on with the party and the open bar and the dinner as though they were there. It's been paid for; it shouldn't go to waste and everyone has time off from work and has traveled so many miles. Please, enjoy yourselves, the note says.

At first, Karom guffaws. He doubles over in laughter wearing the voluminous hotel robe that, though plush, barely covers his shins. He leans his hand against the wall, holding himself upright, and laughs straight from his stomach, pushing out his diaphragm and enjoying the sensation of feeling heady. The note has been photocopied and slipped under guests' doors and Gita is scarcely awake when Karom starts laughing. Bleary-eyed and ripe smelling from sex and sweat, she stumbles out of the bed toward where Karom barely stands, doubled over in laughter, and snatches the paper from his hand.

The night before, Gita had been drinking with the ladies in the bridal suite, where the bathtub had been filled with ice and splits of cava and frosted champagne flutes had been settled among it. But when the girls dropped off one by one, she politely excused herself, not feeling as if she had the background or the history to fall asleep in the chaise longue or drape herself across the bed as so many of Malina's college friends were comfortably doing. Everyone was perfectly friendly, of course, but there was some protocol as to who you spent your wee morning hours chatting with, and Gita didn't feel as though she deserved to be there, not having shared those embarrassing first days at college or those rat-trap teensy apartments in the Mission District with them. Karom was down at the bar convincing Lloyd to hold at least one glass of brown liquor in a tumbler for the evening so that his friends wouldn't chastise him about not drinking heavily the night before he tied the knot.

"It'll give an illusion," Karom said. "And I guarantee that they won't even notice that you're not drinking it. Hold it, swirl it from time to time and then put it down somewhere."

The boys from college, their friends, were all there in a tight horde, staying close to the mahogany bar while their wives and girlfriends and significant others sat up in their bedrooms or had a polite glass of bubbly with the bride-to-be before retiring to pay-per-view and nail filing in bed. And Karom was right. Lloyd sipped demurely at his one glass of Scotch all night and there were never offers to refill his glass, and no one berated him for not enjoying himself.

After some time, Lloyd leaned in to Karom. "I'm going to check on Malina," he whispered.

"These guys are done," Karom said quietly. "I'll wrap up with them. I'll see you tomorrow." Lloyd set his untouched glass down on the heavy oak bar and walked quickly out of the room. At the doorjamb, he turned back to glance at the scene. The rest of his friends were still entangled in an argument over the greatest quarterback of all time, but Karom gave Lloyd a slight knowing smile before turning back to insert himself into the huddle.

Hours later, somewhere over the Pacific Ocean, with the plane's wing lights blinking assuredly in the black of the night, Lloyd and Malina are going backward in time, subtracting hours from the wedding time, moving against reality. With Malina's heavy head curled up in the reclining chair of business class, Lloyd reaches for the in-flight phone. When he has flown in the past, this phone has always been an anomaly. What kind of a situation would necessitate using this? What emergency would arise that you would need to bleed dollars from your bank account with each ticking second that you were on it? What fool would fall for it? Birth or death? Medical malfunction? Terrorism? And now he realizes that it's not an emergency that requires the use of this phone at all, but a revelation.

Everyone in the cabin is sleeping; the lights are dimmed and there are gentle snores emanating from a vestibule somewhere behind him. Each of the sleeping capsules are hooded enough that this call will be private, but at this point, as their plane barrels toward Bangkok, Lloyd realizes that this flight is the first one where he hasn't imagined an engine failing as the plane gains miles or oxygen masks tumbling forth from the ceiling. As the plane took off, he had sat up in his pod and grabbed Malina's soft hand in his, looking into her large brown doelike eyes, and leaned over and kissed her eyelids as she wept. She was crying as they took off, as they were soaring over the bay and the Golden Gate seemed like a pile of orange cinderblocks beneath them.

At first, he'd been shocked to see her tears, until he realized that he was crying, too. She looked surprised at first to see his tears, but she stopped crying long enough to ask, "Why you?"

"Because," he said, "there's no one in the world I would rather be doing this with."

Malina nodded, fat drops clinging like dew to her eyelashes. "I wish we had done this in the first place. I wish we'd thought of it before." He'd held her tight until the flight attendant had apologetically asked them to buckle up, as they were still ascending.

The phone feels heavy between his hands, but he dials without hesitation. The rings are international and seem more insistent and important than the ones on land; he remembers how the phone purred instead of rang when he studied abroad in London for a semester. And in an instant, he is on the other end.

"Unknown number. This is certainly fishy," Karom says.

"Hi."

"Where are you?"

"Somewhere over the Pacific. Malina's passed out."

"Are you calling me from one of those in-flight jobs?"

"Yep."

"Wow. I'm touched. I don't think anyone's ever called me from a plane before."

"You should be. This costs, like, half my honeymoon, so say something profound."

"What the fuck?"

"Ha."

"Are you guys okay?"

"More than okay. We're going to be great." There is a pause

and Lloyd feels the plane bump over a pocket of air. "What about over there? What's going on?"

"Well, since you ask, your parents are amidst a shit-fest. Gita and I have been with them all morning, making calls and figuring out logistics. Malina's friends are dealing with her folks. We called the justice of the peace this morning to tell her the situation and that she'll be paid. Pretty much your run-of-the-mill scene at an elopement. So what are you going to do when you get there?"

"Eat pad Thai. Get married. Ride elephants. Have sex. Relax. Sightsee. Not necessarily in that order."

"Sounds perfect."

"It does."

"Hang on." There is commotion on the other end of the line and then rhythmic crunching.

"Sorry. Your parents wanted to know who was on the phone. Gita's got them under control. Don't worry about them. They'll be fine. They're just a little…tender right now."

"Sorry I left you with them."

"Please, they're cake. Plus, you know Gita can handle almost anybody. You're the one I'm worried about. You want to tell me what this is all about?"

"I think you know."

"I do?"

"On some level."

"Yeah…I do." And just like that, it is in the air, in the already hundreds of miles between them, lingering there in space like a cloud or a wisp of smoke from a snuffed-out candle or the wish that came before it. It hangs there in the atmosphere suspended outside the plane, suspended in the hallway where Karom stands leaning against a maid's cart, fingering the tiny soaps wrapped in plastic. Karom feels it pricking at the corners of his eyes. And then, just as quickly as it was there, it is gone. Lloyd feels it, too, but on his end like a giant cloud outside the window of the moving plane, following them until the plane reaches a higher altitude, until the cloud is left behind, until it's just Lloyd in his seat with his bride next to him and lots of nameless passengers barreling forward into the sky along with him.

"Karom? When you were in India, did you ever think about looking up your birth parents? See what happened to them? Learn their story?"

"No. What's the point? I had parents. They died. Then I had other parents. And they died, too. I loved my parents, without question, even though they kept this huge secret of my origin and my first near miss. I missed *both* of my parents' deaths by a hair, a *hair*. Someone—or something—has always been looking out for me. Something bigger than me really wants me around."

Malina begins a gentle snore and Lloyd reaches over and brushes the hair lightly away from her face. She shifts in her seat and holds his hand, encircling her fingers around the fleshy part of his wrist. Her fingers cool his skin; it is almost as if he can feel a cool blue line of relaxation where her body meets his.

Suddenly, Lloyd feels a deep rush build up within him. It erupts from his ear across the phone, and unlike the blue line that appears where Malina touches his skin, this force field is bright red and pulsing with anger. He is angry. Angry at Karom, angry that all these years have been taken from him, angry about unrequited love as a theory, angry that Karom has failed to appreciate what he had, angry that Karom may never understand. He grits his teeth, breathes through his nose and speaks.

"I need to say something and I need you not to talk until I finish."

"Okay." On the other side of the phone, at the small inn and vineyard, Karom shifts nervously.

Lloyd opens his mouth again to a flood of words. He can barely stop them. He has imagined saying them in the past but had never had the guts or the timing. He'd never been prepared. But now he realizes that in order to say these words, he could never have prepared.

"I can't do this anymore, Karom. It's just too hard. I can't watch you play this game, even if I just hear about it or know about it or feel you playing it in the backs of my eyeballs from all the way across the country. I can't watch you live your life like this without realizing what's in front of you. I can't talk to you about what you're going through or hear the same story over and over, the same shuffle—two steps forward, one step back. I can't imagine people, conjure up people in front of my nose that haunt me through my days. I felt like I was going mad at times. I felt like I'd lost all control of myself. I couldn't see where I was going.

"Gita is far stronger than me when it comes to you. She knows what she has in front of her. She knows it's tangible and accessible and she wants to keep having it. Whereas I could never have it and I've been passively, uselessly hoping for it.

"I can't do this to *myself* anymore, Karom. I can't absorb your sweat or cry or languish over you or your game or the memory of holding you tight in that dorm room when it felt like there was nothing else but the two of us. I can't do it to myself anymore. I can't do it to Malina, or Gita. It's not fair. I hope you understand, but I won't ask if you do. It's too terrible a fate to be relegated to for the rest of my life. I'm going on my honeymoon. I'm going to get married to a wonderful girl and then I'm going to live happily ever after the rest of my life with her. Without you."

There is a considerable silence after which Lloyd wonders if the in-flight phone has petered out, and they are too high in the atmosphere to connect to land anymore. But he hears a sudden scratching from the other end of the line and he hears Karom clear his throat softly and say, "I understand," and he hears himself move the earpiece of the phone and look at the receiver, as though if he stares long or hard enough, he will see a tiny Karom way on the other end, across miles and miles of phone line like a tin can or a microscope. And then he hears himself lean forward slightly in his seat so as not to disturb his fiancée's slight hand that still encircles his wrist, turns the receiver away from him and replaces it into its holder. Then he turns off his overhead light, adjusts his hand softly and sleeps.

Kamini

~~~

Miles away in Delhi, Kamini stands back and surveys the slim woman in the pressed khaki pants and the button-down shirt. The woman has her back to her as she inserts a small placard into the groove in the windowpane and wipes her hands on the backs of her knees. She cocks her head at her handiwork and turns toward Kamini, who sits mildly in the chair by the door, lacing her fingers together in a steeple.

"Mrs. Pai? Auntie?"

"Hmm, yes?" Kamini looks up and smiles at the girl. This girl reminds her of Savita in her youth: ebullient, sweet, unchallenging.

"We're all set. We've posted an ad on the Net and we'll have an open house in a few weeks once we gain some interest in the flat, but with the market being what it is, you should be out of here in no time."

"Wonderful."

"Where will you be relocating?"

WHERE *Earth* MEETS *Water*

"To America. Ohio. To be with my daughter and her husband."

"That's nice. It's good to be with family."

"Mmm. Thank you for everything on such short notice."

"It's not a problem at all." The woman picks up her briefcase and holds it to her chest. She sticks out her hand before she lets it float back down and envelops Kamini in a loose hug. "I'm sorry. I just thought you needed that. I'm sure it can't be easy getting rid of this place. I'm sure you've lived here for a long time, that there are memories caught in the crevices and the corners. You're doing a very brave thing."

"It's not brave, actually. It's quite cowardly running away from this place. But I have no use for it anymore—had no use for it for quite some time. Somehow there were always loose ends to tie and a reason to stay, and I suppose I made excuses for far too long," Kamini says, adjusting her glasses.

"Well, I think you're brave," the woman says, moving toward the door. "Good for you for moving on, whatever the reasons are. Shall I leave you, then? We'll be in touch."

"Thank you." The door clicks shut and Kamini looks around the room. The ceiling fan has been removed and the walls and the paint above her have been replaced. The new air-conditioning unit hums busily in the corner. The furniture has been reupholstered and the floor polished to a shine where if she peers low enough to the ground, she can see her face against the tile. The woman had suggested all these cosmetic changes. *It will appear more appealing,* she'd said. *It will help potential buyers envision a life here, a home here. It's a great starter apartment.*

But Kamini is finished. Over the years and years when Savita had requested she move to their sprawling home in Columbus, Kamini had resolutely refused, first on the basis of inconvenience, then because she claimed that America didn't understand her, didn't get her—the shopgirls could barely understand her accent—and then because she was far too settled to uproot everything and start over. But at this stage in her life, starting over isn't an option. She will continue her life where the plane touches down in Columbus—her *seventh* plane ride, for the record. She will continue cooking and making meals for herself—and now her daughter and Haakon. She will continue living, surviving, as she has for the past eighty-two years of being shuttled back and forth between homes and then hostels and then finally this house. She has done it for Savita, because although Kamini knows that she can care for herself in this house—in fact, other than writing, it's the one thing she knows how to do—she knows that Savita is uncomfortable with her old mother living here alone, without family members dropping in every day, without someone here for company. Savita is insistent that Kamini is lonely though she doesn't realize it. And what's more, in Columbus Kamini won't feel beholden; Savita has been very clear on that distinction. "You're not staying in my house, Amma, you're staying in *our* house. You shouldn't feel like a guest here. I don't want that. I don't want you to move here if you're going to feel obligated. Promise me you won't." And Kamini had promised, because she is tired of being lonely, because it would be nice to live with her daughter and her daughter's kind, solid husband. And she is tired of needing to feel beholden. In fact, after all these years, she has forgotten just how to do that.

On her small wrist, there is a reassuring ticking. It is gentle, unobtrusive, yet it is still there, reminding her of the gift Karom left her when he and Gita left Delhi a few months before. When she found the Rolex hidden between the sheets that had comprised Karom's bed while he stayed in her living room, she'd instinctively jumped up and attempted to run after the rickshaw that had taken them off to the airport before realizing that Gita and Karom had left hours before. She'd opened the laptop and tried to fire off a quick email to Karom, letting him know that she'd found his watch and would send it to New York through the very next person that might be flying there. But she'd been surprised by a fresh email in her own in-box.

Subject: "Talisman"
Dear Ammama,
Please take care of this for me. It is both my most prized possession and my most mortal enemy.
Thank you.
Love, Karom

From that moment, she had slipped it onto her hand, but her tiny wrist was no match for the strap and it had swung this way and that. The following morning she had taken it to the leathersmith's down the road, where she had two more holes punched into the alligator watchstrap so that it now fit snugly against her wrist. She had never worn a watch before, and certainly never a man's watch. At first, it felt heavy against her body, but after some time, the large face with its tiny little crown and gentle ticking served as a rhythm for her day. It set the tone for her morning ritual and she began listening for the tapping of the second hand as she meditated after lighting the lamps in her shrine. She would take care of it, she told herself. She would see to it that the watch lived its life out to the fullest. She would ensure that Karom never had to worry about what it meant again.

Now she moves toward her computer, where it lies hidden

underneath a dust cloth. Delhi is so dusty; everything valuable has to be protected. Ohio isn't like this, she remembers
from her three visits in the past. She opens the computer, and
the document she'd started before the Realtor arrived springs
open. She taps away at the keys, finishing a thought, adding
some color to the last sentence, before she presses Return and
faces a blank page. When she'd first started writing, blank
pages had scared her, actually frightened her because she'd
felt intimidated by what could be. So she'd seasoned herself
to begin, begin anywhere, to see black ink on the pages or
perfect letters on the screen even if she had to scratch it out
or, when she got a computer, delete it later on.

Whiteness looms before her and she takes a deep breath,
disturbing the wisps of hair that surround her face. She puts
two fingers to the keys and begins a new chapter.

Karom

~~~

As a New Yorker, there are things one knows. There are specific separate pieces of information unique to those who inhabit the city. The sun rises past the East River and sets beyond the Hudson in the west. Downtown is south and uptown is north. If you're a woman, you can comfortably wear high heels to certain train lines, but for the ones that are farther away, you do the New York Changeover, carrying your heels in a purse and slipping off your sneakers or flip-flops around the corner from your destination. You know which subway car to enter for perfect alignment with the exit for your mad dash on a late morning to work. You know to feign sleep when a panhandler slides between the doors on your train. You know which fruit-stand guy—and there is one on every corner of every main thoroughfare—has the best deal on bananas. You know which gutter consistently gets flooded each time it rains. You know which city block smells the most rancid in the summertime.

But somehow, even though you know all these tiny pieces of information, it is still baffling to think of what is in there at each moment, scurrying through the streets, bustling in the thousands of buildings—people pulling vacuums along dusty carpets, taxis floating along the avenues. The street-cleaning trucks shuffling along the road, their tough bristles scuffing against the earth. There is something delicious sounding about these brushes to Karom. He has always wondered if it was somehow Pavlovian, as every time he's heard that sound, he's yearned to bite into something textural, like hair or an acrylic sweater. There is always something going on within the mazelike architecture. There is always something alive and indefinite.

There is something alert within the streets today, as Karom holds his girlfriend's hand in his left one as he locks the door of his parents' brownstone with his right. Gita's fingers are loose and cool, unlike when they arrived in the morning, Karom watching the tears glimmer in the corners of her eyes because she knew what an invitation into this house meant. She knew that it was the last hurdle to scale that would enable the two of them to move forward once he had introduced her to the mausoleum that held painful memories of Karom's previous life intact inside.

Karom remembers the words in *Fairytales of Freedom,* in "The Invisible Husband, Parts I and II." He remembers how Janaki, Kamini—he's not sure because they blur into the same person in his brain—had been so strong but had faltered when she recognized how isolated she'd been, how alone. He had thought to himself that he couldn't allow the same thing to happen to the two of them. He had thought to himself that something had to change. Something had to give. So he'd asked Gita into this last vestige of his past so that they could both move forward together.

When the door had creaked open hours before, she'd collapsed against it, weaker than Karom had been a few years before when he had arrived with the box of photos that reunited him to his first past, the one he couldn't remember. He'd sunk down next to her, cuddling her head into the crook of his neck, letting her sob hard and long before she gathered herself up and walked toward the entrance to the house, fighting with all her will to move forward but sniffling with each step. Inside, after Karom had placed surgical masks over their ears as protection from the dust, Gita had walked slowly, solemnly, as if she were in a museum, taking everything in: a signed framed glossy photo of Dharma Sen on the landing, Mohan's editing trophies, Rana's cookbook collection, the brassy pots and pans in the kitchen hanging from hooks.

Karom had followed her around silently, not saying a word, not even directing her one way or another because there was nothing that was off-limits to her—she could look and touch everything; she could open closets and ask questions. But there had been none of that. She'd opened every drawer in his parents' room without touching anything within them, and when she got to their bedside drawer, she'd looked at him quizzically and he'd nodded, soundlessly conveying to her that, yes, that was the drawer in which he'd discovered the letter to himself.

She gets choked up again in Karom's room over a Kurt Cobain poster, and when he moves toward her, she shakes her head and holds her hand up, continuing to cry quietly on her own, wrapping her own arms around herself and insisting on moving forward. She inspects every single book title on the shelves, the sports paraphernalia under the bed, the grunge

T-shirts hanging in the closet, the piles of CDs stacked like Stonehenge on the ground.

Tears stop leaking from her eyes as she winds her way down the stairs and into the living room, the one room in the house she has overlooked until now. The carpet is still thick with dust, and there is a faint imprint of Karom's body where he'd lain on the ground and let the spinning world overwhelm him years before. The photographs are still taped on the wall, though some have fallen off as the tape's adhesive lost its strength, and she walks from one end of the wall to the other, stopping at each and every photograph, reading the protest signs, memorizing faces and architecture. She picks up the fallen photographs that have curled over with age and props them on the couch so she can survey them one by one. Karom licks his lips repeatedly; he's not quite sure what to say or to do. But once she's examined all the thousands of photographs, she turns to him questioningly and he realizes that there is nothing left to say, there's nothing left to do. So he looks at her, he watches her, just as patiently as she's examined the artifacts of his past. He watches her face and recognizes how for the first time it appears relaxed, but he can make out circles beneath her eyes and tiny wrinkles at the corners of her mouth. He realizes what a toll this all has taken on the woman he loves. And he recognizes that he doesn't want to be responsible for that anymore. He wants to take in her beauty and shed the responsibility for her pain.

When he first approached Gita on the street that morning at the flea market, it wasn't because of her light eyes and her dark hair, her olive skin, a perfect olive mixture that combined the darker paint of Savita's skin and the fairness of Haakon's, her taut cheekbones that created hollows above her jaw, her plump lips that looked as though they might burst if flicked.

Or maybe it was those things, but it was a deeper attraction, a somewhat Freudian one. He imagined that this was what his mother had looked like, the one he's never seen. The one who either had expired with a soft exhaustion of breath after her lungs had collapsed like a deflated balloon or was still living a new life in the tired streets of Bhopal, with a new husband or maybe even the old one, dressing her new son for school or perhaps her old daughter—his sister—for her wedding day. He imagined that his mother, regal but soft, with ruined hands from hard labor, was reflected in the same hollows that dipped under Gita's collarbones and in the gentle webbing between her fingers. He imagined the space between her nose and her lip, that gentle dimple, that groove where his pinkie finger fit so perfectly, was the same distance on both women.

Of course, the moment they stepped into the bar together and drank the gimlets that would render them both giddy and helpless, he knew that there was nothing about this woman that was like his mother, because he would never know. So he released it from his mind into the air, just like the chemicals that had consumed his family, letting the idea catch in the wind and disappear forever.

As he descends the steps after locking the door, he looks at her face the whole way down, partly because he needs to focus on her right now, partly because he knows the number of steps—nine. He feels buoyant, weightless as he hails a taxi on the corner and they slide in together, ready to emerge to their lives on the other side of the river from Brooklyn. As soon as the meter clicks on, Gita falls asleep on his shoulder, overcome by the morning's emotions. He lets her body collapse against his, the weight of her head bobbing as the cab traverses cobblestones. For the first time in his life, he doesn't want to take his eyes off her. He doesn't want to lose sight of what's important.

Just as the cab enters the tunnel that will rejoin them to their lives, she stretches and pokes his ribs.

"Sorry," she says. "How long was I out?"

"About five minutes," he says. "Don't worry about it. You can sleep."

"No, that was perfect. I guess I was overwhelmed."

"Understandably."

"Thank you for that. You have no idea what this morning meant to me."

"Don't thank me, Geets. It was long overdue. And I'm working on it, every day. You have to believe that," he tells her.

"And I do. For the first time I do. And I'm here, I'm always here. I'm going to help you. Don't forget about me."

"I'm not. I haven't. I won't."

As the yellow lights of the tunnel tick past them, Gita sits up.

"Hey, look. It's coming, Karom. Get set. Wish!"

Karom and Gita close their eyes and hold their hands and their breath as they pass the tiles that demarcate the difference between Brooklyn and New York.

"That was a good one, I could feel it," Gita says, gripping his hand tightly, so hard the bones in it ache.

"I hope so. I need it."

She leans back into him. "What time is it?"

He glances at the clock on the dashboard. "Twelve-fifty."

She leans over and moves a piece of hair out of his eyes. In the shadows, he watches himself in her eyes, her gaze as soft as her touch. Her skin smells unwashed but not unpleasant, tangy and yeasty, like Gita always smells. Karom can just see the glow of morning at the curve of the tunnel ahead. It is his exodus, welcoming him home. As she kisses him gently, her mouth tastes sweet, as though she has just eaten grapes. She looks at him tenderly, holding his face between her palms before she leans forward and whispers softly in his ear: "To-gether, we learn."

★ ★ ★ ★ ★

Acknowledgments

First and foremost: thank you to the readers. Writers would be inconsequential without you.

I wouldn't be here today without the support of Leonore Waldrip and the entire MIRA team, or the keen eye of Susan Swinwood. Just when I thought my book couldn't possibly get any better, the inimitable Erika Imranyi entered the scene, editing this novel into a leaner story fit for publication. I am grateful for your tenacity and the lesson in humility.

The tireless Priya Doraswamy redefined the role of agent in my eyes. You showed me the possibilities and continue to lead me to them.

Much like a human, a book needs to be nurtured and coaxed along. Countless friends and family supported me along the way. My early readers Maya Frank-Levine and Shomit Mitter believed in the story and gifted me with invaluable insight to push it to its true potential.

Borrowing the words of E. B. White: it is not often that

someone comes along who is a true friend and a good writer. Kamala Nair is both. Thank you for reading and challenging, engaging and sharing, laughing and crying alongside me on this journey. Your support means the world to me.

One of my most effusive cheerleaders: my prolific brother, Neil, whose encouragement and commitment to read and respond to anything and everything never flagged even from the other side of the world.

Salman Rushdie wrote that your parents allow you to become the person and the writer that you have it in you to be. There are no words that can convey my gratitude to my parents, Maitreya and Nina Padukone, for all they have done to support me in immeasurable ways. A reverberating shout-out to my mother, who painstakingly pored over each and every draft, questioning motives and brainstorming solutions. I think this book became as much a part of you as it was of me.

My loving Rohit, who helped train my eye on the prize by sating my stomach and feeding my soul. You don't put up with my idiosyncrasies; you embrace them, always reminding me to place writing ahead of everything else. *You are my strength.*

WHERE EARTH MEETS WATER

PIA PADUKONE

Reader's Guide

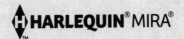

QUESTIONS FOR DISCUSSION

1. Karom struggles with the idea of his invincibility throughout the book. How does he ultimately overcome this struggle? How does reading Kamini's book help him?

2. Do you believe that Karom is truly invincible or do you think it's just coincidence that he escaped these disasters? Discuss your thoughts about fate.

3. What do you think motivated Lloyd's decisions to abandon his wedding and cut off ties to Karom? Do you agree with them? Why or why not?

4. How does ritual play a role in the book? How do each of the characters utilize rituals?

5. Discuss the role that Karom's watch plays in the way he lives his life. Does it help him or hurt him? What are some of the talismans or lucky charms that help you?

6. How does Gita become Karom's strength? What does she do for him? What are the sacrifices she makes in order to help him?

7. Karom's adoptive parents gave him a unique name—after a carom board—which means "to ricochet." Discuss how the meaning of his name shapes his life and journey.

What inspired the ideas for the story and characters in *Where Earth Meets Water*?

I originally wrote the first section of Where Earth Meets Water as a short story. But I felt there was more to the characters that I wanted to explore, so I kept writing to see where the story took me. I believe that every story has autobiographical influences, and Where Earth Meets Water is no exception. The book was inspired by my own realization of how marginally I have escaped tragedy. The last day of my summer job in Tower 1 of the World Trade Center was just three days before 9/11. I stood on the beach overlooking the Bay of Bengal while the 2004 tsunami crashed into the shoreline a few hundred miles south. I walked past the finish line to meet my husband, who completed the 2013 Boston Marathon an hour and a half before—and a few feet away from where—the bombs exploded. These events forced me to recognize how accidental, how coincidental life can be. The characters were ones I discovered through the first short story I wrote, and the more I wrote, the better I got to know them.

Many of the characters in *Where Earth Meets Water* are Indian, and much of the novel is set in India, yet the novel is really a universal story about fate, love and our inherent desire to understand the meaning of life. In what ways did you intend for culture to inform your novel, and what was your broader intention for writing?

I appreciate that observation because that's exactly what I set out to do. When you first start writing, you write what you know. As you get more comfortable, you begin to stretch the limits of what is possible, exploring unknown territory. Could it have been any other country or culture? Possibly. But there is no denying that I am an American writer of Indian origin—born and brought up in America—who inherently understands and appreciates both her cultures. India is incredibly versatile: Gita's grandmother's Konkani family has a completely different culture than that of Bhopal, with different customs, food and even language. But simultaneously, Indians have so much shared heritage, as the country has undergone so much historical, political and even industrial upheaval. It was important to me that Karom seek a partner with whom he could share some of that inherent understanding. Ultimately I wanted to write a book that embraced a few ideas: (1) that you'll never know the source from which you might derive solace; (2) the world is a powerful, over-whelming place; (3) when you love someone, you have to believe in them no matter what.

Our connection to our familial roots is a powerful theme in the novel. Have culture and family been important forces in your own life? If so, how?

My brother and I were raised with a strong connection to culture and I have always been very close to my family, both my nuclear one in New York City, where I grew up and continue to live, and my extended family in India. So I do owe my family deep gratitude for guiding my formative years and molding me into the writer that I am today, influencing and inspiring me in ways I may not even be aware of. Whenever I visit India, the outpouring of love from family and even family friends always overwhelms me. It's in many ways how I learned that love comes in many forms. It's how I realized that Karom didn't necessarily need his own personal family in order to heal.

You've created such a rich cast of characters in the novel, especially Kamini, a passionate and wise sage who is larger-than-life. When you started the book, did you have the characters' journeys and personalities already in mind? How did they surprise you along the way?

While we're probably not supposed to play favorites, Kamini holds a special place in my heart. She is very much the marriage of both my grandmothers: the independent but fiercely loving characteristics of my mother's mother and the gentle, supportive spirit of my father's. I didn't know where I wanted her to go, but I did know that she would struggle constantly, and that she would only feel peace at a late stage in her life. I let Karom, Gita and Lloyd write their own destinies and was sometimes truly surprised at what those were. I was pleased but also saddened that Lloyd ultimately acknowledged that there was a force larger than him and that the only thing he could do to fight it was to abandon it altogether. It sometimes frustrated me that Gita staunchly never gave up on Karom, and I sought solace in the fact that Karom allowed the country that haunted him to be the place that ultimately healed him.

Do you read other fiction while you're writing, or do you find it distracting? What do you enjoy reading most?

I am a voracious fiction reader and am rarely without a novel nearby. I find reading while I am writing incredibly helpful to the process. It helps me realize other avenues that I hadn't explored with the characters I am working with. Like the characters in the book I'm reading, could mine also go on a journey? Could they also have an unrequited love? Could they also lose a loved one? Maybe, maybe not, but novels are a gold mine for ideas. Beautiful writing is always inspiring. When I read a great book, I get excited about the prospect of writing one.

I am guilty of reading mostly fiction but I love narrative nonfiction, as well. I love the writing of Jennifer Egan, whose novel A Visit from the Goon Squad inspired me to write Where Earth Meets Water in the format of intertwining lives, stories, letters and inset short stories. Some of my other favorite authors include F. Scott Fitzgerald, Dave Eggers, Vendela Vida, Dinaw Mengestu, Gary Shteyngart, Lionel Shriver, Curtis Sittenfeld, Louise Erdrich... The list goes on.

Can you describe your writing process? Do you outline first or dive right in? Do you write scenes consecutively or jump around? Do you have a schedule or a routine? A lucky charm?

I wrote Where Earth Meets Water in the mornings before I left for my job as a copywriter at an advertising agency. Perhaps it was knowing that I had only a few precious hours before the distractions of the day would take me away from Karom's world that forced me to home in on the story and write furiously. I dove in without an outline, without even knowing the beginning, middle or end. All I knew was that there was a story there, and I would fall out of bed bleary-eyed and sometimes still middream but almost immediately fall under the spell of my story. It was a really exciting time in my life, because I was taking myself on an unknown adventure. Once I was deep in the throes of the book, the story would start to overtake my mind: I would find myself scrabbling for a piece of paper to write down an idea for Gita while I was jammed between bodies on the subway. For the most part, I wrote scenes consecutively, but since the novel relies on so much flashback and memory, I did move scenes around after I'd finished the majority of the writing to decipher the holes and identify which parts of the story needed some bolstering.

I am still very much a morning writer. I thrive in the serene early hours before the rest of the world wakes up when it's just my laptop, a cup of coffee and me. Once my brain turns on for the rest of the day, it gets more difficult to focus.

At my writing desk, I have a collection of things that keep me motivated: a photo of Nora Ephron, who was so passionate about the written word that she continued working throughout the pain of cancer; an autograph from Christopher Reeve, a man of tremendous strength both on and off camera; a painting of Kali, the Hindu goddess of female empowerment, as well as one of Pele, the Hawaiian goddess of the volcanoes, who also harnessed creative power and passion. I have a framed quote by Henry James about the persistence of being an artist. A family friend gave me a dandelion encased in glass that helps me remember to always keep dreaming.